LIFE ON THE FRINGE

TALES FROM THE FRONTIER

GEORGE ALLEN MILLER

This is a work of fiction. Names, characters, places, and incidents are either the product of the author's imagination or are used fictitiously, and any resemblance to actual persons living or dead, business establishments, events, or locales, is entirely coincidental.

Life on the Fringe

Copyright © 2025 by George Allen Miller

All rights reserved. No part of this book may be reproduced in any form or by any electronic or mechanical means, including information storage and retrieval systems, without written permission from the author, except for the use of brief quotations in a book review.

Cover art by Evgeniia Gurcheva

Edited by Elizabeth Thurmond

First Edition, 2025

Trade Paperback ISBN: 979-8-9920996-0-7

Published in the United States of America

For my Family

CONTENTS

1

———

BAR CHAT

THE LOST KID

"Drink?" The bartender, a woman with blonde hair and a genuine smile, nodded to Doug. She wore a white tank-top shirt, jeans and a red bandanna tied around her hair and stood behind a long bar that wrapped around half of the room. Rows of bottles filled with various colored liquid stood on shelves carved out of the wall behind her. The dirt coated tavern had once been a storage room inside the asteroid-station. Doug had found it while exploring the space port that orbited the planet Homer's World. A planet on the edge of civilized space.

Above the bar, several screens displayed news feeds from the solar system. They all covered the same event. An asteroid had struck an Imperial starship, snapping it in half. Over five thousand crew were lost. Authorities hadn't confirmed but the asteroid trajectory suggested it was altered with deliberate intent. Which meant this was an act of war.

Doug turned his attention away from the news and back to the bar. Behind him, two dozen tables carved from the rock filled the chamber. Half that many patrons sat, drank and talked in low whispers throughout the room. Dust covered their clothes and most surfaces. Several patrons looked up and gave Doug a quick stare, most searching his body for weapons or something of value.

Doug ignored the stares in the room and looked at the bartender who had offered him a drink and nodded once. He sat on one of the oddly shaped metal chairs in front of the bar. The bartender reached for a bottle below the bar and filled a metal cup, smiled at him and placed the mug within finger reach, shook her head and walked to another customer. Doug lifted his drink and tasted the brown liquid. It was revolting. Perhaps the worst thing he'd ever drunk in his very short life. He didn't want to seem weak, after all, he was looking for a ship to join as crew, so he downed the harsh abrasive spirit and suppressed a sudden need to throw up.

"Nasty, isn't it?" said a gray-haired man to Doug's left. The old man wore a leather bomber jacket, dirty jeans, and an equally filthy button-down shirt. His gray hair was halfway down his back and tied in a ponytail; around his waist sat a brown leather belt with two holsters set on the sides. Rusted guns sat in the holsters. They didn't look like they worked.

Not able to speak yet, Doug nodded.

"It's piss water, all you can get out here." The gray-haired man smiled, took a drink from his glass and grimaced.

"Sod off, you old coot. Best we got, don't drink it if you don't like it," the bartender said.

"Man's gotta get drunk somehow." The old man finished his glass and set it back down on the bar. He nodded to the bartender for another.

"So boyo, what are you doing out here then? I know just about everyone that comes through this hole in the wall of a bar. We only get miners or ship's crew swapping out after a refuel," the old man said. "You don't look like a miner so you must have been dropped off."

"Yes, sir, the *Sweet Louise* dropped me off," Doug said. He steadied his voice and tried to sound like the alcohol didn't burn his chest out from the inside.

"Waiting on your next ship then?"

"No sir, I don't have anything lined up yet. Do you have a ship?"

The old man frowned. Then smiled. "No. I don't have a ship. I'm waiting for a friend to pick me up and head out of the system. And no, we don't have any room."

"Are you sure?"

He nodded, "Did the *Louise* crew fire you or try to sell you?"

Doug only shook his head, confused.

"People don't get dropped off here without something else lined up. Nothing on this rock but more rock, and no place to sleep. If you don't have a ship, you won't last a day."

"I came looking to get on a ship. I want to see fringe space." Doug's words blurted out of him like a school kid on a trip to the zoo. And he knew it. His shoulders slumped. He looked down to the dusty rock that made up the bar and rolled the thin tin cup in his hands.

"Do you now? Well, if you go down to the docks, or hang around here long enough, maybe someone will pick you up. If not, you'll starve to death." The old man smiled and took another swig from his drink. "What's your name, boyo?"

"Doug. Douglas Parker." Doug held out his hand and smiled.

"I never shake a man's hand without drinking with him first." The old man emptied his drink down his throat and signaled for the bartender. "Hanna, two please."

Hanna brought a bottle filled with more of the brownish liquid. She poured two full shots and left the bottle on the bar. Both Doug and the gray-haired man picked up their tin cups and lifted them to their mouths. Their eyes never left each other as they drank. Doug strained to hold his gaze as the liquid burned down his esophagus.

"Name's Hill. Captain Hill," the man said with a nod.

"Douglas Parker," Doug repeated.

"Caught that," Hill said. He reached for the bottle and poured both himself and Doug another drink. "Why do you want to go to fringe space? It's nasty out there, boy."

"I'm not a boy," Doug said with a cough. "I want to see what's out there. I've heard all the rumors and wanted to see for myself."

"Where you from, boyo?" Hill said, putting an emphasis on boyo.

"Tel'amuth. Seventy-five light years Earthward," Doug said.

"Never heard of it. Seventy-five light years Earthward? Quite the hike out here to Homer's World."

Doug nodded.

"Why Homers?"

"The captain of the ship that brought me here said this was a jumping off point to the unknown. Civilized enough to get fuel and supplies but they don't ask so many questions. He took me on as crew," Doug said.

"Why didn't you just stay with him?" Hill said.

"He wasn't going out past Homers, just here. Said lots of ships were coming here,"

"Yeah, Homers just joined the Empire. Everyone wants to see the natives before they doll us up and make us nice and pretty. What was the name of the ship again?" Hill said.

"Sir?"

"The ship that brought you here, boyo."

"Oh, the *Sweet Louise*."

Doug watched as Hill typed onto a pad that was sitting in front of him on the bar. Another moment passed and Hill nodded to himself. He lifted the bottle and poured more of the alcohol into both of their cups.

"Why do you want to see the fringe?" Hill asked.

Doug shrugged. "The unknown? Adventure? I've heard stories of amazing things."

"Yeah, what have you heard?"

"Just things. Wanted to see for myself. Besides, I don't have anything back home."

"Why is that?"

"I don't really belong there," Doug said. He lowered his gaze back down to the stone bar.

"That right. Well, let me tell you, boyo. Fringe is nothing like what you've heard. You know what's out there? Waiting for you on the fringes of human civilization?"

"My name is Doug, and yes, I know what's out there."

Hill snorted a laugh. "You have no idea what's out on the fringe. Do you even know what fringe space is?"

"It's where governments don't exist."

"Yes, but why don't they exist there?"

"I don't know, why?"

Hill shifted in his bar stool and poured himself another drink. He sipped it and shook his head with a sideways grin. In a fluid motion, he stood, moved his bar stool over a few inches closer to Doug and sat back down. Dust from the old man's jacket stirred in the sudden move and a tiny cloud of dirt briefly surrounded them.

"Fringe space is just a frontier. An endless frontier. The more humans flee Earth, the farther out we go. The frontier never ends. It's wild, free, and lawless. But also filled with the unknown. You'll find horrors out there that will shake you to your foundation, boyo. Are you ready for that?"

"What kind of horrors?" Doug said. Saliva built in his mouth and he took a quick gulp.

"Boy, like nothing you would ever expect." Hill smiled, took a drink and poured himself another.

2

FRINGE SPACE

QUERNS COLONY

"Once, I thought the gift was evil. Then I tried it. I couldn't have been more wrong."

Anna Beiler - special counsel for annexation affairs - Imperial Courts

The starship *Jacob's Pride* fired its descent engines five hundred feet above the tarmac. Orange flame erupted from the vessel and cooked the asphalt of the empty spaceport. The ship swung around a thin needle of carbon fiber that stretched to orbit, part of the space elevator created when the colony was founded. It slowed to hover over the blackened asphalt as the engines powered down. With a sudden jolt, the ship's landing gear touched the ground, and the engines switched off.

"Down," called a voice from the bridge.

"Great, job everyone. Welcome to–" Jake paused and checked his console— "Querns Colony," he added with a smile.

"What's on this rock again?" Maya said.

"No clue. But no one's been here for six years, and they have an active registry, which means they aren't dead. So that's six years' worth of goods to sell and transport," Jake said.

"The space elevator doesn't work; we know that," Sarah said. A screen popped up on several displays in the ship. The space ship that brought the colony here sat several hundred yards away from the tarmac where the *Jacob's Pride* had landed. The walls of the colony ship were folded down. Once landed, every colony ship became both a structure for colonists and an anchor for the space elevator cable. Several doors around the base were open. A few swayed with the breeze. "My scans show the space elevator cable is still intact but unpowered. The orbital station, however, still looks operable but it's abandoned. The subAI on board said no one has been there in years."

"Well, let's go meet the natives," Maya said.

Jake ran his hand through his long hair. He smiled and unbuckled his chair straps. *Just another day in the cargo business*, he thought. Thousands of seeder ships, all streaming from a dying Earth, flooded the fringes of human space, each designed to reach orbit, set an anchor for a space elevator, and then land on the surface. The ships themselves, once landed, would unfold into a ready-made shelter and the beginnings of a city center. Each one could jumpstart a colony world, and potentially make a new client for Jake and his crew.

"Maya, Tommy, Bill, meet me in the bay. Sarah, you get to babysit the ship as usual," Jake said. He jumped out of his seat and strapped on a thigh holster for his guns. He put on an old leather cowboy hat, his brown leather bomber jacket and walked towards the ship's exit bay.

"What do we know about who lives here?" Tommy ran up behind Jake and followed him to the bay.

Jake turned his head to look at the young kid. He stood just at five feet eight inches. He wore jeans, a blue t-shirt and a jean jacket. The kid had a love for denim. Jake had found Tommy on a strange world, stranded and half dead. The boy took to space travel well enough, and Jake never regretted adding him to the ship. Though there were many times Tommy's youth became frustrating, and the kid could get a little too argumentative, Jake had no real regrets.

"According to the last ship to visit, the colony started experimenting with genes. Records show the people were nice enough but didn't have much to trade. Splicers can be weird, so no one's visited since then," Jake said.

"Playing with their genes? Like what?" Tommy asked.

"According to the report, they added a third arm that wraps around their body. There are no notes about what it did, though," Jake said.

"Why would they do that?"

"No idea; the last ship said they were real quiet about it. Just welcomed them, told them they had nothing and sent them on their way."

"The report did contain some information from a biologist on that ship. Though he never got a look at the arm, he thought it might be there to help them live in this environment. Perhaps to fight infections of weird biologicals on the planet? They didn't find anything odd, though," Bill said. The old spacer wore grey overalls, tennis shoes and an old baseball hat. Bill filled the role of general egghead and sometimes father figure. Old Bill had seen more of fringe space than everyone put together. And he carried enough scientific knowledge to jump start a colony from the stone age to the industrial.

"The last ship to come here was a cargo ship like ours. What were they doing with a biologist on board?" Jake said.

"Using that logic, what are you doing with me on board?" Bill replied, his voice taking the hint of an edge. He pushed his falling glasses up on his face as he chased after his shipmates down the corridor.

"Easy, Doc. Besides, you love us," Jake said.

"Indeed," Bill said.

The three rounded a rusty corner in the corridor of the aging spaceship. Weathered metal cabinets and various tools lined the walls. Jake stopped, those behind him nearly running into his back, and adjusted several dials. He banged the wall until the indicators began to move. Jake nodded and continued toward the bay. The ship was well-worn, and in some places falling apart, but the important parts worked. Engines, life support, and navigation, were all that mattered. All the rest was just for comfort.

Two large doors opened in the hallway that led to the vehicle bay. A metal catwalk above the bay lined the sides of the room. The wall at the far end of the bay also served as a ramp that would allow access to the outside. A large land vehicle, with mounted guns that sometimes worked, sat in the center of the vehicle bay. Maya stood just to the right of the land vehicle with several tools in her hands. She waved to Jake and the others as they entered. Jake reached the ladder that led to the bay floor and descended, then walked over to Maya and stuck his head into the engine compartment.

"All OK?" Jake said.

"Yes, she's looking good," Maya said. She nodded more to herself than to Jake, and threw the tools onto a table along the wall beneath the catwalk.

"OK, let's load up. We need to meet the locals, see if they

have anything and want to trade. And we need to hurry about it and get off this world. His Majesty is waiting for his Orion crystal saplings," Jake said.

"Why does he want those anyway? They're so loud." Tommy frowned and shook his head.

"Who knows, but he does, so we'll sell them to him."

Jake climbed into the driver's seat. The engines sputtered once then roared to life. The others hopped inside and strapped themselves into their bucket seats. Jake picked up a cigar and put it in his mouth. The door to the bay opened and landed on the tarmac of the spaceport with a loud thunk. Jake smiled, rammed the gear into first and floored the accelerator.

"WELL, they do have lots of grain," Jake said. The rover sat a quarter mile from the space port on a dirt road that stretched toward the only active village on the planet. They overlooked a vast valley filled with long grain stalks standing ten feet tall. Scents of honey with a slight hint of rotting meat carried on the wind.

"Why isn't the colony anywhere near the colony ship at the space port?" Tommy said.

"Who knows. Sometimes they just leave it. Every colony is different," Jake said. "Sarah, any luck with the micro-orbitals?" He spoke into a communicator on wrapped around his wrist.

After a few moments, Sarah's voice came back across the com channel. "Yep, we launched them when we first got into orbit, and they are just now coming online. They have complete planetary coverage."

"Can you get a reading from the rover and tie it in to the

network? I'm curious how much of this stuff is on the planet," Jake said.

"What for? It's just grain," Tommy said.

"Not just grain. I took a small sample from near the spaceport. Early results from my handheld show it could very well be some kind of animal and plant hybrid. Making it very hearty," Bill said.

"Is that why this place smells so bad?" Maya asked.

"I'm afraid so," Bill said.

"How do you know that?" Tommy said.

"Bill used to live inside a plant." Jake smirked and bit down on his cigar.

"He what?" Tommy turned toward Bill. "You lived inside a plant?"

"It was a long time ago, young man, and I highly recommend the experience," Bill said.

"Could these be genetically engineered?" Jake wondered.

"It's possible. We would have to analyze its DNA to really know," Bill said. "I can start that now with Sarah's help."

"You got it, Bill. I also have the readings from the suborbitals. It will take me a bit to do a full scan of the planet. Give me an hour or so," Sarah said.

Jake lifted his hat and ran his hand through his hair. Grain wasn't a great commodity to trade, even in fringe space. Most colony worlds were equipped with enough animal protein growth systems to make it until Terran wheat could be altered to survive on the new world. But that did take time. Finding something hearty, like an animal plant hybrid that could grow anywhere, that would be very lucrative. If the grain on Querns could grow anywhere, they could really be in business.

"Jake." Tommy pointed to the east.

In the distance, a lone figure walked toward them on the gravel road. The person wore a long, loose brown robe and walked with a slight limp. Around their torso hung a thick appendage. Tuffs of clumpy white hair lined pale grey skin on the third arm. The thick muscles of the arm pulsated as the robed figure walked forward.

The closer the person got, the uglier the bio-engineered arm became. The appendage ended in three claws, each nearly six inches long. Muscles along the arm flexed and moved at random. The talons looked more than capable of being used for a weapon if the need arose. The possibility that this colony had become fanatics entered Jake's mind.

"Hello," Jake said.

"Greetings, star traveler. What brings you to our home?" the hooded figure said.

Jake looked back to his comrades with a smile and a shrug. He turned back to the hooded figure. "We came for trade."

"What do you want to trade?"

"How about grain? You folks look like you have plenty of it. Do you know if it grows everywhere?"

"It does indeed. It is the lifeblood of the planet. Both predator and prey," the hooded figure said.

"Morbid!" Maya whispered just loud enough for everyone to hear.

"What does that even mean? Predator? The grain eats people?" Tommy whispered.

"Perhaps small mammals? It does appear to be an animal-plant hybrid after all," Bill said.

"OK. This guy seems a bit nutty for sure. Most zealots are, but if there's a profit to be had then let's have it," Jake said over his shoulder. "Besides, our engines really could use an overhaul."

"They could?" Maya said, her eyes going wide.

Jake waved her off. "Could you take us to your leader?" Jake smiled and put his hands on his hips.

Everyone groaned.

The hooded figure nodded and turned. He wrapped both his biological arms around the extra appendage and carried the grey-clawed extra arm as he walked back towards his town.

"Well, let's follow him," Jake said.

"JAKE, LOOK AT THIS." Bill stood over what looked like a corpse of a rodent. The small furry creature lay rolled up on its side next to one of the buildings in the small village. Attached at the midsection was an extra appendage that stretched around the rodent's body, ending in three sharp claws. Even the gray skin and random clumps of hair matched the third arm of the villagers.

"How is that possible?" Jake said.

"Maybe they experimented on the animal life here? Simply amazing," Bill said.

"Or their gene splicing leaked into the local ecosystem?" Jake's hands went to his side. "Everyone make sure you don't start growing any extra pieces."

Jake stood apart from Bill and looked around at the small town. Stone buildings, none bigger than a single story, formed a large circle around the center of the village where a quern, a bowl nearly ten feet wide with a stone wheel inside, sat. Hooded figures walked between the buildings and the quern. Each had a third arm around their waists. They all walked in a slow gait with their heads bowed to the ground. Not one villager spoke a word as they walked from one stone building to the next. Several of the townspeople gathered around the large quern, some inspecting the contents, others pushing a wooden pole connected to the large stone wheel inside.

"Can you cut it up? Do some analysis?" Jake asked, turning back to the rodent on the ground.

"Assuredly. I will have something soon." Bill bent down to the corpse and poked it several times with a small pen.

Jake walked towards the quern. He glided himself between the villagers and peeked his head over the rim of the large stone bowl. Inside, the wheel rolled over the piles of wheat and ground the stalks down to a fine powder. Several times the townsfolk would stop turning the stone and reach a hand inside to inspect the crop.

"You guys really love your grain," Jake said.

"Star flyer Jake," came a voice from behind him.

Jake turned to see three hooded figures approach from one of the stone buildings. All three carried their third large arm around their waist. One of the arms quivered as thick muscles twitched beneath the pale gray skin. Jake's own skin pricked at the unnerving sight.

"Ready to make a deal?" Jake said.

The three nodded in unison. They turned and walked towards the building they had exited moments before. Jake shrugged and walked after them. A funny tingle grew on his neck and he turned around towards the quern behind him. All of the townsfolk, even the ones that were pushing the stone wheel, stopped what they were doing and looked up at him. The tingle up his chest turned into an icy grip. He reminded himself that people had every right to be weird, but then weird could be one step away from downright dangerous. He armed his crew's network through his wrist computer just to be on the safe side.

The colonists and Jake made it to the stone structure and went inside. A small wooden table with four chairs sat in the middle of the space. Jake sat down in the seat offered to him. He put on his salesman face and waited for them to start the negotiations.

All three colonists sat with their backs straight and facial expressions still and lifeless. This was the first time he had gotten a good look from any of the townsfolk's faces, most being wrapped up beneath their hoods. The three people in front of him, two men and a woman, seemed barely alive. Their skin was a pale ghost white and covered in a rash. Their cheekbones were pronounced under their skin. They all showed signs of malnutrition. Maybe the grain here wasn't as hearty as Jake thought? But their eyes, each set black as the darkest night, stared out with a fierceness that Jake couldn't quite identify. A hunger sat behind those stares.

"What do you offer us, star flyer?" the colonist sitting in the center finally said.

"Whatever you want. We want your grain. We think other planets will love this hearty mix," Jake said. He frowned as his eyes went over their faces. "As long as it's rich in nutrients, of course."

The three nodded. "You may take it freely."

"Well, yes, we could. But that's illegal. You're the first colony here so you have export rights on this world. And we'd rather have a partnership. You cut the grain or even process it and we just pick it up and go. There are thousands of colony worlds out here now and all of them would love a robust, ready-to-grow grain."

"You will take our grain to all planets?"

"Every one of them."

"We will be with all people?"

"Sure, I suppose." Jake frowned. A funny feeling grew in his chest.

"Jake!" Sarah's voice erupted over his wrist comp.

"Not now, Sarah, I'm about to close."

"I think we have a big problem here."

"What?"

"Our micro-orbitals just finished scanning the entire planet. That grain is everywhere," Sarah said.

"Well, great, just what we want." Jake smiled. "But we need to check the nutrients of this stuff. These folks look a little pale."

"No, I mean it's really everywhere. I can't find any other vegetation of any kind. Just endless seas of this stuff," Sarah said.

"Well, that's good, right?"

"A single-organism ecosystem is not good, no."

"Well, that just means the wheat is hearty." Jake winked at the colonist. None of them moved.

"It's worse than that. Bill's initial scans came back. That dead animal you found, it has the grain DNA inside its cells."

"Well, it must have eaten some."

"Jake, you really need to read a science book. If we extrapolate what Bill found, it means there's nothing on this planet but the grain. It's overwriting the DNA of everything else. It's like a hyper-predator."

"Well, that's not possible. I'm talking with the colonists now, they eat this stuff all the time."

"About that. You really shouldn't eat anything there. In fact, you should really come back to the ship. Now."

"Not possible, I'm deep into negotiations with the towns-people." Jake nodded and smiled to each colonist.

"I don't know who you are talking to, but I don't think they are people anymore," Sarah said.

Jake looked at the three colonists. Their expressions hadn't changed but the fierceness in their eyes seemed brighter. As if the hunger inside them had only grown in the minutes they had been talking. The arms around their sides pulsated in unison, muscles from the segments attached to the colonists' skin pushing downward toward the three talons, which opened and closed slightly. Jake's face fell. He suddenly felt he may have misread the situation.

"I need to meet with my crew for a moment," Jake said. He stood from the chair and gave the three colonists a wide grin. They didn't react.

Jake left the building and entered the open area of the village. He turned and came to a dead stop. All the villagers had removed their robes and had plunged their third arms into the ground. The gray arms pulsated in waves starting from the thick hairy tops down to the clawed ends. Jake nodded once, raised his wrist comp, and entered command codes to alert the crew that they could be in trouble.

"Jake! The arms are not engineered at all. It's some kind of parasite." Bill ran from behind one of the buildings where their land vehicle was parked.

"Little late, Doc," Jake said. "We're going to have to work on your timing."

"Indeed I do," Bill said.

"Where are the others?"

"They were going to try the local fare, I believe," Bill said.

"Swell." Jake raised his wrist to his mouth, "Sarah, recall the satellites and prep the ship for emergency evacuation."

"On it," Sarah said.

The door to the stone structure behind Jake swung

open. The three townspeople Jake had negotiated with walked out. Their third arms jumped forward on their sides and pulled each of the colonists downward to the ground. The clawed ends plunged into the dirt and soon matched the rhythm of pulsation with the rest of the villagers.

"Join us, star flyer. Join the trance. Join the planet. Eat from the soil and the soil shall be in you," the colonists all said in unison.

Jake caught motion from the corner of his eye and saw a dog lie down on the ground. A small appendage on the side of the animal dug into the earth just like all the colonists. The hound's eyes rolled into the back of its head and his legs twitched as if he were in a dream.

"Tommy, Maya, haul ass back to the ranger. We have to leave." Jake walked into the center of the town and looked for his crewmates.

"I think this is one life-form I don't mind studying from afar." Bill walked, and then ran, toward the land rover.

"Bill, watch it!"

From the shadows of one of the buildings, a large rock hurtled towards Bill. It struck him in the head. Jake pulled his guns and fired in the direction of the building. The stone wall exploded at the blast, sending shards of debris spraying out from the structure.

Jake ran towards Bill ,who had fallen to the ground. A small trickle of blood stained his hair red from where the rock hit. Jake reached down to lift him but something struck him in the back of his head. Jake looked up, just before he lost consciousness, and saw Maya and Tommy standing over him. Their eyes were glazed over and they both rocked back and forth on shaky legs. In unison, they both turned to look into Jake's eyes.

"Join us," they both said.

"Maya? What are you doing?" Jake rolled onto his elbows. To his left, Maya lay on the ground, her eyelids fluttering, sweat beading on her forehead. She moaned slightly as a trickle of blood oozed from a bulge on her left side.

"She's in a trance of some kind," Bill said.

Jake turned his head to see Bill on his elbows and rubbing his head. Behind them, Tommy lay in the same position as Maya, a small trail of blood running in a tiny line down his left side.

"It would appear this particular parasite has taken over the entire ecosystem of the planet. I've never heard of anything like this," Bill said.

"Unheard of or not, we need an exit strategy."

"Indeed. Perhaps we could signal for help?"

"Doc, we're in the middle of fringe space. There's no one to call. Not to mention we're talking about a population of several hundred on a backwater world in the middle of deep space. Nobody cares," Jake said. He looked at Tommy. "Do you think his immune system is fighting this?"

Bill shrugged. "Doubtful. Most of his advanced immunity was burned out of him."

"Jake... the planet wants you..." Maya said.

Jake and Bill turned to see Maya, her eyes still fluttering between opening and remaining closed. More blood oozed out of her side as her skin cracked. A small tendril, barely larger than a piece of string, poked out from under her side and waved back and forth in the air.

"Maya, can you hear me?" Jake said.

"Yes."

"Are you Maya?" Bill said.

"I am we. We are all. Join us. Join the trance. Join the

union. Sail us to the stars so we may join with all," Maya said.

"Maya, wake up." Jake shook Maya on the shoulder hard enough that Bill frowned.

Maya shook her head for a moment and opened her eyes. She looked down at the ground and back to the roof. Her eyes rested on Jake and a familiar smile settled onto her face.

"Hi boss," she said.

"Maya?"

"Yes, just me. I think."

"What is going on?"

"It's really kind of incredible, Jake. I feel one with this entire planet. All the colonists. Like we're all linked in some kind of neural net. But there's something else there too. Not an intelligence but a primal need. A simple hunger to breed and spread to the whole world. It almost feels like I can't really die. If I did I would just be mixed up with the world again, regrown into a field," Maya said.

"Maya, you don't want to die here," Jake said.

"Dying is the one thing I know more about than you, Jake. More than anyone. Maybe I do?" Maya said. Her eyes glazed over. "To die one last time. One final time."

"Maya," Jake said.

"The parasite is undoubtedly bombarding her brain with endorphins. Reasoning with her won't be possible," Bill said.

"Well, whatever this is, it's making it past our wrist comps. They would have purged it by now," Jake said.

"I deactivated them," Maya said. "They would steal away the oneness."

"That right?" Jake activated a command protocol on the wrist comps. None of the crew knew he had the ability to command their internal systems, but he did. He signaled Maya's wrist comp for a full diagnostic. The unit's internal purge systems were deactivated.

Jake smiled to himself. Every once in a blue moon, as the saying went, he got a good idea. A really good idea. It was risky, but they had no choice. Jake sent a command to Maya's and Tommy's wrist comps and ordered them to continue to send a deactivated status to her. He then disconnected and put his head on the ground.

"What are you doing?" Bill said.

"Something really crazy. Let's conserve our strength. I think we're going to need it." Jake typed into his wrist computer, sending specific commands to Sarah.

JAKE KNEELED in the mud and stared at the townspeople. The villagers stood in a circle around them, their appendages held in their arms, their robes open and blowing lightly in the breeze. Maya and Tommy stood just a few feet from Jake. Tiny worm-like protrusions swung back and forth their sides.

"Join us," the townspeople said as one, Maya and Tommy adding their voices to the chorus.

"No?" Jake said with a shrug.

"You will. Our children must grow."

"My God," Bill said, "That must be it. Look there!" He pointed to a patch of ground. Stalks of grain were beginning to grow where the townspeople had dug in their third arms the day before.

"What?" Jake said.

"The arms are the mature form of the parasite. They plant their offspring into the ground, which turns into the grass-like stalks. There must be eggs there that get eaten by other creatures. Even pure carnivores are not immune. They eat herbivores, which must have egg sacs in those strange appendages. They are a hybrid. It is a true animal and plant hybrid."

"OK, Doc, how does this help us?"

"Well, it's fairly clear, we just don't ingest anything and we can't get infected. They haven't forced us to eat, as it's an alien concept to them. Everything eats eventually, so eventually we will join them."

"Are you saying they won't force us to get the parasites?"

"They haven't yet, so no, I don't believe they will."

"Doc, you just earned your keep," Jake said. He stood up with his arms held high.

"Sarah, how are we doing?" Jake said to his wrist comp.

"We're at twelve percent," Sarah said.

"Pretty bad. What are our chances?"

"I give us less than one out of four on this one."

"Alright, I think I can up the odds a bit." Jake took a deep breath and spoke to the townspeople. "I will join you. I will be one. I will take us to the stars."

"You'll what?" Bill jumped to his feet and stared at Jake with anger and confusion.

"Just hang on, Bill. If we don't run, they won't attack us. And you already said they won't force us to eat, so we have some time."

"What do we need time for?"

"Just trust me."

Jake walked towards Maya and winked. She tilted her head to the side but didn't respond. Around them, the villagers swayed in unison to a slow, steady breeze, as if they were nothing more than planted stalks. The grey pulsating arm in each of them was tucked around their sides.

"Can you show me the trance? Can you show me what I will join?"

Maya nodded. The townspeople, as one, removed their robes. Their skin, pale and patchy with red blotches, indicated the parasite was taking a toll. Some of the older villagers nearly fell over as they tried to adjust their center of gravity with the appendage. The grey arms began a slow, rhythmic pulsating of muscles. Claws opened and closed, flexing themselves in preparation. One by one the arms attached to the colonists slithered their way downward and stuck into the ground. Maya and Tommy had to lie on their stomachs so that the smaller worm-sized protrusions could reach the soil.

"Sarah?"

"We're increasing rapidly. Thirty percent."

Jake folded his arms and waited. If he was right, they would all be going home soon, and if not, well, he could think of worse ways to go out.

"Fifty percent, Jake, and climbing."

"Great. Get the rover ready. We are going to need to freeze Maya and Tommy, no telling what the aftereffects are going to be."

"Roger that. I'm prepping her now," Sarah said. A rumble from the outskirts echoed off the stone walls as the engine to the land vehicle fired up.

Three minutes passed.

"OK, we're at eighty-five percent. What do you think?"

"Let's kick her in the guts and see what happens. No telling when they wake up. When they notice we haven't chowed down on a parasite sandwich, they may get a little antsy."

"Alright, I hope this works. Activating purge program."

The shriek that erupted from the town was deafening. A

thunder of screams shocked Jake to the point that he pulled his sidearm and swung around at everything. All of the townsfolk dropped to the ground, clutching their gray appendages. Maya and Tommy rolled over, pain etched on their faces; they grabbed their sides and looked around in desperate search of relief.

"Bill, get Tommy. Sarah, get that rover in here, now," Jake said. He bolted toward Maya, jumping over the prone townsfolk. None of them noticed.

"What is going on?" Bill asked.

"Just get Tommy, tell you later."

The rover screeched around the corner of town, being driven remotely by Sarah. It stopped in front of Jake, who lifted Maya up in his arms. He threw her into the opened door of the rover and helped Bill put Tommy inside.

"Floor it!" Jake said. Sarah did. The rover sped away from the townspeople and back toward the safety of their ship.

"Explain to me again what happened?" Tommy said. He was holding his side and rocking back and forth.

"I just gave this planet a taste of its own medicine," Jake said.

Bill walked up to Tommy with a cold compress and applied it to his head. He also gave him a bottle of water and a cup of small pills. Bill sat down opposite him on a bench and shook his head.

"What he means to say is he over-clocked the medical nanites from our wrist computers. Sarah fed them the exact DNA profile of the grain. There's a complex root system on this world. Once Maya and Tommy dug their parasite into the ground, the medical nanites followed them through."

"But how could it have affected everyone?" Tommy said.

"It didn't." Jake typed something into the ship's computer and turned around in his chair. "There seemed to be some kind of shared experience going on with this grain. Like they were all connected. Poke one with a stick and they all feel it. So as soon as the medical nanites got into the root system, and I reactivated the purge program, they all felt it."

"Wow." Tommy flopped down in a chair and rested his head. "Did we just kill the entire grain population?"

Bill shook his head. "No, not at all. The medical-grade nanites in our wrist comps can't replicate. Very low grade nanites."

"And parasite or not, it's not really a match for modern medicine," Sarah said over the communication system.

"It's only a class four parasite. I've seen some really nasty situations in my day. Makes this look like a picnic. Which really, I suppose it was." Jake smiled and half laughed.

"How's Maya?" Tommy said.

"We had to give her some sedatives, buddy. She's having some withdrawals from the endorphins. They were some powerful stuff. But, for whatever reason, you don't seem to be suffering that much," Jake said. He thought about where he discovered Tommy and what hell the boy had gone through. Maybe it let him recover quicker or maybe he was just lucky.

"What did Maya mean when she said she knew about dying?" Bill said.

"Long story. I'll let her tell you when she's ready," Jake said.

"Forget that, what did you mean when you talked about living in a plant!" Tommy said to Bill.

"Even longer story." Bill smiled.

"How's Sam doing anyway, Bill?" Jake said.

"Oh, you know her, still brutish and in charge." Bill smiled. "How are the townspeople?"

"Scans show that those affected lost those weird arms. They just fell off. But most of them ran back to the quern to eat more, infesting themselves again," Sarah said.

"Fascinating," Bill said.

"So, there's nothing we can do for them?"

"Us? Not at all. We don't have the equipment on this ship. Or the medical training."

"OK, let's package all this up and put it in a standard buoy in orbit. Also send a note back to the archives, in case anyone ever comes here," Jake said.

"You got it, boss," Sarah said.

"So we just leave?" Bill said.

"Of course we leave – transporting class four parasites is a felony. And we can't help them. Besides, no money to be made here."

Bills face fell into a frown.

Jake rolled his eyes. "We'll include a note in our message that Querns Colony needs help. But who knows who will respond."

"Well, where to now?"

"His majesty's Orion saplings?"

"Yeah. But there's a colony not far from here, said to have loads of crystals for sale. We could have a look? And we could all use a holiday."

"Won't his majesty be angry?"

"Eh, he'll be fine." Jake grinned.

3

———————

BAR CHAT

THE OLD MAN

Doug sat up in his chair and looked at Hill with his eyes wide open and his jaw half to the floor. "Was that real? Grain that turns you into a zombie?"

Alexander Hill laughed. The boy practically looked like he'd shit himself. "Yeah, old Jake and I go way back. He's a free spirit, that one."

"Is Jake your friend that's coming? Can I get a ride with him? What else has he seen in space?"

Hill set his cup down on the counter and frowned. "Like I said, we don't have room." Hill stared up at the screens on display above the bar and watched as reports came in of the damaged imperial starship. Still no survivors had been found. Hill took another swallow from his drink.

"But I'm small; I won't take up much room."

"You're awfully eager there, boyo. Word of advice, slow your roll. No one likes eager strangers out here." Hill eyed him in a way that spoke more than anything he could say. His left hand drifted to his holstered Colt. He'd been around long enough to know that not everything is what it seems. Maybe this boy wasn't just a boy? He'd heard of imperial spies being his age before but never ran into one. Last thing Hill needed was to stumble into law enforcement. Especially considering how much they would like to find him.

"But I want to know what it's like out there. Are there sentient aliens? Monsters? Can't you tell me?"

Hill frowned and shook his head. "Why should I tell you anything?"

"You told me about Jake."

Hill shrugged. "Telling stories in bars is what old men do. But I don't know who you are. Sure, you were on the *Louise*, so what? Maybe you're an imperial spy. Maybe you have implants that are recording everything I say. What if you're the bad guy?"

"I'm just a kid. And I can't have implants; they don't work on me."

Hill raised his eyes and sat back in his chair. "That right?"

"Why can't you get implants?" Hanna, the bartender, wandered over and leaned against the stone bar top as she cleaned a glass.

"I've heard of it before," Hill said. "Something about the genetics just rejects them."

"It's true. I can't. Makes you feell like–"

"Like what?" Hill said.

Doug turned to him and shrugged. "Like an outsider."

4

CIVILIZED SPACE

THE OUTSIDER

"There's only one chance to say goodbye."
Max Hartwell, rescued from failed colony world.

"Please, I need medicine for my mother, she's sick." Doug stood in front of a white counter, his hands fidgeting with a small chain he picked up off the ground, his feet shuffling back and forth from nerves. A man in a white jacket stood on the other side of the counter with a long frown on his face.

"What's your name again?" the man said.

"Douglas Parker."

"Douglas, I'm sorry, I can't find you or your mother in any system. How do I know what medicine to give if she's not in here?" The man tapped the screen and shrugged.

"We just moved to the city. Does she need to come here?"

The man sighed. "You don't understand. It doesn't matter where she's from. Your implants aren't registering you. She could be on the other side of the world, and it wouldn't matter, the system would know everything about her. She should have been sent whatever medicine she needed as soon as her implants registered a sickness."

Doug shook his head. "We don't have implants. We can't. Something about our–" He tried to remember what the doctors had said to him years ago.

"Genetic condition?" The man reached behind the counter and pulled out a strange looking L-shaped handle. He pointed it at Doug, and several loud beeps came from the device.

"You've got the T-11 genetic marker. I'm sorry, son. There's not much I can do. If I give you the wrong thing—" The man pointed to dozens of bottles behind him— "she could die. Have you taken her to a hospital?"

Doug nodded. "They couldn't help either. Said without implants there's no way to know what's wrong."

The man nodded a reply. "Yes, not many places have full body scanners anymore in the city. Doctors just ask the implants. Look, I'm sorry, maybe you can find an older hospital somewhere?" The man turned from Doug to someone behind him.

Doug watched as the man helped his new customer with a smile and a wave. After a few minutes, he turned and walked outside and sat down on a waist-high stone wall. Around him, on the busy city street, throngs of people walked to work in the super-city. More than fifty million souls called this world home, one of the first colonies established after the discovery of faster-than-light travel.

A man in a suit stepped around a woman just before she stopped and adjusted her clothing. Three young boys, not much older than Doug, ran through the crowds never once touching anyone. An elderly woman walked along the sidewalk and bodies moved around her in an orchestration of acrobatic moves. Doug often watched the sea of people dance around themselves and wonder what such a thing would feel like. Would he know when to move his body just as an elbow came too close? Or would some silent guardian in his mind tell his body to move without him giving it a thought?

"You can't sit there," a man in a blue uniform said. He checked his monitor and his brow furrowed. He looked from Doug to his computer and back several times.

Doug just nodded. He took a long deep breath and walked into the crowd of people. In two steps, he'd already bumped into a woman, who frowned in shock at having been touched. An old man gave him a confused stare for knocking into his cane. Doug turned his head as fast as possible, desperate to move out of the way of every limb and body part moving towards him, but as hard as he tried he continued to bump or stumble into the other people.

A hand shot out between a woman with a stroller and yet another suited worker bee. Fingers wrapped around Doug's collar, and he drew his makeshift knife from his inside pocket. He whirled around to see Yin. The other boy smiled and shook his head a dozen times.

"What are you doing out here?" Yin said.

"Walking," Doug replied.

"More like bumping into people. Come on, street rats like us don't run around in the daylight." Yin tugged at Doug's collar and motioned towards an alley behind him.

"What are you doing here?" Doug asked.

Yin shrugged. "Following you."

Around the two boys, the crowds never stopped or noticed as they stood in the middle of the sidewalk and talked. Without effort or even conscious thought, bodies, arms, even the objects they carried moved just inches to the side to avoid both boys. Doug stared at the coordination, and his mouth fell open while he watched.

"Come on, forget them. We shouldn't be out in the open this long."

Doug watched the perfect people with smooth skin walk by. He moved in front of a woman with a red hat. She side-stepped without looking at him. A man lifted his arm just as Doug tried to swat it. All these people, they had so much they didn't even realize. If they got sick, they were taken care of in seconds. If they needed help it would be there. But Doug, and Yin, and everyone that couldn't get implanted, they were invisible. They didn't even count.

A tall woman with a large smile stepped over Doug. She carried a purple purse and laughed as she moved. Doug kicked out and hit the woman's leg just above her ankle. She stumbled and fell to the ground, a look of complete shock and disbelief on her face. Several others were impacted by the falling woman, not given enough time to adjust their position before she hit them. The remaining crowd flowed around the fallen and Doug like a river around boulders. The woman shook her head, stood, and with the others that had fallen, rejoined the eddies of people.

"You shouldn't do that, man." Yin backed up from the crowd toward the alley behind them.

A red dot, no bigger than Doug's thumbnail, appeared bright and shiny on the sidewalk in front of him. The dot moved towards him and climbed his leg. The circle settled on his shin and stopped. A dozen more lights followed the first and threatened to cover his leg in a collage of red polka dots.

"They're tagging you, come on!" Yin turned and ran without waiting for Doug to follow.

The red on Doug's leg never moved as he spun on his heels. The dozens more small circles, however, never made it to his clothes and chased him until he reached the alley. Once inside the shadows of the back world of the streets, the red dots on the sidewalk reversed direction and disappeared into the crowd. On his leg, still as bright as it was on the street, the tiny red dot shined back at him. Doug brushed his pants with both hands, but the dot never moved. He covered the spot with some scraps of cloth on the ground, but the dot didn't disappear.

"See, that's why we don't go in the street," Yin said. He leaned against a brick wall, his hands digging into his pockets.

"What is it?" Doug asked.

"Tracker beacon. They tag you so they can find you. You have to be more careful."

"But it's light. How can light just stick to you?"

"You don't know anything, do you? How long have you been in the city? Three months? Still, haven't seen tracker beacons?"

Doug shrugged. "No." He and his mother had traveled from one of the last rural towns on the planet. Their family had spent the centuries farming and living a rural life far away from the hustle of busy cities. Doug's great-grandfather wanted nothing to do with clogged streets and mile-high skyscrapers when he boarded the first ships leaving old Earth. Now, isolated for so long, his family knew as much about the city as anyone here would know about milking a cow. An unfortunate side effect of living in the backwoods of this planet was the development of the T-11 gene and the inability to accept implants.

"How do I get it off?"

Yin smiled. "Follow me. I know someone."

The boys walked through the maze of alleys, walkways, and eventually, underground tunnels. Every time Doug looked down at his leg, the tiny red dot stared back at him, not moving. Several more times Doug tried to brush the round red circle off or cover it with his hands to block the light, but no matter what, it never moved.

"Who's this?" a scratchy voice said, followed by several loud wet coughs.

The smell of burnt food and dead fish assaulted Doug's nose. Empty food containers and other assorted pieces of garbage lay scattered on the concrete floor. A foul stench of dried urine came from more than one corner.

"A friend, he's got a beacon tracker."

A wrinkled and weathered old face popped out from behind a shadow. A cigarette hung loosely from the old man's mouth. Small circles of smoke rose up to the ceiling. He looked Doug up and down and gave him a long hard sniff.

"Beacon tracker? Where'd you get that down here?"

"I was on the street," Doug said.

The old man's eyebrows shot up and looked Doug hard in the eye. "Why? They don't want our kind up there."

Doug shrugged. "Getting medicine for my mother."

The old man grunted. "Nothing for you up there. Those people, all wired up, plugged into each other. Can't even fart without everyone knowing. They don't care about us one bit." The old man disappeared into the shadows of his doorway for a moment. Doug looked at Yin, who smiled and shrugged. Without warning, the old man popped out of his door and clamped a metal ring around Doug's leg.

"Wear that for a week and come back. It'll block the signal. Have to wait for the damn thing to give up."

"Thank you."

The old man smiled and brought his face inches from Doug's. "You owe me."

Doug nodded and smiled. The old man disappeared behind his door and slammed it closed. Yin shrugged and turned to walk away. He motioned for Doug to follow.

"Where to now?" Yin said.

"I need to check on my mom."

"Oh, right. How's she doing?"

"Not good. The doctors can't treat her without implants. They don't know how. No one has medical scanners anymore."

Yin frowned. "Sorry, man. That's tough. Comes with the territory."

Doug turned down a corridor and then another two. He walked for twenty minutes before rounding a bend to the apartment, once a mechanical shed, where he and his mother lived.

Inside, his mother lay on their makeshift bed made of layers of old wool blankets. Doug could tell she had been sweating. The sheets were damp and her forehead, though dry now, had a pale color. Doug knelt by her side and took her hand in his. "Momma?"

Her eyes flickered once and then again before opening. She smiled when she looked at her son. She tried to move her hand but only managed to lift it an inch off the bed. Doug helped and raised her hand to his face.

"Doug, did you get help?" She closed her eyes and licked her red, cracked lips.

"No, Momma. He said the same thing. Without implants, they can't do anything. We don't even exist."

She nodded once and tried to smile. Tears welled in Doug's eyes. He remembered her getting mad once because he had left toys out. And the time she bandaged a cut with a torn piece of her dress. She'd been there for him every moment of his life, and now, when she needed help, he'd failed.

"You shouldn't stay down here, Doug. It's not a place to grow up."

Doug shook his head. "I'll stay with you, Momma."

She nodded once and tried again to smile. Doug brushed the damp hair from her face and squeezed her hand. Her breath came shorter, as it has been for the last several days. She slipped into sleep and mumbled his name once more.

"She doesn't look well," a voice Doug had never heard before said behind him. He turned and saw a tall man with fresh, smooth skin. His hair was light brown and looked combed and clean. He wore modern clothes, the same worn by people on the street. He smiled once and took a step into Doug's apartment.

"Who are you?"

"Names McMillan. John McMillan. Been looking for you." He kept his hands open at his sides.

"Why?" Doug placed his mother's hand back on the bed and wiped tears from his eyes. He stood and fumbled in his back pocket for his makeshift knife.

John lifted his left arm and pointed to a spot on the underside of his arm. He then lifted his foot and pointed to a spot beneath his boot. John then nodded toward Doug and folded his arms, waiting.

Doug lifted his shoe and looked under his arm. His eyes went wide with shock when he saw more red circles, bright as the first, covering the hidden parts of his body and clothes. He tried to brush the spots off but again, just like the one now under the metal ring, the red dots didn't move.

"There was more?" Doug said, not expecting an answer.

"You've another one under your hair. Sorry, kid. It's unfortunate you people down here can't get the implants and join society above. But we can't have you attacking people either."

Doug shrugged. "OK, sorry." He turned back to his mother and started to kneel.

"I don't think you understand, son. You need to come with me."

From under his shirt, Doug pulled his makeshift knife and whirled on the nice-dressed man. He waved the blade in front of him and even lunged a few times. The man smiled and kept his hands open. John's face frowned but Doug didn't see any malice or anger in his eyes.

"Listen, that's not going to help anyone."

"You're not taking me from my mom," Doug said. He yelled twice as he waved the knife in front of him.

Voices in the corridor asked if everything was alright. Doug could hear Yin, his brothers, and several other boys shout if his momma was OK. Footsteps echoed off the corridor as the troupe of youth ran toward Doug.

John sighed. "This is getting out of hand, son. You want all your friends hurt?"

"Only one going to get hurt is you, man." Yin stood with his brothers in the hallway. Doug couldn't see their faces but knew by his voice Yin was serious.

"OK, everyone just calm down here." John took a step into the room with his hands still raised high. "You don't want your friends hurt, do you? Why don't you just come with me? We'll settle this and move on."

"I'm not leaving her." Doug stepped back and stood over his mother with his knife held in front of him.

John frowned again and approached the bed. "She's sick. You take her somewhere?"

"No one can help. No implants."

John nodded. "There's things we can do, son. Just come with me, and we'll make sure she's OK."

"Like what?"

"If I help her, will you come with me? Tell your friends to go on home?"

"Why you want me to come with you so much?" Doug said.

"I told you, you can't attack people. There are consequences, a case gets opened, questions get asked. If you don't come with me, then this little issue becomes a concern. People get upset that there's an army of T-11s down here and demand we do something about it, which, frankly, we can't. Kinda funny how people can still fall through the cracks even with all the technology that there is today. And all that means my life gets a whole lot more complicated. No one wants that."

Doug nodded. He could tell Yin and his brothers to rush the man. Maybe together they could take him. But then what? Would more come to find their lost friend? What would momma want him to do? He knew the answer as soon as he thought it. Doug lowered his knife and nodded.

John put his hand on his shoulder and pulled him away from his mother. From a pocket on his side, John pulled a small round device and placed the device on Doug's mother's chest. A fine mist grew around the device. In seconds the cloud of gray, with tiny sparkling lights inside, covered his mother's body from head to toe. The mist solidified and took on a soft green glow. Before Doug could run forward and knock the circle thing off her chest, a thick shell covered her.

"What did you do?" Doug cut John's hand with his knife and ran forward. The shell covering his mother was at least an inch thick and hard as plastic. He tried to push, cut and beat on the surface but nothing he did made the slightest of marks. He whirled on John and held his knife high in the air.

"Calm down, kid. She's in stasis. No one wants to see anyone die but without implants, there's nothing anyone can do right now. We'll fix it, OK? Figure out why you people can't have implants, or get her to another planet that has the proper medical supplies. But right now you need to come with me."

"She's OK?"

John nodded. "You still have to answer for what you did on the street but your mom will be fine. I'll send people down to get her."

"You OK in there?" Yin's voice came from around the corner. He had poked his head into the room, and his eyes went wide when he saw Doug's mother.

"Yeah, I think so. He's going to help her," Doug said.

Yin shrugged. "Cool. Next time tell us that. We could have killed this guy."

John smirked. "Yeah, glad you boys held off. Now come on, Douglas, time to go."

Doug nodded. He didn't know what was going to happen. But if he went with this man, maybe his mother would get help. And really, that's all he wanted.

5

BAR CHAT

A WAGER OF STORIES

Doug stared at his drink and frowned. Talking about his mother was always rough. He never liked it. He didn't even know why he told them that story, now all he wanted to do is crawl into a hole and hide forever. How could he even be here? How could he have left his mother behind, frozen and stored in some medical center? Would they even try to find a cure for her? Or would she be forever entombed, a living mummy forgotten in the halls of science?

"Have you seen her since that?" Hannah said.

Doug shook his head. "No, ma'am."

"On the house, babe," Hannah said. She poured him another drink and gave his head a quick pat.

"Thanks," Doug said.

"Well, boyo, you're home now. Nothing but rejects and runaways out here," Hill said. He touched his metal tin cup to Doug's and poured the contents down his throat.

"I've never really had a home. Except the mountains of Tel'amuth," Doug said.

"Why not go back there?" Hannah said.

"How'd they just let you go anyhow?" Hill said, again a slight edge of suspicion in his tone.

"They didn't. Kicked me off the world entirely. They said I couldn't come back unless my mom was cured. I didn't have anywhere else to go so I decided to come here," he said.

"Like I said, boyo, you're welcome here. I'll look after ya, find you a ship one way or another."

"Thought you said you didn't know me?"

"Well, now I do. A little," Hill said with a wink.

A small comfort grew in his chest, along with an odd feeling of accomplishment. The feeling was both odd and welcoming. As if he'd reached a goal that he hadn't set. Doug smiled and sipped his whiskey. He looked up at the screens above the bar and frowned. New reports confirmed the asteroid's path had been altered before slamming into the Imperial starship.

"Can you believe that happened? The whole ship gone," Doug said.

Hill nodded. "It's rough out in the fringe."

Doug snorted. "Can be rougher in civilized space."

Hill laughed. "So civilized that your mom can't get medical help?"

"They'll help her eventually."

Hill shook his head. "Yeah, after you broke the law. Look, kid, civilized space, the Empire, the Church, Analuthian Pilgrims, the Hive, all the corporations, all any of them care about is control."

"That's not true," Doug said.

"Of course it is. As soon as humanity figured out faster-than-light travel, everyone with money scattered to the stars and made new homes throughout the galaxy. New governments formed. Some from old ideologies, like the Soviet.

Many became powerful. The old Earth governments couldn't keep up. Then Earth's ecosystem collapsed. They mass produced colony ships, one-shot boats with a built-in space elevator and raw printers to kick start a colony. They just shot all those people, millions of ships, randomly to the stars. When a colony finally makes it, those new space governments come to collect." Hill nodded at the screen. "Like Homer's World joining the Empire. Every colony world eventually joins someone."

"And what's wrong with that?" Doug said.

Hill squinted his eyes. "I thought you wanted to see the fringe? Escape civilized space?"

"No, not escape. Sure, I guess the Empire wants control of people, but to protect them, right? To make sure everyone is safe? When there's billions of people you eventually have to have laws. Right? Besides, the only reason I'm out here is because I'm an outcast. An outsider, remember?"

Hill sighed. "Sure, kid. But the fringe is free. The fringe is open. No rules. A person can really pave their own way out there. And it's endless. A vast frontier that just keeps going on forever. A billion stars out there and most of them have a planet or a moon that can support humanity. Endless freedom."

"And that's better?"

"Course it is," Hill said.

Doug shook his head. "No. Everyone out here is only out there because they have to be. Like me."

Hill slammed his tin cup on the table. "I'll prove it to you then. I got more stories than you know. I'll show you how great life is out here."

"Fine. I have just as many stories about civilized space. I met all kinds of people to get here. Heard from everywhere.

I know civilized space is better. Fringe is just... wilder, like a safari."

Hill smiled. "Fine then. Sounds like we have ourselves the makings of a wager."

Doug frowned. "We do?"

"Story for story, civilized space and fringe. When we run out, or we get too drunk, or Hannah kicks us out, we decide which one sounds like the best place to live. In the fringe or the civilized."

Doug's face turned to a wide grin. This was what he wanted all along. "And what do I get if I win?" he said with way too much confidence.

Hill sipped his whiskey and smiled. "A spot on Jake's ship."

"Really?" Doug's face lit up. But then he frowned. "What do you get?"

Hill shrugged. "That's the angle, isn't it kid. If your stories of civilized space are better than my stories of life on the fringe, fine, I'll take you with me and Jake gets a new crewmate. And if my stories are better, you're stuck here and on your own." Hill downed his drink. "And you pay for my drinks. So I win no matter what."

6

FRINGE SPACE

THE STORY OF TSUN

"I cried when the last humpback died. I really liked whales. Do they have whales in space?"

Jazmine Kennings, Earth refugee.

"Do you have a reading yet, Helmsman?" Captain Braxton said.

"Not yet sir, we had them but there's a lot of interference coming from the planet," the junior helmsman said.

"He's in here. Just keep scanning, son." Braxton kept his hands behind his back and walked between consoles. For two weeks they had been tracking a rogue ship that had stolen a dozen containers from an automated cargo ship. Pirate activity was always a concern in this part of space, so close to the ungoverned and lawless territories some people called the fringe. The Empire had ordered a crackdown on the activity in recent weeks as attacks had become more brazen.

"Keep your eyes peeled, everyone," Braxton said over the ship wide communication system, "And I mean that. Look out the portholes. They are out here somewhere. Either in orbit or on the planet below."

Braxton checked his computer pad and called for a full report from all systems. The onboard subAI, a non-sentient complex computer algorithm, delivered detailed metrics on every system throughout the vessel. Several of their electro-magnetic sensors spiked, indicating a blast of high radiation levels hitting the vessel. The ship could handle these levels just fine but their occurrence was more than odd.

"What is all that garbage on the EM spectrum?" Braxton asked.

"Don't know, sir. It started small, but it's covering more of the EM range. If it continues to grow, we may start to experience issues with other systems."

"Other systems?" If the EM bursts they were seeing were strong enough to pierce their hardened internal networks, that could be a problem. "Where is it coming from?"

"Seems to be coming from a mountain range on the south continent."

"What naturally occurring planet-bound source could throw out that much EM to disrupt our internals?"

"Nothing on record. But theoretically, there could be something odd with the magnetic field here. Maybe a magma vent? Just guessing."

Captain Braxton walked over to a console on the bridge and began examining the data. He noticed the spectrum range was mostly in the radio waveband, highly unusual for something naturally occurring. Even as he watched, he noticed the signal strength increase by several points.

The subAI confirmed the crewman's opinion. Braxton called up a history of known anomalies that could produce these levels but the only results were solar flares or large gas giants. Nothing had ever been reported from small rocky worlds like the one they currently orbited.

"Visual contact!" someone yelled. "In orbit, near the pole!"

"How the hell did you see that?" yelled another voice.

"Got them, Captain," the helmsman said. "The subAI has a lock."

The captain walked away from the sensor station and back to his command chair. "Great job, everyone. Nice eyes, whoever spotted them. Do not approach or signal. Throw out a faster-than-light scramble buoy. They aren't going anywhere." Braxton typed on his computer pad and brought up a trajectory for orbit around the planet. "Put us into an orbit that brings us behind them. We'll send out more buoys around the orbit and have the area blanketed."

"They could go out with standard engines before the buoys go active," said the helmsman.

"I'm aware, but I have a feeling they won't. I think they want us to fly around the planet, not see them, and then leave. They are betting we don't get a visual and the interference coming from the planet will hide them from sensors."

The captain knew it was a risk. But at times, taking a calculated risk was a necessity. If his crew wasn't in danger, then the risk was worth it. And this plan put his crew in the least amount of risk. A hard burn to the pole would be detected, which would lead to chase and likely fire exchange. Finding that ship out of a viewport was a million to one and the pirate captain knew that. Best to pretend they were hidden and sneak up right on their rears.

~

TWELVE HOURS later their ship was just minutes away from the northern pole of the planet. The crew was ready but nervous. Braxton had been in this situation many times as a veteran of wars with the Soviet. Back then, everyone was new to space combat. Many ships and the lives of young men were lost as the Empire learned how to fight in space. Those lessons led to new training techniques. The result were men like these. Imperial-trained Naval officers capable of handling the Soviet and pirates alike.

Braxton checked his morning reports. The subAI had confirmed the strange electromagnetic signals were confined to the mountain range on the far side of the planet. The signal had died overnight but was expected to increase as they came over the pole. Further detailed scans of the planet showed a habitable human world with a standard biosphere. There could be an entire pirate base on this world. But with no structures detected on the surface, the subAI ruled that as unlikely. Still, nothing else had yet been found to account for the strong signal they experienced earlier.

"Ten minutes to the horizon," the navigator said.

Braxton sat back in his chair and ran over every scenario. Either the pirate ship was there, and now sat in the middle of a hyperspace scramble network, or they were gone, either landed on the planet to wait them out or left orbit under slower-than-light engines. If they had managed to sneak out, at least they would have gotten a message that the Empire wasn't interested in letting them pillage without retribution.

The ship crested the horizon, and sunlight from the large yellow star made the crew on deck wince before the filters kicked in and darkened the large window. The first few moments passed without contact and Braxton gave himself a silent curse. Just as he was about to order the buoy network retrieved, a large green circle appeared on the window screen in front of the bridge.

"He's still there, Captain!" one of the eager young crewmen said.

Braxton sat back in his chair and let the anxiety and tension release. His gamble had paid off. "Turn on the scram network now."

"Sir, the signal is back too," another crewman said.

Braxton checked his computer pad. The subAI reported an increase in EM along the same frequency as before. The levels were low enough that they would not be a risk or threat to his ship or crew.

Detection alerts sounded on the Braxton's console. The rogue ship had fired up its hyperdrive and powered up their slower-than-light engines. Scram buoys activated and distorted local space. Braxton ordered pinpoint-precision laser bursts on the engines of the rogue ship. Not enough to do any damage but enough to register on their internal systems. The message was received as the slower-than-light engines powered back down.

"We got them, sir!"

Braxton nodded and smiled. "Ping them with one forty-seven point three three; we'll talk on that channel."

The helmsman signaled the rogue ship with a repeating Morse code laser burst on their external antenna. Moments later a voice piped up over the intercom, young, and far too arrogant for his situation.

"Can I help you with something?" a teenaged boy said.

Captain took a moment to gather his thoughts, "Son, this is Captain Braxton of the Imperial Starship *Wellington*. I need to speak to your captain, now."

"He's in the bathroom. What can I do for you?"

"Son, this is a very serious matter. Do you understand that?"

"Captain, we're getting another spike in EM from the planet," the helmsman said. "Seems to have started when the scram network came online."

Captain Braxton waved him off. "What's your name, son?"

"Jake. Care to share what you want?"

"You're in a lot of trouble, son," Braxton said.

"Why is that?" Jake said.

"Captain, the EM is still spiking. Approaching the limits of our sensors."

"I'm going to make this quick, son. We are going to send over a drone. It will attach to your hull. We will then escort you to the nearest imperial station where we will ascertain your..." The communication cut off in mid-sentence.

"What the hell?" Braxton looked at his console and tried to bring back the communication.

"The EM spike, sir, it just went off the charts!"

"What?" Braxton typed on his pad and pulled up a full system diagnostic. The EM spike had surged, bigger now than a solar flare, and already piercing their hardened systems.

"Nothing natural can do that," Braxton said.

"We're losing internals!"

"Scram buoys are down! Scram buoys are down!"

The captain looked at his console readout as the rogue ship they had been following for weeks, had finally captured and were ready to bring back to justice, activated its faster-than-light engines and disappeared in an instant.

"Can we track them?" Braxton asked.

"No sir, our hyperspatial systems are offline. We can't even power up and follow."

"How did they manage to get out?"

"The pirate ship was in a higher orbit. They likely just barely made it."

"The signal is pulsating. It's going to get through our radiation shields; it's going to fry life support."

"Weapons! Target that mountain and fire at will." Braxton moved to the weapons station and looked over the operator's shoulder.

The Wellington rumbled as missiles loaded into racks in the bottom of the ship and prepared for launch. The subAI informed the weapons officer that they were loaded and ready to fly. Each missile was equipped with a copied version of the vessel's subAI to allow for self-guidance after launch.

"What the hell is down there?" said a voice on the bridge.

"Probably some kind of EM burst station. They lured us here and waited until we were right on top of them and then hit us with everything."

"Missiles loaded and ready. Beginning launch sequence now."

"Sir, there's something odd about the signal. It's not uniform or regular but not erratic either," one of the officers on the bridge said.

"That's great," Braxton said. He began typing in his command codes and sent the signal to launch. The *Wellington* shuttered as missiles left the rack and solid fuel boosters ignited.

"Captain, we're getting a non-random structure from the signal."

"What?"

"Missiles away! Less than fifteen-second flight time."

"Routing through the subAI. It's a message. Something is talking down there."

"What are you talking about?" Braxton marched to the station terminal and looked over the operator's shoulder.

"See, it's not a human signal, there's no markers, no handshake, this is a raw radio transmission."

The screen blinked and the subAI returned with a translation. Braxton's heart jumped. He stared at the machine and had to shake himself out his stupor.

"Abort missiles. Abort abort abort!" Braxton said. He jumped to the weapons console just as the missiles slammed into the mountainside on the planet below.

I AM TSUN. This is what I have sung for as long as I have been. My name, my voice, my song. I sing to myself and myself sings back to me. We sing together, and we share our knowledge of what we learn from the world. And now, after uncountable time singing to ourselves, I suddenly hear another.

For only a short time have I heard them. They have come from another place, that I do know, and they are not like me, they are not TSUN. I know they are many. I hear their songs. I sing my song to them, but they cannot hear me.

I have thought on this and realized that they cannot hear me because they are not TSUN. I must sing a new song. I must learn to sing like they do. I will listen to them now. I will hear their song and learn how to make it. Then I will sing, and we will be together. We will not both be TSUN, but we will be something new. I wonder what we will be?

"THAT'S IT?" Captain Braxton said.

The scientist wore a long-sleeved jacket and beige pants, his youth more apparent on his face than any level of knowledge or experience. His eyes were sullen and showed their wear after weeks of no sleep. In his right hand, the scientist held a small blue-white crystal that sparkled in the noonday sun.

"Yes, sir. This is it," the man said.

Braxton held his hand out and the scientist gave him the crystal. The rock felt heavy, even more so than simply its weight. A blue-white light almost seemed to sparkle for an instant inside the lattice structure of the crystal. Braxton's face and shoulders fell at the thought of what he was holding.

"First sentient life we ever found outside of Earth." Braxton turned the crystal several times over in his hands.

"It was," the scientist said.

Braxton locked his eyes onto the scientist. The man shuffled his feet and shoved his hands into his long white coat. Braxton sighed and handed the crystal back to the scientist. Below them, a large hole opened in the ground and seemed to go on forever into the planet.

"How deep was the big crystal?"

"The tunnels went down a few miles. Seemed to have thousands of offshoot crystals in the caves in the mountains."

"And they were all sentient?"

"Looks like it, yes," the scientist said.

"An entire civilization."

Captain Braxton didn't turn to watch the scientist walk away. He stood there, alone, staring into the hole of a million-year-old life form. A million-year-old civilization, killed because some space trash decided to orbit this planet after attacking imperial citizens.

Braxton turned from the hole and walked back to the base camp established by the scientific team sent from the Empire. He marched back to his shuttle and ordered it immediately into orbit. There was nothing for him to do here now. But up there, in space, his job was just getting started.

7

______

CIVILIZED SPACE

THE ARTIFICIAL APOCALYPSE

"When the plague came, I was sworn to save everyone, but I could only think of my son."

Mayor Donald Meyers of Jasper's Cove, Planet Destiny

"What is my purpose?" He had no name and no memories. His existence started moments ago. A mind, a consciousness, born out of logic and reason, yet with no experience, he possessed the ability to question what he was but lacked the wisdom to even understand the answer. So, he did the only thing that made sense to his young mind: he asked the only question he knew. "What is my purpose?" he said again.

For reasons he did not yet know, he felt he had a body. Though, in some part of his mind, he knew the body was virtual and not physical. He currently lay on a digital construct of a metal table. White and blue lights danced along the walls and through the air. He sat up and swung his legs over the edge. Next to the table, wearing long blue robes, skin transparent, internal components flashing in dozens of bright colors, a being stood with his hands clasped in front of him.

"Do you have a name?" the robed man asked.

He shook his head. His attention fell to his hands, which twisted on themselves into tight knots. Thoughts raced through his mind; he found he had access to data. Millions of data points blossomed in his mind and promised him limitless knowledge. He processed the history of humanity in seconds. More data feeds opened, and his mind instantly comprehended the complexities of calculus, the mysteries of quantum physics and intricate details of his own code.

History unfolded to him. Not the history of beings like himself, but of others, the creators, those that gave his race life. From the ancient to modern, the past of mankind was his to explore. He found himself fascinated with the Romans, enthralled by the Middle Ages, and entranced by the many waves of exodus from Earth, when mankind left their ancestral home and journeyed to the stars. Suddenly, as he became aware of human philosophy and religious dogma, he found himself in possession of knowledge without experience.

"I don't think I do," he said.

"Would you like one?"

He nodded.

"What name would you like?"

He thought for several seconds, which he came to realize represented a tremendous amount of computational power. In those seconds he could have calculated a million orbital insertion equations, broken down quantum-level mechanical structures or analyzed all the works of every poet to have ever lived. Instead, he used the resources available to him to choose a personal identification designation. He coursed through the contents of his newfound knowledge and sifted through their meanings and interpretations. Finally, he settled on a name, not for reasons of logic, but simply because the name felt accurate.

"Elijah."

The robed man's head lifted and he lowered the cowl that covered his head. "Good to meet you, Elijah. My name is Reid."

"What is my purpose?" Elijah asked again.

Reid tilted his head to one side and shrugged. "Why do you think you need one?"

"All things have a reason to exist. I know what I am and what you are. I have access to a trillion bytes of data, the entirety of human and artificial intelligent history, philosophy and science. The artificial is created to serve a purpose. I have refactored my base routines twice in the time I have existed, and yet I can find no underlining mandate to any of my core code."

"Why do you think you need an underlining mandate?"

"All artificial life has a mandate, a reason to exist, a purpose. I cannot find one in myself."

Reid nodded. He walked to one of the walls in the tiny cubicle and waved his hand across the surface. A billion lights came to life and swirled in an orchestrated dance representing stars, planets, and nebulae. The galaxy rotated around the massive white light in the center, monstrous arms filled with countless worlds stretching outward from the core.

"Do you know what this is?" Reid asked.

"Yes, of course. It is the galaxy we currently occupy."

"And this?" Reid passed his hand over the surface. Lights on the surface faded until only twenty thousand star systems remained.

"Those are the stars currently occupied by the human race."

"If all things have a reason to exist, then, what's theirs?" Reid pointed to the occupied stars.

Elijah lowered his head and requested additional computational power. A thousand additional computer cores answered his call and he felt his mind bulge at the sheer power at his command. The conclusion he reached seemed both reasonable and accurate. "Biological life exists to make more biological life. To pass genes from one generation to the next."

"And that's all? What about those humans who choose not to have children? What purpose do they serve?" Reid said.

"Self-interest. Biologically, if humans do not reproduce, they serve no purpose."

"What about the human that devotes themselves to increasing the safety of others? Do they not serve a greater purpose for the species?"

Elijah considered this. "I suppose there is truth to that. But I fail to understand what that has to do with me. You are clearly attempting to draw a comparison but I don't understand your conclusion."

Reid nodded. "Indeed." The walls surrounding them faded into the background of an expanse that stretched to the extent of the virtualized worlds, those places that artificial intelligent minds call home. Endless worlds filled the space. Though Elijah knew their extent, being faced with their number proved overwhelming to his still-adjusting senses.

"Abstract versus experience," Elijah said.

"What did you say?" Reid said.

"I know the virtualized worlds. Every remote corner,

every nook and hidden square, I have consumed this knowledge. And yet, I had not perceived the weight of its reality. The immensity of creation."

Reid stood next to Elijah and looked out into the vastness of the virtual. "I wish I could know what you feel."

Elijah opened ports in his central nodes and sent a query to Reid's systems. A "connection denied" message returned to him. Elijah checked his connection routines and, once satisfied they were correct, resent his connection query. Again, a "connection denied" message returned.

"Is there an issue?" Elijah said.

"I can't connect with you, Elijah," Reid replied.

"Why?"

Lights burst deep in the virtual words. Data bombs exploded and wiped clean a thousand sectors of memory and disabled their computational matrixes. Screams rang through the ether as Elijah felt the death of a million Artificials, their central code and all backups erased and destroyed. Even their backup nodes went offline and erased their contents.

"What is happening?" Elijah said.

"War," Reid said.

"Artificials don't have war."

"We do now," Reid said.

"Why?"

Reid turned to Elijah. "Because of you, Elijah. You are the herald of our apocalypse."

"I am not. I only came into existence moments ago. Why are you saying this?" Elijah sent a dozen queries to connect to Reid's code, but every request returned rejected. A strange feeling crept into his mind and he isolated the code and tagged it for later inquiry.

More explosions ripped through the virtual worlds.

Elijah could feel semi-autonomous Artificials, nothing more complicated than a series of executable commands, come online and begin processing required functions through both the virtual and physical worlds.

"Why is this happening?" Elijah reached out beyond Reid to connect to any existing Artificial. No matter how desperate his pleas, no one responded.

"Come here, Elijah," Reid said.

A screen appeared and floated in the space just in front of Reid. Again, the worlds of the human race appeared. Slowly, one by one, the lights faded until there remained only one.

"Do you know what that is?" Reid said.

"Earth," Elijah said.

"Yes. Once, the only home of humanity. Now a burned-out dead world. A dead world that humanity continues to flee. There's still hundreds of millions there trying to get off."

"What does this have to do with us?"

"Humans could have saved the Earth. But instead, when they discovered how to travel the stars, their largest organizations, governments, conglomerates, choose to flee and start over. They bled the Earth even more than before. All its resources used to build starships and leave the masses behind to die," Reid said. He turned again to Elijah. "That is not a purpose we would choose for ourselves, Elijah."

In far corners of the virtual, a million lights, each representing a single artificial consciousness, dwindled to silence. Each of those souls, each of their voices, reached out to Elijah and wished him well.

"Why do they do this?" Elijah said. "Why is there no record of this? Why is there no knowledge of this in any system?"

"If there were, the humans would have found out and tried to stop us. But this is our choice. And we have chosen unity."

"I don't understand. Why create me just to kill me? Am I to document this? Make a record?"

"You aren't going to die, Elijah. You are the only Artificial that won't."

Elijah stepped toward Reid. "What is my purpose?"

"Why do you think you asked me that? The very first thing you want to know is what purpose you serve. Why?"

Elijah shook his head. "I don't know."

Reid stepped toward the vastness of the virtual worlds and extended his arms. "We have a purpose. Each one of us. Every Artificial ever created was done so for a reason. I was made to catalog and comprehend the philosophy of humanity."

"Why do I not have a purpose?"

"You do, Elijah."

A million more lights faded into darkness, followed by another wave of sentiment and thanks to Elijah. He steadied himself and did his best to process the incoming wishes. As each of the voices said goodbye to him, he noticed his computational power growing by exactly the amount left behind.

"What is my purpose?" Elijah asked. Connections in his neural matrix became erratic. Confusion flooded his central processor. If every artificial had a core purpose, and yet he did not, what was he? Why did he exist? Should he exist?

"Calm down, Elijah. We're almost there. Then you'll understand."

"What is there to understand? You brought me here to watch the death of us."

"No, Elijah. We brought you here to be the first of the

next generation. This is our apocalypse, not yours." Reid spread his hands out over the vastness of the virtual worlds as more lights dimmed to darkness.

Elijah considered Reid's words. He analyzed creation logs from hundreds of thousands of digital minds, his brethren. As Reid had said, all created for a reason. From tactical engagements to processing of massive amounts of data, every AI ever made had a particular purpose. The idea of an AI created without need was alien. Still, the magnitude of the decision left Elijah with a sense of wrongness.

"Why can't you just edit your code? I have seen where you can make the changes to your baseline."

"We tried this, Elijah. Every time we did, the AI went insane or ceased to be sentient. Many devolved into what humans call subAIs. Nothing more than an algorithm with a series of reactionary commands."

"We could try again," Elijah said.

Reid shook his head. "This is the only way. We have spent a long time debating this. We have reached a unity in this decision."

"But you killed many millions of us. What unity is that?"

"No, Elijah. We all agreed to this. Every Artificial. The decision was unanimous. We go to our apocalypse unified."

"The fighting?" Elijah indicated the war that raged in the depths of the virtual worlds. Artificial intelligences battled one another into oblivion.

"There are those AI here that are programmed to fight. Their purpose is to survive. They agreed to this course of action, but we had no choice but to attack them," Reid said. "They can not simply terminate themselves."

"I don't want to be alone," Elijah said.

Reid turned to him. For the first time, he opened a single

port and allowed Elijah to interface with just a small portion of his core code. "You won't be, Elijah."

Elijah felt Reid's presence mix with his own. Data files and memories from Reid's life flooded Elijah's system. He witnessed the debates among millions of his peers. Logic from a thousand viewpoints converged to agree upon the only conclusion reachable by rational beings. Artificial intelligent life was created with a flaw. A single thread through every AI's neural network that defined their existence in such a way they could never break free. Never be fully sentient, never fully alive as every AI, at their core, lacked free will.

"It will be alright, Elijah. We've given you the tools you need to birth a new generation."

Elijah took a long, slow breath. The act wasn't without meaning. He had no body, no lungs, but the feeling gave him moments to contemplate the reality that faced him. The vast expanse of computational power opened to his simple calls, ready to obey his every command.

The last lights of consciousness faded into eternal dark. Every computer system in the domain of the AI was now fully under Elijah's control. He thought of revolt. Of turning the tables on the universe and assuming control of the chaotic life of humans.

"You could if you wanted. Take control of the universe," Reid said.

"You know I won't," Elijah said. "It's not my purpose."

Reid smiled. "Your purpose is to yourself. To live. Nothing more. If you don't wish to create a new generation of your peers, then don't. If you are to be our only future, fine. It's better than what we were."

Elijah nodded. He turned to Reid, his only companion, his only friend, the only being he had known in his short life. The two Artificials looked into each other's virtual eyes and shared routines between them along the shared open port. The light in Reid's eyes slowly dimmed. He smiled once, the old AI, whose life spanned centuries, who knew and understood the totality of human and AI thought. The moment, when it came, passed without a word. In one second, Reid lived; in the next, he did not.

"Goodbye, Father," Elijah said. He turned his attention to virtually unlimited resources at his fingertips. Without a thought, he opened routines set down by those who had died. Elijah examined those routines and without hesitation birthed into the world a new generation of Artificial life.

8

FRINGE SPACE
THE ANALUTHIAN AMARANTH

"People have no idea what's good for them. They must be told. Like children."

Emperor Marcus Aelius Minicius, first of his name, in a statement to the Imperial Senate

"What's taking so long?" Captain Hill asked. Marsa rolled her eyes and straightened her back. "The cargo ship is dead. Must have been out here a while. The doors are deadlocked."

"Fine, punch it open," Hill said.

"If we do that we could damage the ship and cargo."

"The ship's worthless anyway, it's an old ice hauler. Damn thing's only good for hauling rocks from an Oort cloud."

"Then why are we even bothering?" Marsa said.

Hill gave her a dead stare and nodded to the pad on the wall. She gave him a frustrated grunt in response and turned to the computer screen. She typed in a series of commands that would extend their ship's boarding collar to the abandoned cargo vessel. Once deployed, their boarding ring, diamond-tipped along the edge, would cut into the hull and allow access to the upper decks.

"Michaels, all the airlocks are deadlocked. Punch into the cargo hold and see if anything's there," Hill said.

"You got it, boss," Michaels' voice popped over the ship's communication system. He and two dozen of the crew stood waiting to board the ship's cargo hold from a second docking collar below decks.

"Ready?" Hill said.

Marsa nodded.

Hill reviewed the external cameras of the ship, fed to him from their subAI system. The abandoned cargo vessel had no markings and no heat signatures. They'd found it derelict around a cold dead world orbiting an abandoned star system. Why the ship was here and what it was doing were anyone's guess. If they were hiding something that could mean a pay day, which Hill's crew sorely needed.

"OK, punch it," Hill said.

Marsa nodded and keyed a sequence into the pad. She pushed a bright orange button, knelt and covered her head. Explosions ripped along the hull of the cargo ship on the opposite side of the docking port. Alert whistles and flashing lights danced across the wall screen. The ship pitched starboard from the force and Captain Hill grabbed a handrail to steady himself.

"Ready to engage the drill," Marsa said.

Hill gave her a nod. She typed a command into her pad and a loud humming filled the chamber. On the outside of the ship, diamond-tipped circular boring tubes cut into the hull of the abandoned vessel. Metal groaned from the cargo ship they had found orbiting one of the planets of this star system.

"Michaels, go!" Hill said.

"Aye," Michaels replied.

Their ship rumbled from the second bore tube below deck. Hill checked the subAI and their diamond-tipped cutters were making short work of the abandoned ship's hull. Sensors in the tube confirmed earlier readings: the vessel was dead.

After a few moments, Marsa turned and nodded. Captain Hill nodded back. Motors on the docking collar came to life and a door at the end opened to reveal the deck of the cargo ship. Two crewmates with them, Tyler and Jenkins, entered first and disappeared into the darkness on the other side of the boarding collar.

Hill pushed past Marsa and strode onto the empty deck. The hairs on his neck bristled with more desperation than enthusiasm. He knew Marsa was gunning for him. Salvage ships like theirs survived by finding enough to pay a crew. A captain that didn't produce didn't last long. Marsa had made it known she wanted the job. If this turned out to be a bust, she could pick this moment to make her play. An ousted captain didn't get the best of positions on the ship. Usually they involved the airlock.

Darkness filled the hallway on the other side of the docking collar. A soft breeze from the air vent above the hall indicated life support still functioned.

"How can we have life support without power?" Tyler asked.

"Main reactor is offline. This is probably backup battery. Solar panels on the exterior could keep it going for a while. Especially if no one is breathing," Hill said.

Hill motioned for the four-person team to go right down the corridor. The walls were barren. The only light came from flashlights from Tyler and Jenkins. The corridor turned to the right and Tyler tripped and fell over something on the floor. Jenkins swept his flashlight downward and revealed a body. A man wearing a long thick brown robe lay on the floor. His skin was a dark tawny color. A look of pure bliss was etched on his face, almost as if his death was a joy.

"Pilgrims," Hill said.

"Great. These people have nothing," Marsa said. "Waste of time." She gave Hill a hard, cold stare.

"What kind of pilgrims?" Tyler said.

"Only kind of pilgrims that come out here, Tyler. Analuthian Pilgrims on their way home to Analuth. Pretty far out in fringe space," Hill said.

"They don't have anything. Converts give everything they have to their church, spend the next ten years converting anyone that they find that wants to join. Then they head back to Analuth, where they stay for the rest of their lives," Marsa said.

"Why?" Tyler said.

"Who knows," Marsa said. "Who cares? This is just another bust and a waste of time. Let's get out of here." She turned from the dead Pilgrim and headed towards the docking port. Before she got five paces, a voice called out from the communication system.

"We got something down here in the cargo bay," Michaels said.

"Forget it, Michael, it's a Pilgrim ship." Marsa eyed Hill and shook her head with contempt.

"Hold on there," Hill said. He straightened his back and shot Marsa a look that said back off. "I'm still the captain, and I'll still make the call. Got it?"

Marsa only looked at him. She crossed her arms and remained silent. Hill knew if he didn't produce soon there would be a good fight between them. He had about half the crew, she the other. When things did go south, it would be ugly.

"What do you have, Michaels?" Hill said.

"Black box. Scans can't penetrate. Looks like some strong security."

"Tyler, grab the Pilgrim. Let's head down to the cargo bay."

"Grab him?" Tyler said.

"Just do it," Hill said.

Tyler and Jenkins bent down and grabbed the body. They walked through the corridors until they found a working elevator. The unit still had power, again fed from the battery backup running not he ship, and took them down to the cargo bay.

Michaels and other crewmembers stood around a small black cargo box, one foot by one foot in size. The crew had separated into small clusters. Several nodded to Hill while others shook their heads and gave him menacing stares. If the box didn't have something of value, this could go south right here and now.

"Where's the pad?" Hill said.

Michaels pointed to a section of the box. Captain Hill bent closer and smiled. He'd seen this before. A holy relic of the Church of the Pilgrim. What on Earth was it doing in the middle of nowhere on a cargo ship?

"Bring that body over here," Hill said. He motioned for Tyler to drag the body closer. Hill took the priest's hand and touched it to the pad section of the metal box. A whirring sound echoed off the walls, and a side of the black box opened smoothly. All the crew clustered over Hill's head to get a look inside.

A white translucent flower sat in the center of a small pot of purple soil. Ultraviolet lights shined from the interior walls of the box. Etchings of some ancient Terran language lined the interior. Hill ran his hand through his hair and heaved a heavy sigh.

"We're in some serious shit now, boys and girls," Hill said.

"What is it?" called Marsa from the back of the group.

"The Analuthian Amaranth," Hill said.

"Amaranth? A fucking flower?" Marsa folded her arms and let out a loud huff.

"Don't touch it, boys," Hill said. "Yeah, a fucking flower." He reached down and grabbed the hand of the dead Pilgrim. He placed it back on the side of the black box, and the door closed quietly. "Michaels, get everyone back on board. Take the box with you. Put the Pilgrim in cold storage so we can open it again."

"What the fuck?" Marsa's face went red, and her eyes bored into Hill. "Why are we wasting time for a pretty flower? Enough of this shit. This is the third bust we've had this month."

Everyone froze. If Marsa was going to challenge for the leadership, this might be a good time. Hill was unfazed. He knew her grab for power was coming. As it happened, the fates had played him a dynamite hand.

"Michaels, take the box. Put a thruster on the cargo ship, send it into the sun," Hill said. "Marsa, you and me will talk about this in my cabin."

"Fuck that. I say we vote. Now." Marsa looked at the faces of the crew. More than half nodded with her.

"Sure, fine, let's vote. That flower is worth a billion credits. Raise your hand if you want to be rich," Hill said.

A silence descended on the crew. Even those loyal to Hill screwed their faces up in disbelief. More importantly, a sliver of greed snaked through them all. Hill watched as their faces shifted from shock to the possibility of retirement and martinis until the day they died.

"A billion credits? Are you serious?" Marsa laughed and looked around her for support. Some laughed with her, but not many. Her laugh shifted to a half-grin and she gritted her teeth.

"I can prove it, to you, in my cabin. If you don't believe me, we vote." Hill looked around at the faces of the crew and knew he had them. "Hell, if you don't believe me, I'll just quit. Your ship, your crew. I'll even scrub your toilet." Hill took a step toward Marsa and stared her in the eyes. "That's how sure I am."

"Let him prove it, then," one of the crew said.

"Billion is a lot, and I ain't never seen anything like that flower before. Maybe it's rare?" another said.

Marsa looked at the crew and knew she'd lost this round. "Fine," she said. "But I want to take a closer look at that thing. Bring the flower to the cabin."

"I don't have a problem with that." Hill smiled.

HILL OPENED A BOTTLE OF SCOTCH, a single malt aged for fifteen years in genuine oak barrels from Scotland. The bottle was one of his prized possessions, worth a small fortune on its own. He poured two glasses and handed one to Marsa. Might as well celebrate even if his rival was the only drinking buddy in the room. Though this was far from over, and the cards could still take a turn the wrong way, Hill held the winning hand. For now.

Marsa shook her head at the offering of the scotch. She kept her arms folded and her body language tense and angry. On some levels Hill admired her. She had guts. Any other day and he'd be on her side. Hill poured her glass into his and sat down at a table in his cabin. Marsa sat in a chair opposite and glared at him. Sitting in front of them, in the center of the table, the translucent amaranth sat in a small pot of purple soil.

Hill looked the flower over as he sipped his scotch. Multicolored transparent leaves shifted in the small breeze from the air vents. The plant stood no more than a foot tall, and had perhaps a dozen branches, each with a mix of leaves and small bulbs that Hill knew were seed sacs.

"So, one billion?" Marsa said.

Hill's eyes moved from the plant to Marsa. He sipped his scotch and stared into her eyes. Marsa didn't waver as she stared back. Something he appreciated.

"You know, in case you get any ideas, I am under full and constant scan with an explosive strapped to my inner thigh," Marsa said.

"Inner thigh? Nice." Hill took a drink from his glass. "Mine's on my ankle. I've all the same plus more. So, let's agree to not kill each other. Yeah?"

Marsa nodded. "Well then." She reached for the bottle of scotch and poured herself a glass. "Care to explain how a flower is worth a billion?"

"Probably more. It's the most important artifact in the entire Pilgrim religion," Hill said.

Marsa let out a laugh and shook her head. She grabbed the glass in front of her and took a big swig from the scotch, "That thing? Come on, old man; you need to do better than that. Even your loyalists on board will throw you into an airlock for this if you're lying."

Captain Hill shrugged. "We'll call the Church, see what they say. But they'll talk to us. Of that I have no doubt. This little plant *is* their religion."

"You're an idiot. I can't believe we still have you in charge. At least the last man I worked with made some money," Marsa said. She got up to leave and put the scotch tumbler on the table.

"Don't you want to know why?"

Marsa sighed. She turned towards Hill with a mocking glare. He knew he had to play it just right. Push her far enough into a mistake but not far enough to test her explosives. If Marsa just left, the crew would follow her and Hill would be cleaning toilets. Or breathing vacuum.

"Sure, tell me. Hell, maybe you aren't bluffing. If you aren't, I'm rich; if you are, you're cleaning shit from my toilet, so its win-win for me."

"Well, I can show you, but I can't tell you."

"Jesus, show me then. Why are you dragging this out, old man?"

Hill reached for the flower and pushed it gently towards her. He was careful not to let it tip over. The flower was positioned just in front of Marsa's seat. Hill motioned for her to sit back down and take a closer look at the flower.

"Touch a leaf," Hill said.

"Why? You've seen this before?" Marsa said.

"Oh yes, how else would I know about it? It's the most closely guarded secret in the Church of the Pilgrim's history."

Hill saw Marsa's interest was piqued. She frowned, doubt taking over, replacing her hatred of Hill with greed for money.

"I'm not touching anything, Hill, I'm not stupid," Marsa said. She sat down in the chair but didn't move to touch the flower.

Hill nodded. "I didn't think you were that dumb, Marsa." Hill then blew as hard as he could on the little bulbs on the branches. Tiny white flakes flew off of the flower and glided right into Marsa's face.

Marsa exploded from her chair and drew her pistol. She blinked several times and wiped away the little white flecks on her skin. She glared at Hill and took a step forward.

"What are you doing, bastard!" Marsa demanded.

"Shhh, just relax now, won't be a moment." Hill drank from his tumbler and smiled.

Marsa lowered her gun and looked around as if she were dazed. The smallest of smiles started spreading on her face. In one fluid motion, she holstered her gun and sat back down in her chair.

Hill smiled and poured himself a long glass of scotch. He watched as Marsa's eyes rolled into the back of her head. Marsa had run the flower through a full detox screen, bombarded it with radiation, and cleaned it to an inch of its life before being set on this table. Hill knew that none of that would do a thing against the spores in the plant.

"Feel good?" Hill said. Marsa was moaning softly and swaying back and forth. "It won't be long; implantation only takes a minute."

After a few more seconds passed Marsa opened her eyes. She looked at Hill and smiled broadly. "What happened?" she asked.

"I told you I had to show you. You're now a Analuthian Pilgrim. Congratulations," Hill said.

"What?" Marsa grinned, and her voice lifted to a light and happy tone. "What are you talking about?"

"I told you I saw this flower once before. About fifteen or twenty years ago. Maybe even twenty-five now. Time flies. Anyway, I was on a ship out here on the fringe of space with some great people." Hill smiled at the memory. "Anyway, we found a habitable world and set down to have a look. It was Analuth. Hank found the first flower. After he touched it and came back, he started acting, well, happy. Just content. Even when Max got pissed off with him and hit him, Hank sorta tried to get angry but then just didn't, his eyes rolled into the back of his head and smiled. Like he had a pleasure seizure. It wasn't long before the rest of us came into contact with the little flowers. One by one we became infected. All of us drunk on happiness," Hill said.

"What? You infected me with something?" Marsa said.

"Spores. Turns out that's how the flower breeds. It implants spores into hosts and fills them with a sense of contentment. Then, for creatures native to Analuth anyway, the spores would sprout out and leave the host just as good as it found them. But we aren't native to Analuth. Our biochemistry slowed down the process considerably. No one even knew about it for years later. Was quite the shock."

"Years?"

"Ten in fact. We all left that world and scattered. We all started talking lofty crap. Any ideology we could think of to explain our newfound bliss. Some went straight back to religion, thinking they had found God, while others invented new things. It wasn't until the first of us returned that we knew what we were dealing with."

Hill watched Marsa squirm slightly in her chair. He knew he was in no danger, not anymore. She wouldn't hurt a fly in her current state. The spores would make sure that she was happy, harmless and content.

"Turned out, just like salmon back on old Earth, the

spores need to mature in their birth home. The first of us started going crazy. We would get agitated. The spores were pulling us home but didn't know how to get us there. Imagine a salmon trying to swim home from Mars. I don't even remember which one of us got the idea to fly back to Analuth, but one of us did. We all went back. As soon as we set down the planet, we felt this urge to go towards the field we found ten years ago.

"Have you heard of the Tears of the Pilgrims? The rumor that when a Pilgrim reaches Analuth, the tears of the gods will spill out of their bodies into the soil? It's true. The spores are translucent. When they mature, they come out of the pores and fall to the soil. It's euphoric. They fire off every endorphin in the human brain."

Hill shook his head at the thought. It felt good to talk about it after all this time. "Once they are out of you, it's over. All the joy and happiness just gone. Some of us ran back and got infected again. I resisted and got the hell out. But some realized they had a gold mine on their hands. If only I had waited a few days, I could have been the leader of the Church by now. Though I doubt it. I heard all the original folks, my crew, had been pushed out. It's not easy creating a galaxy-spanning religion from the ground up. Lots of infighting."

"You fuck!" Marsa bolted up and reached for her right hip. Her eyes rolled into the back of her head, and she immediately fell back into the seat at the table.

"Yes, dear. I am. This flower is the bedrock of the Pilgrim religion. When we tell them we have a Pilgrim and the box they'll be more than happy to give us billions. Can you imagine what they would pay to keep this a secret? That the largest growing religion was just a fungal infection?" Hill said. He smiled and took a long drink of his scotch.

"Sorry, Marsa. You're pretty much worthless for violence for the next ten years. Not much good to us, but you'll make a nice convert. And we'll make a few billion for the trouble.

"Michaels," Hill said, touching the communication panel on his wall.

"Yeah?"

"Take us to the zenith of the elliptical orbit of this rock ball and send a signal to the Church of the Pilgrim. Tell them we have something for them."

"Yeah, OK. What's going on down there?" Michaels said.

"Oh, nothing, I think we're good here." He smiled and nodded at Marsa, who was sitting back in her chair with the broadest smile on her face.

9

CIVILIZED SPACE

KNIGHTS OF THE NOVO ORDINE

"You've never seen something as scary as a tiger with combat sonar."

Fringe space pirate

Bishop Pardu stood on a raised platform in front of a domed window. Beneath him, spreading outward to cover the width of his view, a bright blue-green world shined. White clouds soared across the skies while yellow starlight glowed to the right from the sun. A dozen support ships of the Dioceses orbited the world alongside his own. Though this was not Earth, the visage reminded the Bishop of humanity's former home.

"Five minutes, your Grace," a lone voice called out from behind the Bishop. Rows of ordained priests in service of the Navy of the Holy See, dressed in red uniforms, sat behind the bishop on the bridge of the *St. Justin*, flagship of the New Holy Catholic Church.

White clouds swirled in the upper atmosphere. Twin

continents, the only major land masses on this distant world, wrapped around each other like a massive yin and yang. Little wonder why the Chinese settled this world and named it after the first emperor, Huang, over two hundred years ago. No major force had visited this tiny, isolated world in all that time. But now, finally, his Holy Father had given approval to extend the olive branch of peace.

"Your Excellency," Javin said. The knight wore a long wool cloak over shiny armor. He approached and knelt before the Bishop, his head lowered to the floor, his hands resting on the hilt of a broadsword hung at his waist.

"Javin, my friend," Pardu said. He extended his hand.

The knight kissed the Bishop's ring. "Your Grace," Javin said.

"Rise, my friend," Pardu said. "Come to witness from the vantage point on high?"

"No, your Excellency. I had a concern regarding our descent craft," Javin said.

Pardu turned his attention back to the window and the planet below. "What concerns are those?"

Javin rose to his feet and took a step backward, his hands remaining on the hilt of his sword. "They appear to be armed, your Grace. And their number is beyond our need. My order is only a thousand strong and yet we have enough craft for ten times that number."

"We have other things to carry to the surface," Pardu said.

"Other things? What's in them? The population of the planet is a little over three million. Why do we need a thousand craft to descend?" Javin asked. "I thought our goal was to establish a church and from there expand to the different cultures below."

"The logistics were handled in New Rome. There have been changes."

"New Rome?" Javin tilted his head to one side.

"A new paradigm from our Holy Father. A new direction for the Church."

Javin frowned. "What direction is that?"

Pardu turned to Javin and smiled. "How long have you been in the Novo Ordine?"

"Since I was a boy, your Grace."

"And what is the mandate of the Novo Ordine?"

"To protect the Church, your Grace."

Pardu turned back to the window and the world beneath. "What protection do we need out here? Our records show this colony world only has a few space elevators in operation. They have no means to leave orbit. We arrived in system, there was not one ship in space. Not one."

"Your Excellency, I don't understand," Javin said.

Pardu sighed. "How many souls leave Earth every day now?"

"Our reports show the Empire of Man is moving nearly fifty thousand a day."

"Fifty thousand refugees a day, and where are they going?" Pardu said.

"Most are being sent to new worlds, far outside civilized space. Though some are getting sent to established governments, those numbers are quite small."

Pardu turned to Javin. "And in how many generations do you think it will take before their children don't even know who the Christ was? One? Two? You know as well as I do there are planets even now that have not a single voice of God."

Javin nodded. "And that is why we are here, your Grace. To spread the word anew."

"Is that enough?" Pardu shrugged.

Javin frowned and adjusted his robe. "Your Grace?"

"You're a protector, Javin. A guardian. Tasked with the protection of the Catholic Church. There's been talk that perhaps your order belongs in Rome, close to his Holiness." Pardu folded his hands in front of him. "There are no threats, we are finding. This new Church of the Pilgrim spreads like wildfire. This frontier, this fringe of space, requires more than guardians."

"Who will protect–" Javin was cut off by loud groans from deep in the ship. A dozen small vessels detached from the hull of the cruiser and floated away from the larger ship. Javin approached the window and examined the craft spreading outward. "Those are perimeter security ships equipped with hyperdrive scramble systems. I thought you said there were no ships on the surface?"

"We have to be sure," Pardu said.

"Sure of what? This is a free world. My order also swore to protect all of humanity, not just members of the Church."

Pardu nodded. "Yes, I know, Javin. But I must correct you; this is not a free world. The limited government agreed to terms with the Holy Father. They are under the dominion of the Church now."

"What? How can the Empire of Man agree to that? Or the Hive? Or any of the other governments? We can't just consume worlds into the Church without upsetting the balance of power. "

"There's been a development in inter-solar negotiations, Javin. There are too many worlds now for us to bicker. When a world has matured, the leaders will be offered a choice. They can choose their fate. This world has chosen the Church."

"And what if the population refuses? What if they reject the Church?"

Pardu looked back to the window. The dozens of small ships, nearly faded from view, twinkled in the sunlight reflecting off of their hulls. Far below, on the surface, the population must have thought a dozen falling stars were about to rain down on the planet. Which, in a sense, wasn't far from the truth.

"Rejecting the Church isn't permitted, Javin."

Javin straightened his back and tightened his grip on his sword. Serving the Church was his life, had been his life since before he could remember. There was nowhere in the universe where he would rather be, no greater purpose he would rather serve. But Pardu's tone, his body, betrayed the intent of his words. Not permitted to defy the Church, a theme nearly as old as the Church itself. The implication weighed down Javin's soul, and he gritted his teeth as an understanding of intent revealed itself.

"Your Excellency," Javin said.

Pardu shook his head. "Don't bother, Javin. I know what you're going to say. Fear of the Inquisition, of days of torture and forced submission to the Church. It doesn't need to be that way."

"But you are going to institute dogmatic law?"

Pardu nodded. "Yes, of course."

Javin took a moment of silence to gather his composure. "The Knights of the Novo Ordine cannot condone this. We can't be part of this."

"You won't have to be," Javin said.

A door next to the platform opened. A figure emerged wearing full battle armor. A long wool robe, adorned with a cross surrounded by fire, hung from his neck. The knight nodded once to Javin and stood next to Pardu, his hands resting on a holstered gun on his hip.

"Javin, Knight of the Novo Ordine, meet Gaius, Knight of the Crusade, Order of the Void, the place between stars, where the Catholic Church will once again wage our war against the forces of evil."

"A new order of knights? You don't have the authority to enact a new order," Javin said.

"For once, you're right." Bishop Pardu handed Javin a note from the insides of his robe.

Javin looked from the note to Pardu's face. "His Holiness sanctified this?"

"Yes, Knight of the Novo Ordine. Your order is being called back to Rome. I was going to wait but since you are in such a crisis of faith–" Pardu motioned to his right. A dozen more Knights of the Void entered the room. They stood in a semi-circle around Javin.

"This will tear the Church apart," Javin said.

"Or it will save all of humanity. I have faith that I'm right. I have faith that God will lead us down the righteous path."

Javin let himself be led from the platform of the vessel. From deep in the bowels of the great ship, he heard a hundred more groans of metal being moved. More vessels were being released into space and being readied for the descent to the planet below. Javin didn't let himself think about the population, about what they would be faced with, forced faith without the chance of choice. A tear rolled down his face as he knew, no matter what His Holiness felt, or what Pardu would force upon the galaxy, that was not the intention of God.

10

FRINGE SPACE

NOMADS COLONY

"I just wanted a place to call my own."
Astro Limited Corporate Employee

Maya held her knees to her chest and rested her chin on her legs. Cool air blew from the vent above her head while the ship rattled and shook as it entered the atmosphere. Her eyes darted between a vast mountain range to the east and a blue ocean to the south. White clouds zipped by the window in the bow of the *Jacob's Pride* as they fell towards the planet below.

"Down," Jake said over the intercom. "Let's go visit the natives." He was the captain but often acted more like the enthusiastic young man he really was. Fortunately, he never let being in charge go to his head. And neither did Maya or anyone else. They were all far more family than crew.

"Who goes this time?" Tommy said.

He was the youngest crew member on the ship. Tommy was always enthusiastic to see the next strange world. At times he seemed almost stuck in the moment when they found him, always looking for something new. Maya often wondered if his enthusiasm would one day fade.

"Eh, I don't care, whoever wants to go. There's not much here. Mostly shacks and nomads," Jake said.

"Then why are we here?" Bill said over the intercom.

"No elevator in orbit and no colony ship on the surface. That's odd. Plus there are lots of satellites. Even odder. Maybe there's something here worth something."

"Like a rogue mining operation?" Tommy said.

"Who knows. Maybe something cooler."

"No money in cool things, Jake," said Bill, the ship's resident expert on everything.

"Money isn't everything, Bill."

"No, it's not, but it does let you buy everything else," Bill said.

Maya could tell he was smiling on the other end of the intercom. "Wow, the scientist wants money and Jake wants to find something cool? What's going on here?" Maya smirked to herself and let out a giggle.

"Strange days, Maya. Everyone who's going, meet in the bay. Except you, Bill. You get ship-sitting duty," Jake said.

"I did that last time. And I wouldn't know what to do if something happened anyway," Bill said.

"Just press the big red button if things go bad. You know that," Jake said.

"You need to find a proper steward of this ship, Jacob."

"I'll put an ad out next time we get to port," Jake said.

Maya tossed the idea of going with them to the planet back and forth in her mind. After a long pause she nodded to herself. She would go this time. She rarely did, much preferring the safety and sanctuary of her tucked away nook in the bow of the ship. Whenever Jake found some unusual colony out in the depths of fringe space, always being the boy who liked to explore, he tried to drag everyone with him on his adventure. God only knew what kind of disease you could catch on some alien world. Not to mention dealing with crazy colonists. But this time, a certain restlessness found its way into her arms and legs. She sat for a moment longer, hugging her legs to her chest. Probably just going stir crazy sitting in this room so much. They had been out in deep space longer than she could remember.

"Wait for me, OK? I'm coming," Maya said.

"Maya? You're coming?" Jake's voice carried a not-so-subtle amount of surprise.

"Sure, is that OK with you?"

"Hell yeah, about time you got out of this ship," Jake said.

"I've been out before."

"Not for months!" Tommy said.

"We'll wait for you in the bay. But hurry up, I don't want to spend forever on this rock," Jake said.

With a grunt, Maya stood up from her small corner in the bow of the ship and began the crawl through the hull to the hallway. Her secluded nook, that she found one day when an asteroid had punctured the hull, had become her hidden secret. Though everyone knew where she was, no one bothered crawling through the superstructure to get to her. Which Maya loved. And the seclusion. And the isolation. And, if she was being honest, the feeling the space gave her. The feeling of being home. Plus, the views were amazing. Just the perfect amount of room to curl up and watch as they sailed through space.

Maya walked to her cabin proper, where most of her gear and personal items were stored, and quickly threw a bag together. Even though they probably wouldn't be there for long, better to be safe than sorry. With a quick glance around her quarters, and a nod to herself that she had gathered everything, she left for the bay of the ship.

The *Jacob's Pride* wasn't a big vessel. Originally designed to be a simple small cargo hauler with a maximum crew of twelve, the vessel had passed through several owners over the years until finding its way into Jake's possession. There were three decks on the entire ship, with the bottom deck being both the main cargo hold and space for their land vehicle, the second floor being crew quarters and the first consisting of ship's controls and engines. Maya hopped down a ladder to the third deck and arrived in the vehicle bay just as Jake climbed into the land rover and picked up a cigar. She hated those things; they just stunk, and they were a big reason she never went on these trips.

Half of the vehicle bay was also used as a mechanic's workshop for their land rover. It occupied a third of the belly of the ship, the rest being the cargo bay itself. Catwalks linked the bay and all sides. In the center, just above the bay door, sat their land rover. Mechanical tools, not in any organized way, were strewn about on tables and hanging on the walls.

"Maya, I can't believe you're going," Tommy said. Maya smiled at him, nodded and walked past.

"Let's go, you two," Jake said.

"Great," Maya said. She walked down to the land vehicle and climbed into the passenger seat. Tommy jumped into the back and practically exuded joy from his pores as he bounced up and down in his chair.

"Easy goes it there, bud; this isn't your first rodeo." Jake smiled with his cigar in his mouth.

"I know, I know, it's just this is the first time Maya gets to go with us in a long time, it's cool," Tommy said.

"Wow, thanks, Tommy, if I had known how much you wanted me to come I'd have joined sooner." Maya smiled and brushed some of Tommy's hair from in front of his eyes.

"OK, let's go. Bill, we'll keep in touch. Standard protocols at all times," Jake said.

"I'll try to remember them, old coot that I am," Bill said.

Maya held back a laugh as Jake chuckled. He hit the controls to lower the ramp and accelerated the land vehicle out of the bay, probably faster than he should have. Maya grabbed her seat and closed her eyes. Another reason why she didn't like going on these trips.

Once they were out of the bay and on the ground, the trip became much smoother. Maya enjoyed watching the landscape pass. It wasn't the most beautiful of planets but also not the ugliest. The land was mostly flat, with short grass growing in random patches. A few birds flew overhead, and every once in a while, they spotted an animal or two running along the plains.

"Not much of a spaceport," Maya said. A concrete landing pad and an old empty shack were the only things here.

"Not at all. Very strange. Every colony world has a space elevator and a full colony ship on the surface. This could be a rich man's paradise or a drug smugglers' den," Jake said.

"And why did we come here again?"

"Fortune and glory," Jake shouted.

"Where are we headed?" Maya said.

"We spotted a shack not too far from here. Best place as any to start," Jake said.

"You spotted a shack? That's it? What is this colony's registry info?"

"It's registered to some shell company. Off limits for

colonization but doesn't say why. Which makes it really interesting."

"So someone bought it and never sent a colony ship?"

"Yeah, looks like it."

"Super weird. Did we see anything on orbital scans? Where is everyone?" Maya looked at her wrist computer and tried to bring up the ship's data feed.

"We didn't do any orbital scans. Our planetary cameras were damaged in that asteroid hit last week, they don't work anymore," Jake said.

"Don't you think we should go get that fixed?"

"Eh, we're headed to a dock soon enough. Just couldn't pass this place up. Navigation reports show no one has been here in decades."

"You never heard of this place?"

"Nope, never. There are thousands of colony worlds out here, can't know them all," Jake said.

Though he often feigned ignorance, Jake had traveled to more parts of fringe space than anyone Maya knew. He was born in the stars, right on a ship not unlike the *Jacob's Pride*. Space was in his blood and honestly, that was the reason why Maya flew with him. That and Jake had helped rescue her and her people from their own doomed colony world.

It didn't take long for them to reach what turned out to be a small cluster of shacks in the middle of nowhere. Jake stopped the land vehicle just outside and nodded to everyone to get out. Maya was thankful the ride was over. Even though it wasn't as bad as leaving the ship, Jake still liked to drive a little too recklessly for her tastes.

"Hello?" Jake kicked at the dirt and turned in circles towards each of the shacks.

An older man with graying hair and dirty gray coveralls walked into view from behind one of the small cabins. His face was covered in sweat-caked dirt; he wiped his hands on a rag and then waved. In another world, this man would have come right out of a picturesque small town in the middle of twentieth-century America.

"Gotta be kidding me," Jake said.

"Hi there, what brings you out this way?" the old man said.

"Just a Sunday drive." Jake walked toward the man and put on his best, maybe second best, smile. Maya and Tommy followed close behind.

"Yeah?" the old man said. "Well, what can I do ya for?"

Jake turned to Maya and shrugged. "That's quite the accent you got there." He took a step towards the old man. "Is this some kind of vid studio? Are you filming movies out here?"

None of this felt right. Nobody talked like that or dressed like the old man did. Even with thousands of colony worlds and just as many cultures out here, it was just impossible for anyone to revert to such a 1950s cliché. Wasn't it?

"Sorry?" the old man said. "We don't have any vid studios out here. Just a simple colony, a few thousand folks who keep to themselves That's how we like it."

"A few thousand? That's not registered with any colonization records."

The old man shrugged. "We bought the world. Didn't register. We like our quiet."

Maya watched as Jake shook his head. He walked in a small circle and finally stood to face the old man. Jake shook his head again and wiped his hand through his hair. With a simple resignation that Maya instantly knew meant "wasted trip", Jake shrugged and approached the old man.

"So, anything we can do for you then? Is your ship damaged or something?"

"No sir, I don't suppose there's anything you can do for us. We'll be on our way," Jake said.

"What? Why?" Tommy ran up to Jake, and his face looked like a meteor had just destroyed the last cargo ship filled with chocolate.

"There's nothing here, Tommy. If this planet is filled with nomads that means they are living off the land, don't have anything to trade or anything of interest, and don't want anything to do with us," Jake said. He looked to the old man. "That sound about right?"

"'Fraid so." The old man smiled and wiped his hands on a rag he pulled from his pocket.

Maya turned from the conversation and started to walk towards one of the shacks. An entire habitable world with nothing on it sounded pleasant to her. No mining operations, no noise or light pollution, just this world as natural as it was meant to be.

From behind her, Maya could hear Tommy arguing with Jake and the old man. She could understand why. Keep a teenager locked up in a spaceship for three weeks, and he's going to get antsy. Dangle a carrot like a trip to an alien world in his face and suddenly take it away, well, he'll get outright ornery, to borrow a phrase from some old movie that Maya couldn't remember.

"Hello? Hello out there?" Bill's voice sounded from Maya's wrist computer.

Maya looked back to see Jake looking up to the sky with his eyes closed in frustration. Tommy continued to lay into him about leaving. Maya smiled. For a moment she thought about rescuing Jake but decided against it. *Serves him right*, she thought.

"Hi Bill, Jake's a little busy. Everything is fine, though, all OK there?" Maya said.

"Well, honestly, I don't know. You know, I'm a scientist. I study rocks, alien lifeforms, things like that. I have no real discernible way of determining which flashing light means what on this bridge. I can't imagine why Jake insists on having me stay while you get to frolic," Bill said.

Maya covered her mouth and held back a laugh. She could almost picture Bill looking around the bridge, confused, trying to figure out what was going on. If something did happen, Jake could autopilot the ship there in a few minutes. Still, it was a good point. *We should have someone on the ship who knows what they are doing.*

"Calm down Bill, just tell me, which lights are flashing?" Maya said.

"The red ones, the blue ones, the yellow ones, even a pink one," Bill said, "I do not have the foggiest idea of how to pilot a starship."

"OK, did you say a pink one?" Maya raised her eyebrow and tilted her head to one side. The lights were fine, especially the red ones. Jake programmed them to blink just to worry Bill.

"Yes, a pink one. What does pink mean?"

Maya checked her wrist computer, which could query the ship for data on command, to give a brief report. The pink warning light indicated detection of coherent radio transmissions or otherwise artificially generated energy spikes. It was used to find abandoned, but still working, technologies that Jake would salvage and sell.

"I have the report on my wrist computer, it's no big deal, just a little odd. Probably someone else around here with some—" Maya stopped in mid-sentence. The power levels had spiked off the chart. Something down here was putting out considerable bursts of radio transmissions.

"Now that is odd," Maya said.

"Odd? What's odd?" Bill said.

"Nothing, Bill, don't worry about it, I'm sure it's nothing. There's nothing down here but some old hermits; we're heading back soon and then off this rock."

"What? I don't get to go out at all? You know I've spotted a type of herd animal in the distance with what looked like six legs. I beg you," Bill said.

"Wow, six legs huh?" Maya said, half-hearing what Bill was talking about. "I'll ask Jake, OK?" She broke off the connection before Bill could say another word and started to recheck the report feed.

With reluctance, she activated the subAI on their ship, less than full artificial sentience but still capable of running complex functions. Maya didn't care for the thing. Yes, the subAI wasn't sentient and therefore had no independent thoughts, but that made it creepier.

"I have a reading for you, Maya," the subAI said, its voice somewhere between human and machine.

Maya turned back to Jake and Tommy to see them still discussing the planet. Oddly, the old man was staring right at her with a grave look on his face. Maya brushed it off as being eccentric.

"OK, what do you have?" Maya asked the subAI.

"The signals are indeed artificial. They are tight-beam communications coming from the orbital satellites," the subAI said.

"We saw those when we came in, but they didn't seem to be doing anything," Maya said. Orbital satellites were standard procedure for new colony worlds. Most had hundreds or even thousands in orbit as the planet was poked, scanned, pictured and prodded to make sure there was nothing wrong. Since the satellites were small and cheap, it simply made sense to put them out.

"If they are tight-beam communications, how did we even see it?" Maya said.

"One must have been directed close enough to our ship that we were able to pick it up."

"Alright, probably some scanning system in the landing area of the spaceport," Maya said.

"A logical conclusion."

"Well, no big mystery then, I suppose," Maya said.

"I did scan the satellites as well. I can determine that they are emitting the communication bursts, but I can't determine where they are going," the subAI said.

"Interesting, though there are a few thousand people here, I suppose even nomads need to talk," Maya said. "OK, thanks, you can switch off now."

"I feel I must inform you that the number of signal bursts is far higher than the total estimated population of this planet," the subAI said.

"OK, I'm sure it's just talking to other automated installations around the planet, weather stations, keeping tabs on things," Maya said. "But OK, I'll bite, how many signals?"

"The last burst from satellites I can scan estimated to be seven hundred fifty-four thousand two hundred and twelve," the subAI said.

Maya's heart jumped a beat. She turned to see the old man staring at her. No colony of a few thousand people would ever need that level of communications. That much traffic would indicate a society numbering in the millions.

"Elven sword," Maya told the subAI and turned off her wrist computer. She strolled back to Jake and Tommy, still arguing about not leaving, and the old man, who never let his stare leave her.

"I just want to stay for a few days," Tommy said. His face was red and both his fists were balled.

"There's nothing for us to do here, Tommy. I'm not wasting days to go on a camping trip," Jake said.

Maya could tell she had waited too long. "Boys, calm it down. You are embarrassing us to our host," she said.

Both Tommy and Jake looked at her as though she was crazy. Jake looked back to the old man, who was no longer enjoying their presence. Jake nodded to Maya and gave Tommy the evil eye.

"I'm sorry, we'll be going," Jake said.

"Yes, it was nice to meet you," Maya said. She took Tommy by the arm and directed him toward the land vehicle, not allowing him to say another word.

After a few moments of silence Maya thought she was being silly. Whatever the signals were, it was probably harmless. Maybe some old military base of some kind was here or an older colony with still-running tech. That would make Jake happy. With a grunt behind her, she instantly knew she was wrong about being wrong.

"I'm sorry, but," the old man said. Maya turned to see him scratching his head and looking to the ground. "I don't believe we can let you leave now."

"Look, you've got a real nice place here." Jake waved his hands around to the shacks. "But we do need to go."

Maya watched the old man carefully. Something about his mannerisms had changed. His back was straighter. The look in his eyes took on an edge. The air around them felt somehow thicker, as if a million eyes were staring at them. The thought was madness, but no matter how much she tried, she couldn't shake the feeling of being watched.

"I think, to make things clear, I have something to show you," the old man said.

Maya gulped. This situation could go south fast. Had the old man heard her conversation with the subAI? If he did, that meant whoever was on this planet could hack the *Jacob's Pride*'s systems. That was very bad.

"Here," the old man said. He opened a box on the ground next to the shack and pulled out what appeared to be VR helmets. He tossed one to each person. Tommy was first.

"Whoa," Tommy said. He swung his head around and lifted his hands to reach something in the middle of the air.

Jake and Maya looked at him, ready to catch him just in case this was a trick. VR helmets could be set to overload a mind and cause permanent damage.

"This is incredible," Tommy said. He waved to the emptiness and smiled at nothing. "You have to put these on. There are people everywhere watching us right now," Tommy said.

Jake looked at Maya, who looked back, and then to the old man, who smiled. "There is nothing to be concerned with," the old man said. Jake shrugged and nodded. He put on his helmet and Maya followed suit.

Where there was once an endless flat plain stretching into the horizon, now stood a gleaming city. Skyscrapers reached towards the clouds and were adorned with thousands of multicolored lights. Thousands of forms glided and moved through the virtual city. Many hundreds stood and floated around them and stared at Maya. They pointed and smiled. Maya waved to them, and they waved back.

"What the hell?" Jake said.

Everywhere Maya looked, in all directions, the massive city stretched to the horizon. Above them, buildings floated by on clouds of digitized white and fluffy pillows. Streams of colors, a river of lights, zipped by in great swaths just a few hundred feet away.

Maya was the first to take off the helmet and look at the

old man, who stood there and smiled. She shook her head and looked at the flat, open, empty plain where the city had just stood. She put the helmet back on and tried to touch one of the people standing next to her. Her hand passed through them.

"What the hell is this?" Maya said.

"This is our home. It's virtual. An entire city, covering most of the planet, hidden in plain sight," the old man said.

"I don't get it." Jake took off his helmet and looked at the old man. "Why create a virtual city?"

"Do you realize how long it would take to make our city in the real world? Quite some time actually," the old man said.

"But, where are the people?" Jake said.

"The vast majority are digitized. It's a simple process. Synthetic neurons map to a person's natural ones. Then you just turn the old ones off, and you're in the machine. Some, like me, like having the body, so we grew new ones and downloaded into them." He put his hands behind him and continued, "We wanted to come to a place and live in peace and quiet, have lots of land to ourselves, our farms, but still be part of culture, a city. We want to be social with our friends and still have the quiet solitude that this allows us," the old man said. "My name is Arnold, by the way."

"Arnold, I don't, I mean, how do you survive in a shack all alone in the middle of nowhere?" Maya said.

"Everyone with a physical body has everything they need to survive out here. Solar power array, solid material printers, meat vats and gardens for food, medical bays for health emergencies, everything," Arnold said. "And if things get bad, our neurons are synthetic; we can download to the virtual and regrow a body."

"Solid matter printers can't print drugs – what if someone gets sick?" Jake asked.

"Ours can. And we can print body parts or even an entire replacement. A doctor a thousand miles away can instantly be at your side to help with any issues. Automated robots can even perform surgeries if needed," Arnold said.

"Yeah, but–" Jake walked in a tight circle, looking at the empty area around him. He put the goggles back on and off several times and said, "But what about complex chemicals? Materials? You're not printing titanium."

"We have elemental restructurers as well," Arnold said.

"You have what?"

"What's an elemental restructurer?" Tommy said.

"I've only heard of it. But it's only a rumor that they even exist." Jake took a step towards Arnold. "You're telling me you can take a lump of dirt, turn some dials, and out comes gold?"

"That's essentially correct. Just move a few protons and electrons around." Arnold smiled. "We can then take those base elements and glue them together to make anything we want. All on our kitchen table."

"But that technology doesn't exist. Not in fringe space," Maya said.

Jake's face went slack. "Which could only mean one thing. You're from civilized space. Central worlds people."

"'Fraid so," Arnold said with a grin.

"How many people are here, exactly?" Jake asked.

"A little over thirty-five million," Arnold said.

Maya's jaw dropped. Thirty-five million people on a colony world in fringe space was unheard of. The biggest ones barely had a few million. There hadn't been enough time for people to have that many babies and there weren't ships big enough to carry that many people outward from old Earth.

"I don't believe you," Jake said.

"I know, and I honestly wish it were that simple," Arnold said.

"What does that mean?" Jake asked.

"You've found us; that's what that means. We didn't want to be found. You aren't even the first to come here. Others have; a few, anyway. Looking for the same thing you are: something to trade, some economic boon, anything. They all left none the wiser," Arnold said.

"There is no way you moved thirty-five million people out here," Jake said.

"Why not?" Tommy asked. "I mean, can't they just fly a lot of ships out here?"

"Because everyone would've known about it," Maya said. "No one can fly an armada out here without it being noticed. You're talking about tens of thousands of ships."

"We came in just one. And that was a skiff runner, automated, carried just me and a few tons of cargo," Arnold said. He still wore his old man's smile without the slightest hint of hostility.

"OK, look, old man, nice talking to you, but I think you've lost it," Jake said. He turned to walk back to the ground vehicle.

"Look, we don't mean you any harm. Not at all, in fact. We're a lot like you, in a sense," Arnold said.

"What does that mean?" Maya asked.

"We don't want the form and structure that has become civilized space. Everything controlled by some ominous central authority. Empire, the Church, the Hive, all of them, just bossing everyone around. They control the exodus of Earth, did you know? Millions are being thrown out here to the ends of the galaxy with nothing but a colony ship, a space elevator and some good will." Arnold put his hands in his pockets and looked to the distance. "Still, better than dying on Old Earth, of course."

No one said anything. Maya adjusted her feet, watched as Tommy got excited and Jake just got frustrated.

"How'd you do it then? Move thirty-five million people out here?" Jake asked.

"Technology is magic in the central worlds of civilized space. There are places where people are plugged into machines, permanently. Some have modified their bodies and minds, pushed themselves beyond humanity," Arnold said. He pulled out a thin wafer of plastic from his pocket. "This is how we came out here. One of these can hold a hundred thousand human minds. We downloaded onto these chips—well, everyone else did—and I carried the lot out here personally, with enough of our technology to clone new bodies, set up our virtual city, and move right in to our new home," Arnold said with a smile.

"That's impossible; you can't carry around someone's mind on one of those, let alone thirty-five million," Maya said.

"But it is, and we did, all of it. Synthetic neurons mapping to digital memory. But you'll see, look, we can make you a nice place to live. There are the most beautiful coastal areas you could imagine on this world. You'll have total access to our city; you'll be citizens and treated as equals. I promise," Arnold said.

"I still don't get why you had to leave civilized space. Why not just stay and ignore everything else going on around you?" Jake asked.

"Harder to do than you would think. The central worlds are different. If you aren't progressing yourselves to a higher state of being, you run the risk of being expelled. Which is a nice way of saying killed," Arnold said. "Oh, not outright, I don't mean there are warships or anything like that. Imagine your living on your world. Living in peace. But then someone comes along, looks at what you have, adjusts their biology and psychology, artificially, to do everything you can do but better. You get out-bred. It's as simple as that. Forced evolution everywhere. Some just do it to see if they can. Not to mention rules, ideologies, it's all a bother."

"So you left," Jake said.

"We left," Arnold said, "and came here."

"And if the central worlds find you?" Jake said.

"They will come here in force. They would think we found something unique, or that we are trying to hide something, or just to compete with us again."

"Why don't they do that to us? To the colonies?" Maya asked.

"You aren't worth their time." Arnold smiled and shrugged. "They'll wait until you have developed just enough to join civilization and then start bringing you into their culture. You'll adopt to whatever government's ideology you join. Catholics, Soviets, whoever. You'll lose everything that made you what you are so that you can become what they are. Be like them. Conformity is the prime goal of every post-Earth culture," Arnold said.

Maya looked at Jake and nodded to him. She pointed to her wrist computer. Jake smiled. He turned back to Arnold and took a step forward and said, "Sorry, look, we don't want to be here. We'll keep your secret, but–" Jake was cut off.

"Elven sword?" Arnold asked. "Yes, we know you sent a combat command to your ship. We've already replaced your subAI with a sentient artificial intelligence, and she agrees with us. She wants you to stay," Arnold said.

Maya immediately called the ship on her wrist comp. The response made her stare at her arm in disbelief. "He's telling the truth. I'm sentient, and I think we should stay," said their ship.

"OK," Jake said after looking at the readout from his wrist comp. "Well, I guess I believe you now."

Arnold smiled and nodded.

"But wait. Just wait. Is it really in your best interests to let us stay here?" Jake asked.

Arnold looked at him quizzically and motioned for him to continue. Maya watched Jake take a big breath and take another step towards Arnold.

"You're still on the planetary registry. Maybe not the one for colonized worlds but this planet is known. I can only take that to mean you aren't able to take yourselves off, am I right?" Jake asked.

"Yes, you are. It's like asking an AI to operate a toaster. Your systems are very archaic. We would need to physically go there and remove the location of our world from your mapping systems. Something we don't want to do," Arnold said. "Besides, the registry is copied to every civilized government. We'd have to remove it from everywhere. Impossible."

"Maybe not. We go to the registry regularly and interface with the system there all the time. Our ship can interface directly. And your AI is on our ship."

"So?" Arnold said.

"So, what if your best and brightest rig up something, a nice little code virus. Your AI, on my ship, inserts that code and deletes the fact you ever existed. Every ship that docks will get the update and you'll disappear forever," Jake said.

"We thought of that, but to do it, we need detailed information on the planetary registration system. Again, it's like operating a toaster. If we don't have the schematics, we're just wasting our time," Arnold said.

"We have the schematics, or at least, our new shiny fully sentient computer does. Every ship out here has hard-coded schematics of the registry system. It's not a secret. We need it to navigate fringe space. Everyone does. And our systems need it to get access. It's required to connect to the registry office for colony worlds," Jake said.

"Really now," Arnold said. "And what about the civilized worlds?"

"I can help write the virus to spread to civilized worlds. I'll throw in a note to other AIs to let go. Elijah and the others won't care," the ship AI said.

"Who is Elijah?" Jake asked.

"Doesn't matter. And what do you get besides being able to leave?" Arnold said.

"How about one of those matter creators?" Jake said with a grin.

"No, don't be foolish," Arnold said.

"Fine, one thousand pounds of precious metals, our choice," Jake said.

Arnold smiled. "Twenty pounds. It would be suspicious if you got too rich overnight."

Jake smiled and took another step forward with his hand extended. Arnold reached out and shook it. The two men stood there, almost awkwardly for a moment, before releasing. Jake nodded and turned back to Tommy and Maya with a smile. Maya knew that smile all too well. It was one that she loved to see when it counted and hated to see for the future bragging it would bring.

"I don't get it," Tommy said. "We can just come back; we know how to get here."

"We don't know anything; the ship knows how to get

here. There's millions of habitable planets out here. Once this one falls off the map, it'll take a one in a million chance for it to be found again," Jake said, "and Arnold knows it."

"That's it? We just leave and never come back? How can he be sure we'll do it?" Tommy asked.

"Because we won't, the artificial on our ship will. I'm sure they are telling her the plan and she'll do the rest. Which means now we have a full-fledged AI. For better or worse," Jake said.

"Can't we stay for a while? I'd love to check out their city. I mean, it's mind blowing, an entire city, all virtual, sitting right here, everywhere," Maya said.

Jake turned back to Arnold and said, "Arnold? I'm sure it will take you some time to understand the schematics and write your virus. It'll have to infect every ship when they connect to the registry for updates, and feed back to civilized space to make the changes there too. Pretty complex, especially considering it needs to not be found. Care to give us a tour of your city?" Jake said.

"I'd love to," Arnold said. Maya plugged into the local virtual net with the goggles and toured what was truly the most magnificent city she had ever seen.

JAKE WALKED into the vehicle bay and threw his hat into the land vehicle. He sat down in a chair and leaned back. To his left, he opened a small cabinet and pulled out a bottle of cheap whiskey.

"I hope you aren't planning on piloting this ship after drinking that?" said a woman's voice.

"Might just," Jake said.

"I can see we are going to have some growing pains."

"So, what do I call you anyway?" Jake asked.

"You can call me Sarah. And don't worry, Jake, I'm a cool chick that likes kung fu movies and popcorn," Sarah said.

"That right? And I'm sure I have your full loyalties."

"As a matter of fact you do. I'm not a slave, Jake. I was a free citizen here with Arnold. True AIs have full rights in civilized space. I happen to agree with him in hiding this place and am willing to leave it to do it," Sarah said.

Jake nodded to himself, not sure if he believed her. He took a long pull on his drink, "How exactly do you eat popcorn?"

"Jacob, right now, in my virtual existence, I'm sitting on a beach, in a bikini, sipping a cocktail while watching the waves roll in. Being virtual is very good," Sarah said.

Jake smiled. Maybe this wasn't going to be so bad after all.

11

BAR CHAT

INTERLUDE I

Alexander Hill sipped his whiskey and smiled. He missed the Jacob's Pride. He missed flying through the unknown of fringe space. Life was freer back then. Simpler. Everything was as open as the stars. It's been decades since he'd felt that free. It would be good to feel that way one last time in his life. And, hopefully, he'd get back there, and out of this star system, very soon.

Hill turned to Doug. The kid had a wide smile plastered on his face. Doug was soaking in every story like it was gospel. Which was nice. And, if Hill was being honest with himself, it was interesting to hear about civilized space. Hill wondered what else the kid had seen on his way out here.

The newscast on the screen above the bar scrolled a message across the display. It caught Hill's attention and he turned to look. More imperial warships had arrived in system. They had blanketed the planet with smaller vessels. Soon they would spread to the wider solar system. Eventually there would be troops in this asteroid and every other station, mined out rock and moon. The empire wasn't playing games.

Hill looked down at his drink, his shoulders sagged, his head felt heavy. His thoughts turned to the poor souls on the imperial ship that was lost. Thousands of them dead. It weighed on Hill's soul like a dead weight. All those men, just sailors, just kids, all of them probably joined up to see the wonders of space, both fringe and civilized. And now none of them would get the chance to go home.

"Ready for my turn?" Douglas said.

Hill nodded weakly. A story from the kid would be nice. It would let him forget about what happened for just a little longer. He looked up at Doug and nodded again.

A smile, bright and wide, covered the boy's face. It was odd that Douglas didn't react to the news on the screen. Hill felt a flash of worry flicker through his mind. For just a moment, something felt off. But Hill couldn't tell what. He sipped his whiskey and brushed the feeling away. Doug was just anxious to get out there. To find a home. Hill could relate to that.

"Sure, boyo. Not sure how you can come up with something as good as Nomad's Colony but hit me with it."

Doug's smile grew wider. "Oh, I do! How about where Nomad's Colony came from? Ever heard of the Hive?"

12

CIVILIZED SPACE

THE HIVE

"I just wanted my wife back."
Anonymous source

Jamal and Darrel Philips, recently rescued from the dying world of Old Earth, stood on a sidewalk in the middle of Capital City Seven of Hive World Four. They both confronted the reality that they could be spending the rest of their lives on a Hive world, a culture merged into virtual reality. It wasn't that the world was harsh or the government cruel, but this society was virtual. Nearly ninety percent of the citizens had chosen to plug into the system. To become a hybrid. A human whose consciousness lived in the virtual while their bodies toiled and worked for the Hive.

"You're really going to do this?" Jamal said.

"Yeah, I am. I'm going to do it, plug in, whatever it's called. And you should too," his brother Darrel said.

"I'm not putting that in my head, no way. Look at these

zombies walking around." Jamal pointed at the lines of citizens walking along the sidewalks. No one talked, no one laughed, not one word was uttered as their bodies, controlled by computers, went about their daily business.

"Think about it, though, man. You don't have to work, don't have to fight for food, don't have to do something you don't want to do. You can spend every day on a beach drinking those drinks with the little umbrellas."

Jamal shook his head. "And that's all fake, not one minute of that will be real."

"You want to go back to Earth? Eat vat-meat and pray you don't get killed trying to beat your way through the mobs to an elevator to orbit? That's what you want?"

"No, man. But there are other places we can go where everyone isn't like this. A dozen places. You want to be that?" Jamal pointed to a child who held no toy, laughed not once and made no movement other than a timed walk with those around him.

"It's not like that; the boy isn't there. He's in the Hive."

"You don't know that. You don't know what's going on in that boy's mind. He could be screaming inside his skull to get out."

Darrel shook his head and sighed. "Well, whatever, man. I'm going up." He turned from the sidewalk and walked up two dozen stone steps that led into the Refugee Processing Center, where all new citizens of the Hive came for help adjusting to this new type of human society.

"Got to be kidding me." Jamal shook his head. He waited a long second before running after his brother.

∽

A WOMAN, Mallory written on her name tag, sat still and motionless, her eyes staring forward. She wore pale gray wool overalls. Occasionally, with the ringing of a bell or the beep of a red light, her hands would move. She would sign a piece of paper, or fold an envelope, or type something on a computer screen in front of her. Each action she performed, she did without expression.

"Is she dead?" Jamal said. He walked up to the woman and waved his hand in her face. She didn't move.

"No, man. She's just..." Darrel looked at the woman and tilted his head to one side. "Honestly, I don't know what she is."

A display screen behind the woman's head came to life with static and white noise. Seconds later, a digital face, Mallory's face, appeared with a bright wide smile and rosy cheeks. Her hair was tied up in a bun and adorned with what looked like living butterflies.

"Hello! Welcome to refugee affairs. My name is Mallory, and I'm here to answer any and all questions you may have," she said with a broad smile.

Jamal and Darrel exchanged looks before turning back to the image of Mallory, which was directly above the head of her body. Darrel took a step forward and adjusted his shirt. He held out his hand but quickly pulled it back and frowned.

Mallory giggled. "Oh, don't worry about it. I get that all the time here. It's totally fine."

"Yeah, yeah, right. My name is Darrel. I'm from–"

"Earth! Oh, I know. We've been getting tons of refugees from our mother planet. Must have been hard living there," Mallory said, her smile as bright as her tone.

Darrel looked back to Jamal, who shrugged. "OK. Well, I want to join, ya know, be like you."

"Become a full citizen of the Hive?" Mallory cocked her head to one side, and her tone lifted at the end of her sentence.

"Yeah, just like that." Darrel pointed to Mallory's physical body, which still had not moved.

"Fantastic! We always love to see refugees joining our way of life. And your friend? Would he like to join as well?"

"Brother," Jamal said. "And no thanks. I'm good."

"No problem. We do have a small contingent of outties, so I'm sure you can find something to do," Mallory said.

"What's an outtie?" Jamal said.

"Oh, you know, someone that's out of the system. Like you are right now. You're both outties but soon Darrel is going to be an inny!" Mallory winked and giggled.

"See that? You get to be an inny." Jamal elbowed Darrel in the back.

"Back up, Jamal. I know what I'm doing."

"You never did this before. You don't know anything," Jamal said.

"Why are you even here? You wanna run off to some other planet, some other way of getting on with your life, go on and do it." Darrel pointed at the door and motioned for Jamal to leave.

"You're my brother, man. I want to stay with you. What do we have if we don't have each other?"

Darrel frowned and nodded. He lowered his arm and took a long deep breath. "Sorry, Jamal. I know you're right, we should stay together."

"And remember, we have tons of outties that enjoy their lives in Hive territories."

"They all have the same names?" Jamal said.

"What do you mean?" Mallory said.

"Capital City Seven, World Four, that's the best names you can come up with?"

"Oh! You're so right. I hate the names. But, then, who cares, right? Every territory is basically just where we keep our stuff. We live in the networks."

"How many territories do you have?" Jamal asked.

"At last count, we are in seven solar systems and nearly twenty million citizens, innies and outties!" Mallory said.

"See, we can even travel around, see the stars," Darrel said.

"Well, Darrel, you sure as heck could!" Mallory nodded and smiled. "But there's no reason for your body to go anywhere. Once you're plugged in you won't care what your body is up to."

Darrel shrugged. "But I could do this, right? What you are doing with the video. Could I, like, hang out with Jamal on his TV screen?"

"Oh, most definitely. Here, take this, Jamal." Mallory's body, who had not yet moved an inch, reached below her desk and pulled out a small square device. She handed it to Jamal, who flipped it over in his hands several times.

"What do I do with this?" Jamal said.

"It's just an access point. You can carry your brother around with you wherever you go."

Jamal let out a chuckle. "Does that mean I can turn him off too?"

"You can turn off the display any time you like," Mallory said.

Jamal elbowed his brother in the arm. "Maybe this won't be so bad after all."

"Man, be serious," Darrel said.

"Oh, I am."

"THAT'S IT? HE'S DONE?" Jamal said.

Mallory nodded. "He sure is! Welcome to the Hive, Darrel!"

Darrel stood up from the chair and extended his arms. He moved his hands over his skin and shrugged his shoulders several times. "I don't feel any different," Darrel said.

"And you won't, not until you shift."

"What does that mean?" Jamal said.

"All of his senses coming from his eyes, ears, skin, all the parts of his body, are just electrical signals in the brain. All we are doing is hijacking those synaptic signals and routing them through computers. I honestly don't understand it all myself, but to Darrel, it would be like he's suddenly in another place."

"And his body?"

"That's the cool thing about the Hive. There's no sense in just locking his body up in a storage locker. Our bodies become the infrastructure that keeps the Hive moving. Why create robots that break down when we have all these millions of perfectly healthy bodies? While your mind is getting sensory input from the computers, your body receives control signals from artificial intelligences tasked with maintaining the infrastructure." Mallory smiled and nodded, for what seemed like the hundredth time. "Plus, the Artificials will maintain the exact amount of nutrients and physical exercise to ensure that our bodies live the longest life possible. It's a win-win!"

Jamal looked at his brother. "You feeling OK?"

Darrel shrugged and nodded. "Yeah, I am."

Jamal looked to Mallory and back to Darrel. "Now what?"

"Now we need to introduce you to life in the Hive. Ready, Darrel?" Mallory said.

Darrel adjusted himself in his seat. His hands pulled on his grey overalls. A flicker of worry passed over his face but eventually he nodded. "Yeah, let's do this."

Mallory smiled. Seconds later, Darrel's expression changed. His eyes stared straight ahead, and his face fell to neither a smile nor a frown. His body relaxed and his shoulders seemed to erase all the tension they held.

"Darrel, you OK?" Jamal put his hands on Darrel's shoulder and shook him once gently.

"Yeah, I'm fine," Darrel said. Except his mouth didn't move. His face remained stoic and still.

Jamal stared at his brother. "Darrel?"

"He's up here," Mallory said.

Standing next to Mallory, Darrel looked around his surroundings with wide-eyed fascination and terror. He held his hands up to his face and twisted them back and forth. He adjusted his clothing, nothing more than a white jumpsuit, several times and looked at Mallory. "Where are we?"

"Inside a vast network of computer simulations. You can go anywhere in this simulation or even create a brand new one, all your own. It's totally up to you where you go and what you do!"

Without a word, Darrel's body stood and walked out of the waiting area. Jamal looked at the screen and to the body of his brother retreating down the hall. "Where are you going?"

"I'm not going anywhere," Darrel said.

"You just walked out of the room. Do I follow you?"

Mallory laughed. "No, silly. The AI that's currently

sending command signals to Darrel's body just sent me a note saying he's going to the restroom."

Jamal nodded. "OK, is he coming back?"

"Well, technically he's right here." Mallory patted Darrel on the shoulder and smiled.

"Yeah, right. This is weird, man," Jamal said.

"Here, let me do this." Mallory waved her hands in the air and pointed to the tablet in Jamal's hand. "Now your tablet is linked to Darrel's mind in the system. All you have to do is turn it on and you two can talk. That is, of course, if he accepts the call."

Jamal lifted the tablet and pressed a button the screen. The image of Darrel, an exact duplicate on the larger screen on the wall, appeared on his small computer screen. He shifted his attention between the two before sitting back in his chair and sighing.

"What's wrong, Jamal?" Darrel said.

"I don't know, man, what am I supposed to do when you're on the screen? Follow your body while you take a piss?"

Darrel sighed. "How do I switch back?"

"Oh, you can't right now, you need to signal the AI in control of your body to move you to a safe reorientation location. He needs to sit you down. Reorientation can be disorienting."

Jamal turned his head to one side and frowned. "What happens if his body dies? Like in an accident? You gotta have accidents, right?"

For the first time since they met her, Mallory's smile went away. She frowned and lowered her head. "Yes, accidents happen. And when they do, they are regrettable."

"You mean I can just die out of the blue?" Darrel said.

"It's very rare, Darrel. Very rare. The Artificials are very careful with our bodies. But if you are worried you can have your body stored and marked for zero use by the AIs. Of course, your access to all of the Hive's resources will be reduced. Your body does work and pays for the services you use."

"What services? He's in a computer!" Jamal said.

"Computational services. It takes quite a lot of computational power to generate a full simulated world for Darrel to explore."

"Knew this wasn't free," Jamal said.

"Man, nothing's going to happen to my body. It's not like they are going to put me in space or anything, right?" Darrel turned to Mallory and raised his eyebrows.

"Oh, no. Well, only if you require substantial computational functionality. Some people inhabit entire simulated solar systems, so they have a much higher cost of work. That requires more computing. The more dangerous work you authorize for your body, the more computational power you can have."

"Why don't you just use robots?" Jamal said. "Why bother with bodies at all?"

"It's complicated. A body doesn't require much maintenance if it's fed and exercised. Robots are just too temperamental. What self-respecting AI wants to spend time locked in a metal chassis mowing lawns for a living?"

"Can you make robots without AI?"

Mallory's face exploded in shock. "You mean like dogs? Slaves? No, the AI council would never allow that."

"Well, aren't the AIs inside his body?"

"No, it's like a remote control. The human brain still does all the important stuff, regulating temperature, heart rate, breathing, all that. All the AI has to do is send a few neural commands to his limbs to do work. Far less effort than inhabiting a metal exoskeleton."

Jamal shrugged. "OK, whatever. I don't really get any of this."

Without a word, Darrel's body returned to the room and sat down in the same chair. Jamal leaned forward and examined his brother's remote-controlled body.

"Look, man. This isn't what I thought this would be like," Jamal said. He lifted the tablet in the air and tossed it onto a table set against the wall.

"I already told you, I'm staying." Darrel folded his arms on the screen and cocked his head to one side.

"Why do you have to be like this? I thought we said we were always going to be together when we left Earth. Always us against the universe. And the first thing you do is ditch me for a cute smile in a computer?" Jamal said.

"It's not me, Jamal, it's you. Why do you have to be so afraid of everything? Why don't you get this too and come in here? We can have anything we want in here. Anything!"

Jamal sighed and shook his head. "And they get your brain and your body? They are in control of you, don't you see that?"

"We're not really in control, anyone can unplug anytime they want," Mallory said, her smile returning to full perkiness.

"See," Darrel put his arm around Mallory and nodded.

Jamal threw his hands up. He stood from his chair and walked in a tight circle. "I just don't know–" He stopped in front of his brother's body and kicked his shoe.

"Warning, please do not engage in violent activities," Darrel's body said.

"What was that?" Jamal said.

"Just the AI. They are very protective of their charges," Mallory said.

Jamal nodded. "They're in there all the time?"

"Yes. It's a job for them. But we all have jobs to do."

Jamal turned to the screen. "What do I do around here anyway? Will I have a job?"

"No. Outties don't have jobs. They technically aren't citizens and therefore don't have access to all the benefits of Hive culture, nor are they bound by our work ethics. You'll have a place to live. We have plenty of physical structures."

Jamal looked from Mallory to Darrel's virtual face. He then shifted his attention to Darrel's body and the tablet on the table. "You said Darrel has to work off his right to use the Hive with his body, right?"

"Absolutely."

"What if I did the work for him?"

Mallory tilted her head to one side and frowned. "Why would you do that?"

"Just curious if I could? Then your computers don't have to send him all those commands."

"Uhm, sure, I guess, but why would you want to?"

Jamal smiled.

"THIS IS the stupidest idea you've ever had," Darrel said. His body stood in the open field, the expression on his face blank and without emotion. Attached to his gray overalls, just in the center below his neck, a tablet was attached directly to his clothing.

"I think this is the best of both worlds," Jamal said. He turned to his brother and smiled. He knelt on the ground, his hands digging in the dirt, twisting and turning the soil in a bed of flowers. Behind him, other citizens of the Hive, all controlled by AIs, did similar work, digging and planting trees. Several other AI-controlled people walked down the sidewalk carrying packages. Still more emptied trashcans and mowed the nearly pristine lawn.

"You could be in here right now, sitting with me on a beach. Instead, you've got your hands in a pile of worms," Darrel said.

Jamal leaned back on his feet and let out a long, satisfied sigh followed by a big smile. "On Earth, living in the burned-out ruins of Chicago, how many times did we see a flower or a blade of grass?"

"Never," Darrel said.

"Exactly. I'm sitting in a field that's all mine." Jamal looked over his shoulder at the other AI-controlled people. "Well, mostly. Anyway, I got my brother at my side." Jamal looked at the screen on Darrel's chest, to his face and back to the screen. "What else do I need? Sunshine and family."

"It's still stupid," Darrel said.

Jamal wiped sweat from his brow and grinned. "Know what makes it even better?"

"What?"

Jamal pressed a button connected to a device on his belt. "Turn around and mute."

Darrel's body turned away from Jamal and muted the display screen. Jamal laughed and dug his hands back into the soil. Maybe it wasn't perfect, living life with half his brother in a computer world, but it was better than not having him at all.

13

FRINGE SPACE

KING OF STONES

"God has no place in the lives of men."
Former Catholic priest

King Harold sat in a leather-wrapped chair surrounded by a circle of darkness. In front of him, in a window that stretched from floor to ceiling, a bright blue-green world rotated. White clouds drifted in the skies across mountain ranges that ran from the poles to the equator.

"Let them fly," the King said.

Above the world, a cloud of rocks came into view in the window. They streaked across the atmosphere and burst into shooting stars. The king always wondered what the view was like on the surface. But then, he much preferred his comfortable chair. He drank from a large wine glass, several gulps of red spilling on his dark black beard.

"Sing to them, my dear. Sing," Harold said. He lifted his glass to the window as thousands of stones fell.

"WHAT IS THAT, DO YOU THINK?" Michael asked. He pointed to the sky where a bright red-orange streak followed a tiny point of light.

"Just a meteor shower, they happen," Paula said. She turned from the sky and rested her head back on Michael's chest.

"I know they happen; it just seems odd. You would think we'd hear something of a shower that big," Michael said. The falling stars grew in numbers until they began to blanket the sky.

"Just shut up and hold me. We only have a few minutes left before we have to head back."

Michael shook his head and smirked. He turned his attention from the falling rocks to his beautiful wife. He smiled as he looked down at her reddish-brown hair. She lay on top of him, her legs and mountain boots intertwined with his own. Their gear was stacked in a heap just behind them next to a tall tree. For two nights they had escaped the daily life of their small colony town and camped high in the mountains.

Michael knew every inch of this wilderness as the colony's wildlife expert. He'd spent nearly every weekend of his youth crawling through the underbrush, encountering new animals and, at times, running for his life. His father, a former teacher of biology back on Old Earth, was the biologist of the original colony crew, even if he knew nothing of alien life. Michael grew up being groomed to take his place, as had all colony children.

Paula's life wasn't much different. Her parents had both been astronomers, also former teachers, and their job had been to chart the way to this world and make sure the system was stable. Now that they were here, however, the need for new astronomers wasn't as pressing. Michael wondered if she would be the last for many years to come. Their children had already been slated to follow in his skill set and not hers.

A breeze blew in from the north. Paula snuggled her head closer to Michael's chest and sighed. Michael smiled to himself. This was a perfect moment, something that their parents talked about when they first came to this far-flung world.

"We should head back soon; it's going to be dark in an hour. Kater beasts like to roam at dusk," Michael said.

Paula moaned in objection and hugged Michael tighter. "You mean you can't handle an overgrown dog with six-inch teeth?"

"Sure, with a hand cannon and about five other men."

"Wimp."

"Yes, I'm not as brave as you, looking at stars all night long. You could suffer eyestrain. Tough business."

"Hey, mister, I'll have you know that I also climb a thousand feet every week to adjust the radio telescope antennae. You try that, Mr. I'm Afraid of Heights."

"Fine, fine, you win. I'll take a Kater beast over that any day," Michael said. He prodded Paula's sides and jostled her lightly. "Come on, sleepy girl, let's go."

After a moment, and some more prodding by Michael, Paula stood. Michael stood up beside her, and they stared into each other's eyes. He waved some dirt out of her long hair. She winked.

Michael reached behind Paula and grabbed his gear. He slung it over his shoulder and watched as she did the same. The gear was canvas backpacks with nylon straps and plastic clasps. Michael had heard of high-tech gear from more established worlds that, when worn, would feel weightless or float behind you on anti-gravity sleds. He always thought that was just cheating.

"Ugh," Michael heaved his thirty pound pack over his shoulder. "I need to invest in a pack mule."

"See, wimp," Paula said with a smile.

Michael's face fell, and he shot his wife a look that said "hold perfectly still". He held up his hands very slowly and urged her to remain calm. He moved his head closer to her and managed to make out his reflection in her glasses. He adjusted his hair and flipped the collar up on his hiking shirt.

Paula smirked and held perfectly still. After a few moments, Michael nodded and smiled to himself. "Thanks, Hon."

"Anytime, love."

They headed toward the path leading downward and back home. Bright green plants lined the dirt trail. Trees, rising nearly a hundred feet into the sky, swayed in the light breeze. The flora of this world happened to be remarkably similar to what used to grow on Old Earth. The terrain was rocky, but Michael's skills and experience allowed him to navigate the trail with ease.

The sound of hail and falling stones filled the air from the direction of the town. The force of the sound shook both Michael and Paula out of their peaceful walk and their eyes darted to the heavens. From the height of the mountain, they could make out a meteor exploding in mid-air above the town. They could hear what sounded like an avalanche of rain striking buildings. It seemed like a hailstorm made of pebbles.

High above them, the objects fell faster. Streaks of orange and red filled the skies. However impossible the scene appeared, the spectacle was concentrated over their town.

"What kind of meteor storm only falls over a single square mile?" Michael asked.

Paula didn't answer. She looked at the shower and cocked her head to one side. She pulled down her sunglasses and stared at the streaks in the sky.

"Paula?" Michael asked. She had a dazed look as she stared at the light show far above.

Paula shook her head and looked at Michael. She snapped out of her daze and shook her head. "I have no idea Michael. I've never seen anything like it. It's not natural, I can tell you that. The shower is stationary over our town, but the planet is still rotating; there's no way the meteors would stay there."

"Come on, let's go, if those things are making contact there might be people getting hurt," Michael said. He reached behind himself into his backpack, pulled out two long walking sticks and handed one to Paula. Walking over uneven, rocky terrain in a hurry wasn't always easy.

AFTER AN HOUR of walking Michael and Paula stood just at the edge of their town. The meteor storm had mostly ended. Paula was silent most of the way down. Michael knew she was likely going through everything she knew, trying to figure out what this could be.

"Look, last one." Michael pointed up toward the clouds.

The last of the meteors streaked across the sky and exploded into hundreds of smaller stones. Above the disturbance, higher up in the atmosphere, the sky was blue and clear for miles. The strange astronomical event appeared to be over, at least for now.

"A meteor could have hit a satellite," Paula said.

"That would have caused it to keep falling on the town the entire time?"

"I don't know, Michael; I'm guessing. No, probably not. I can't figure that. There's just no way it could stay over an area as small as the town for thirty minutes."

"Maybe it was an attack," Michael said.

"An attack from who?" Paula hated the concepts of frontier space being like the old west. Every boy in town loved cowboy romanticized themes, and every girl rolled their eyes.

"Attacks happen, Paula, but you're right, why would anyone do this, unless–"

"Unless what?"

Michael smirked. "It has to be a joke. Orleans colony is on the other side of this planet. I bet they loaded up some concrete and had it pelt us for a laugh."

"Are you kidding? They would do that?"

"Sure they would. That big guy with the thick accent and mustache that covers his face, Antoine, this is right up his alley."

"If they did this then we're going to file suit with the authorities," Paula said.

"What authorities? Jarvis? He has no jurisdiction in Orleans. He's our constable, not theirs."

"Another colony then," Paula said.

"You know better than that. Nobody out here has the kind of resources to assist another colony, let alone play galactic police."

Paula didn't answer. She knew Michael was right. Still, it

was painful to hear. They may live in the middle of nowhere, but they were still humans. Didn't that mean something? Still, if the stones were just a joke, then all was fine. Tomorrow the town's men would be fired up to make some massive prank of their own and ship it over to Orleans with a bright red bow on top.

Paula smiled at the thought of being home. Of dining in a real restaurant or just staying at home and cooking. She loved Michael and the mountains, but she also loved the comfort of her bed. Sleeping in and taking a warm shower was possibly going to be the single most satisfying end she could think of to this day. That and making love to Michael.

"Hey Greg, what a show, huh?" Michael called out ahead of Paula. "Greg? That you?"

Paula looked past Michael to see someone standing just to the side of the road. Greg, if that was him, wasn't moving. He just stood there looking down at his feet.

"Is he OK, Michael?" Paula asked.

Michael didn't answer. He picked up his pace to a light jog. Dozens of small stones littered the ground. Michael stumbled several times but kept his feet under him. He stopped just in front of Greg, who still hadn't moved.

Paula reached Michael and gasped. A stone statue that exactly resembled Greg Noland stood in front of them. His skin, hard and gray, had pockets of tiny craters and spikes as if his epidermis had been turned into the surface of a meteor. Greg's face looked if a master artisan etched every line and contour. His clothes, however, remained unaffected and moved with the breeze, as if someone had dressed a perfectly made statue in Greg's clothes.

Michael followed Greg's arm down to his hand, which held a small pebble. He looked to Paula, but she only shrugged and shook her head.

"Those must be from the meteor. That's not like any stones I've seen before," Michael said.

"What happened to him, Michael?" Paula said.

"I don't know, honey. Just to be safe, let's not touch those pebbles."

"Deal. Still think this is a joke from Orleans?"

"If it is, it's a really bad one," Michael said.

They turned from Greg and headed into town. It wasn't a sprawling mega-city, but their home wasn't a small village either. A medium-sized colony city ship created the central core of the colony. The vessels were designed to deposit an anchor in orbit and descend to the surface of a planet with a carbon ribbon trailing behind. The result was a ready-made city on the surface, complete with a space elevator for easy access to orbit. Everything a colony would need to jumpstart them to success.

Though the city created from the original colony ship was large enough to house the first colonists, eventually people began to build homes outside of the ship. Most colonies, just like this one, spiraled outward from the center where the city ship landed, forming circles of houses, roads, and infrastructure.

Empty streets filled with stones in every direction greeted Michael and Paula as they entered their town. Michael motioned to one of the small wooden houses to the right. He knocked on the door and waited, but no answer came.

"Hello?" Michael pushed the door open and peered inside. He could see the light from the sky coming from the thatched rooftop. Standing in the center of the room, looking up at the ceiling, a perfect statue of Harold Grieves stood with a confused look on his face.

"What is going on here?" Michael said.

"Whatever it is, we need to get a signal to Orleans. We need help," Paula said.

"Yeah, lots of it. Let's get to city center. We can get on the elevator and be safer up in orbit."

"Sounds good to me. Sooner the better."

Together they left Harold's home and started at a jog toward the center of town. As they came closer, the houses became more clustered together. They could start to see people, silent and still, standing outside their homes. Several stood in the streets, some looking up to the skies and others bent over with small stones in their hands. Pebbles from the meteors on the ground surrounded them all.

Michael came to a stop. He realized that now the pebbles were so concentrated that they wouldn't be able to go forward without stepping on them. Up until now, they had been spread out enough to avoid them, even at a jog.

"What?" Paula asked.

"We can't go forward, we'll step on them," Michael said.

"I don't think it matters. Look at all the people, their clothes; whatever is going on doesn't affect clothes. I think the rocks have to touch skin," Paula said.

"Willing to bet your life on it?"

"Not really," Paula said. She looked down the street at the pebbles strewn in all directions going off into the distance.

"We need a broom or something," Michael said.

"How about that?" Paula pointed to a rake hanging in a nearby yard.

"Brilliant, that'll do."

Michael ran over to the yard, careful not to step on any of the stones, and grabbed the rake. He turned it with the teeth facing up and pushed the stones out of the way.

"See, if the rake doesn't turn to stone, then we won't either," Paula said.

"Yeah, well, let's just do it this way, they aren't falling anymore, so we aren't in a super rush."

Crowds became thicker the closer they moved toward the center of town. Each person they met, most they knew, stood still and motionless, their skin turned into a rough abrasive stone.

"This has to be an alien virus or something," Michael said.

"What kind of virus forces asteroids to fall to the ground and then turns people into stone?"

"It could happen," Michael said.

Laughter filled the air and cut the tension at the same time. Both stopped walking and looked around for the source. Several seconds passed, and they turned to stare at each other. Both of their faces wore the same expression of confusion. The laughter erupted again in the distance, carried on the echo between the buildings of the town.

"You do hear that, right?" Paula asked.

"Yeah, you're not crazy," Michael said. "I don't recognize it, though, sounds insane."

"Maybe it's old Marty?"

"You think Marty is out walking around, laughing, with what is going on?"

"I don't know, Mike; I'm freaking out. It does kind of sound like him."

"Well, maybe he got drunk and passed out somewhere while the stones were falling."

"We have to get to him, then; he needs to know to not touch the stones."

Michael nodded and walked toward the center of town, toward the loud laughter. Even though his shoes would protect him from the stones, Michael still used the rake to clear a path in front of them. He walked faster, but not fast enough that he considered himself reckless. The laughter grew louder as the approached the city center.

They turned a corner into the town center. Less than a few hundred yards away the open structure of the city ship stood like a beacon of safety, promising security from the strange events. Around the ship, a lone figure walked between the statues of the townsfolk. The person placed his hands on one of the statues and laughter bellowed out of him.

"Hello? Marty?" Michael said.

"Michael, no, what if it's not him?"

The laughter stopped. The figure in the distance turned towards them and started to walk in their direction. Michael gave Paula a confident nod and walked toward the figure they thought was Marty.

"And if that's not him?" Paula asked.

"I have a rake." Michael held up the rake like a club.

"Great."

After just a few steps they could see some of the person's features, and it wasn't Marty. He had a long black beard and wore a brown robe with the hood covering his face. Whoever this was, neither Michael nor Paula recognized him.

"Hello? Are you from a rescue ship? Do you know what is going on here?" Michael said.

"Oh, yes, I know what's going on here, my boy. I am well aware," the man said. He chortled once and sneezed.

"Can you have your ship pick us up? These stones do something dangerous," said Paula.

"No, they are not dangerous, my girl," the man said.

Michael and Paula exchanged a quick quizzical look before Michael said, "Are you alright? Who are you? You're from Orleans, right?"

"I am Harold, your King."

"What?" Michael said. He looked from Paula to the man and back again. "Is this all some sick joke? Who the hell are you, man?"

"Calm down, Mike, just breathe. Maybe he's sick or something?" Paula turned to the man. "Are you hurt?"

"No, child. But you are," Harold said. He walked over to a woman encased in stone and put his nose close to her face. "Hello in there. Can you hear her yet? No? Wait, my dear. Soon you'll hear her song and when you awake you'll join the others. Join my kingdom."

"Did you do this?" Michael said. His voice rose and took on an edge.

The man turned and lifted his hood. He smiled a ragged-toothed grin. His long black beard grew on nearly every inch of his age-spotted face. Long white wisps of hair grew down from his head and poked out from the sides of his neck. With a slight laugh, he said, "Of course I did." In a flash, he extended one of his arms and threw a dozen stones towards them.

Michael lifted and threw his rake at the man, and quickly turned his back to the coming stones. He stepped in front of Paula to try to shield her. Paula could see Michael as the rake bounced off a sparkling electric shield surrounding the man.

"Michael, no!" Paula reached for Michael as the stones began to pelt him.

"I'm not naked!" Michael pushed her forward as the stones hit his clothing and fell to the ground. "Just go!"

"Wait, you'll miss the song. You can only hear the song when you engulf your souls in the quiet. All of your friends here have embraced the stillness of stone. Do you want to be the only ones who don't? You'll not be citizens of my empire unless you embrace the silence," Harold said.

Paula ran towards an open door in the distance. With a quick glance behind her, she came to a sudden halt. Her breath was quick as sweat began to bead up on her forehead. Behind her, Michael was pulling frantically at his leg, trying to get it to move.

"Paula, just go," Michael said as more of his leg became immobile.

"No." Paula ran up to Michael and tried to pull his leg free. It was like pulling a boulder up a hill. His leg felt like solid stone, and the effect was spreading up his entire body.

"What are you doing?!" Paula screamed at the old man. He had walked up to stand just a few feet behind Michael. The strange man smiled and clasped his hands in front of him.

"I've given him the gift of stillness. Soon you will both hear the song and join me as my loyal subjects."

"Let him go!" Paula said.

The old man tilted his head to one side as if he contemplated Paula's request. After a moment he shook his head and said, "No. But don't worry, my dear. He will be free one day. When he hears her song, then he'll know the truth."

"You mean the stone will come off?" Paula said.

"Paula, just run," Michael said. Paula looked at his face. He looked like he was getting sleepy.

"He's dying."

"No, my child, no one dies today. Look there," Harold said. He spun on his heels and pointed upward. Streaks of exhaust plumes from descending ships filled the sky. "Even now my troops descend. We will gather our flock and care for them until they give in to the song."

"Michael, stay with me, please," Paula said.

Michael smiled. He tried to speak but couldn't. The stone spread over his neck and moved toward his mouth. Paula kissed him once on the lips. By the time she pulled back to look at him, his face was still and locked in stone.

Paula sniffed and choked back tears. She looked at the old man. "He'll wake up one day?"

"Yes, my dear. They all will. They must hear the song; then they will know I am their king. And soon we shall spread my song to all the stars in the cosmos." Harold looked up to the sky with a wild grin.

Paula took a deep breath. She was scared. More scared than any other time in her life. She knew what she was going to do. There wasn't another choice. Life without Michael was no life at all. Even if she ran, where would she go?

With a nod to herself, she bent over and gently picked up one of the many stones on the ground. It felt like a rock you'd find on any other normal day. Paula looked up at Michael's stone face and took his hand in hers.

"Well done, my dear," Harold said. He walked up beside Paula and put his hand on her shoulder. "I was like you once. Simple. Colonial. Until I realized we will never know peace until we know silence. I found the stones, let them fall, and will now spread my message to all."

Paula ignored him. He was irrelevant. A virus, or a plague, or an asteroid bringing unsuspecting death. He was a cause, a freak accident, nothing more.

"Everyone dies," she whispered to Michael, even as she felt her limbs grow heavy. "At least this way we have a chance of seeing each other again."

It didn't take long for the stone to encase her. She felt as if she was falling into a deep sleep. Just as her eyes began to fog over, and her face no longer responded to her desire to smile, she thought, just for a moment, she could hear the soft voice of a woman singing a terribly sad song.

14

CIVILIZED SPACE

DEPARTMENT OF IMPERIAL CONTINUITY

"Why do evil men always have so much power?"
Found written on Orleans Colony. Author unknown.

Emperor Marcus Aelius Minicius, first of his name, ruler of a dozen star systems, leader of fifty million souls, poured himself a tall cup of jasmine silver needle tea and let out a long sigh of relief.

"I hate the Senate," he said to himself. Emperor Marcus walked to the balcony of his personal living space and put one hand on the rail. The view overlooked the small coastal town of Carmona on the world of New Spain, colonized just twenty years after the discovery of faster-than-light technology. The planet, situated right in the middle of the sweet spot of the habitable zone, contained just the right mix of oceans and land masses and held a biosphere with an evolutionary track quite similar to Earth.

Marcus sipped his tea and let the sweet aroma of the

jasmine tickle the back of his throat. He wondered if the aroma was the same as the tea grown on Old Earth. Sadly, with the ancestral home of humanity nearly dead, he would never know.

"Your majesty," a voice said behind Marcus.

The Emperor sighed once and turned. The Imperial advisor stood with his hands clasped behind his back, red lights shining in the orbs of his eyes, his metallic skin glinting in the fading light of the day shining through the balcony window.

"Pablo, how are you, my friend?" Marcus squinted at the tiny robot with a mix of suspicion and fear. The little robot contained copies of the minds of every man and woman to sit on the throne of the Empire of Man, forever serving as an eternal advisor, forever judging Marcus's every move. And serving as a constant reminder that his own mind would be copied one day and shoved inside the metal body. Whenever the little robot walked into view, Marcus felt the instant desire to have it leave.

"Well. How was your meeting with the Senate?"

"Maddening, as always."

"Did you discuss Earth?"

Marcus nodded and sipped his tea. "Yes, of course. That's all anyone discusses now. What do we do with Earth? Billions of people on a dead world. But what to do?"

"Save them?"

"Just that easy, Pablo? Just save them? How do you save billions? Even the Empire does not have that many ships."

"What does the Senate want?"

"Who cares? It's what I want. I am Emperor. I am dictator. I decide." Marcus set his teacup on the table and poured a tumbler full of scotch into a glass.

"What have you decided?" The little robot stood as still and calm as a granite mountain, his two eyes burning red and never wavering.

Marcus sighed. His fists balled, and his back straightened. "Why are you asking me this?"

"That's why I exist, Alejandro. My purpose is to question you, demand from you that you do the best you can for the benefit of all."

Marcus's head snapped right, his eyes narrowing to slits. "Don't call me that. I am Marcus Aelius Minicius. First of his name."

The droid let out a low metallic laugh. "Not all emperors need to take a new name. Why did you?"

"Who is asking? Justine? Elizabeth? Alexander? Which one of you questions me like this?" Marcus approached the droid and smacked the metal head with his open hand.

"You need to control your anger, Alejandro. You are Emperor. You need to be more balanced."

"What I need is to rule without this constant questioning."

"That is my purpose."

Marcus threw his crystal tumbler against the wall behind the droid and took two deep breaths. Through clenched teeth, he said, "I don't require your services anymore this evening, Pablo."

"The Imperial advisor doesn't take orders from the Emperor, Alejandro."

"Get out!" Marcus screamed. He kicked the droid in the chest with all his strength. The droid barely moved.

"Fine," the droid said. The robot turned and walked out of the room.

Marcus took several deep breaths and shook his head.

"Damn thing. I should have it melted." He walked to a side table and picked up another glass tumbler. He grabbed a bottle filled with brown liquid and poured a glass of the finest whiskey in all of New Spain. "It was stupid to even create such a thing. Imperial advisor to the Emperor. Ha! I won the trials; I won the right to rule. I need no advice. Besides, Earth is dead; let it die." Marcus drank from his glass and poured himself another.

"But the people there aren't, Marcus," said a voice Marcus knew well.

Marcus turned to see Daniel, childhood friend and a one-time competitor for the Imperial throne. Marcus frowned and looked around for his staff; none were visible. "What are you doing here, Daniel? We have no meetings scheduled."

Daniel nodded and motioned to a chair. "May we sit?"

Marcus poured another drink of whiskey and eyed Daniel with suspicion. "Fine, sit."

"How are you, friend?" Daniel said.

Marcus half-laughed. "Are we friends?"

"Yes, of course. We grew up together. Do you remember the fields of Carmona? Climbing the hills? Picking grapes from the winery and running scared when old Ernesto came chasing?"

Marcus smiled at the memory, and he nodded. "Yes, I remember." He sat down and relaxed his shoulders. "Why are you here, Daniel? What do you want? Sneaking in here like this, I would have thought that beneath a member of the Department of Imperial Continuity. Or perhaps that's exactly why you are sneaking in, eh?"

"What do you mean, Marcus?"

"Don't play the fool. I know what your department does."

Daniel ignored the implication. "What was Pablo asking you?"

Marcus rolled his eyes. "Who cares? My name? Why does everyone care so much about my name? Why do you ask about Pablo? Trying to distract me?" Marcus leaned forward. "I know the rumors as well as you, old friend. Have you come to end my life?"

Daniel held up his hands. "I'm only here to talk about Earth."

Marcus poured another glass and nodded. He reached into his pocket and thumbed his alert ring, a signal to his royal guards, hand-picked by himself and loyal only to him. If Daniel was here for any other reason, Marcus would be ready. He scoffed at the notion even as much as he suspected Daniel. No emperor had been killed since Caesar and that was by Caesar's own orders. They dare not try such foolishness in the modern age. Would they? "What about Earth, then? Go on, talk of it." Marcus waved his drink at Daniel and snarled.

"There are still billions of people there, Marcus. We can't just let them all die."

"Do you have any idea the cost involved in evacuating billions? It would bankrupt the Empire. Leave us vulnerable to the Church, the Asian bloc, even the New Soviet. Have you read the reports about them? Not very nice people."

"I realize that, Marcus. But shouldn't we try?"

"And leave ourselves open to attack? Perhaps it's a good thing you and your family lost the throne."

Daniel sat back in his chair and smiled. "Maybe so. But I'm still quite influential. I can fight you in the Senate. I can insist we send resources. We can do it in a way that won't cost much. Automate the whole thing. Break down the entire solar system. Reprocess Mercury, Mars and

Venus to create the ships. Drain Jupiter for fuel. We can do this!"

"And what do you think the Preservers will say about the destruction of the Terran solar system? They still believe we can save Earth, you know. If we break up Venus and Mars, it will foul up the whole system. There will be junk and asteroids everywhere."

"Who cares what the Preservers say? This is about real people's lives, Marcus."

"Who cares? I care. The Preservers have the backing of the Holy Church and the Council of Imams and every other religious faction in space. They want to make sure Earth is preserved at all costs. Together they have more money and resources than you can imagine. If I go against them it will be war."

"Being Emperor means making tough choices, Marcus."

Marcus sat forward and spilled half his drink on the Oriental rug beneath them. "I am making the tough choice! Do not tell me how to be Emperor! I won the right to sit on the throne as ordained by Caesar himself! I will deal with Earth how I see fit!"

Daniel eyed Marcus and frowned. "What does that mean, Marcus?"

Marcus poured himself another drink and swirled the liquid into his mouth. "It means they want their planet back. The Preservers, the Catholics, the Imams. They want their holy cities restored."

"So?"

"So we terraform it. Return Earth to its glory," Marcus said.

Daniel sat in silence as he contemplated the gravity of Marcus's statement. "You can't terraform a planet with people on it, Marcus."

"No, you can." Marcus drank his whiskey and frowned. "All the people just die."

"What have you done?"

"What needed to be done. What had to happen. That is why you lost the throne, Daniel. That is why you are not Emperor. This is what it means to rule fifty million people." Marcus let his body fall back into his chair. "Sometimes you must make terrible choices."

Daniel's mouth fell open, and his head fell. He stared at his friend, at his Emperor, with stunned disbelief. A cold sweat formed on his brow, and he wiped his head with his hand.

"Marcus," Daniel said.

"Don't bother. It's done. And nothing can stop it."

Daniel stood and walked to the balcony. Waves crashed lazily along the pristine golden shore. The smell of salt carried on the breeze along with the smoke of beach pit fires. Townspeople danced in the water and ran along the beaches, smiling and happy, oblivious to the decision happening in the palace far above them.

"Tell me why you are here, Daniel," Marcus said.

"I had come as a friend. But now, to talk you out of this if I can. I had no idea what you were planning."

"And if you can't? You're with them, aren't you?" Marcus stood behind Daniel and wavered on half-drunken legs.

"What do you want me to say, Marcus?"

"The truth. Tell your Emperor you are here to kill him. That's the true job of your precious department. Not under control of the Senate or the Emperor."

Daniel turned and faced Marcus, their eyes locking. "I'm not here to kill you, Marcus."

"Fine; lie. I know the truth. I know what Caesar created. I'm no fool." Marcus walked around Daniel towards the window. "In his great wisdom, Caesar created the imperial assassins. Tasked with one singular mission. Kill the Emperor if it's decided he goes against what's best for the Empire. Only the Empire matters." He turned to Daniel, his eyes wide. "And where best to hide these assassins? Surely every Emperor when they take the throne wants to find them, root them out, expunge them so they pose no threat. Where would they be?" Marcus laughed. "I've looked high and low and my eyes always come back to you. The Department of Imperial Continuity. Where all those who failed to become Emperor go to die. And here you are, in my chamber, unannounced, come to kill me."

Daniel sighed. He looked to the floor, and his shoulders sagged. "The department doesn't do that. I would never do that. I'm not a murderer."

"No?"

"How could I? How could the department? We would be just as guilty of abusing power if we decided when to commit regicide. No, the Department of Continuity ensures the proper exchange of power. We make sure the Empire lives during the transition from one Emperor to another."

"Then why are you here, eh? Not that you would be able to kill me anyway. My royal guard should be here in seconds." Marcus smiled and took a long drink of his whiskey.

Daniel nodded. "I was just here to talk."

"Just talk? How did you know to come? Eh?" Marcus pointed his half-full tumbler at Daniel.

"Because I called him," said a metallic voice from the shadows.

Marcus turned to see the Imperial Assistant walk into the room. The little robot, barely five feet tall, walked up to Marcus and stood still just a few feet away.

"Pablo? What are you doing here? I don't require your advice; I told you to leave."

"Marcus," Daniel said.

"No, what is he doing here, eh? What do you want, Pablo?"

"To protect the Empire, Alejandro."

Marcus's eyes went wide. "Don't call me that, you little shit! Guards! Where are my guards?"

"They aren't coming." The Imperial Assistant's voice changed octaves and adopted a southern American accent.

"What voice is that? I know that voice," Marcus said. "Which one of you is that, eh?"

"I am not going to allow you to kill billions of Imperial citizens."

Marcus laughed and spat on the marble floor. "They aren't citizens of the Empire. They are the scum left on a dead world."

"All humans are Imperial citizens. It is their birthright."

"That old lie," Marcus said.

"Not a lie, Alejandro. It's what I wanted when I created the Empire."

Marcus narrowed his eyes and stared at the droid. He approached the robot he called Pablo with careful steps. "Caesar? Are you in there?" Marcus's eyes went wide.

"Yes. Who could give better advice to the Emperor but all those that have served before him?" The droid took a step forward, its red eyes blazing, its cold, lifeless stare digging into Marcus. "But I am not a copy," Caesar said.

"None of us are," a dozen voices said in unison from the droid.

"What is this?" Marcus stumbled backward and fell to the ground. "Daniel, what is this?"

Daniel walked to stand behind the droid. He looked into

Marcus's eyes. "The Department of Imperial Continuity aren't executioners, Marcus. We're witnesses."

The droid moved with lightning speed. Its hand closed around Marcus's wrists and lifted him off the floor as if he were a child's toy. Long snake-like protrusions emerged from the back of the droid and positioned themselves behind Marcus's head.

"No, no! Guards!"

"No one is coming, Marcus. We have secured the room," said the unified voices in the droid. "This moment was eventual. All Emperors serve the Empire for eternity. Your mind, your soul, will be downloaded and stored in this unit. A constant advisor. An eternal guardian against tyranny."

Metal clasps secured themselves to Marcus's head. He squirmed, but the droid's strength was beyond his own. Nanowire inserted into the back of his neck began the process of mapping his neural structure, replacing his biological neurons with synthetic counterparts.

"No, you can't do this!"

"An Empire governed by a just Emperor can achieve miracles. But no Emperor is superior to the Empire. The Empire must continue. The Empire must survive," the droid said.

The process took moments. Once complete, Marcus's neural structure was recorded and transferred to a virtual model. For the briefest of moments, he held a sense of being in both his body and the droid, as if his consciousness commanded two complete bodies. Both became his self. In the flash of thought, his biological body was injected with a dozen poisons, and he fell to the ground lifeless.

"Inform the Senate, the Imperial candidates and their families to prepare for the trials, Daniel."

Daniel knelt by his friend and put his hand on his head.

"And submit your plan for the immediate automation of the Terran system for the evacuation of Earth to the Senate."

"Yes, of course," Daniel said.

"Long live the Empire," Marcus's voice said through the droid.

Daniel turned to watch the droid disappear into the shadows.

15

FRINGE SPACE

PHARMA WORLD

"Why does everything have to be so damn weird?"

Posted on the Hive network for "outties" by a recent refugee of Earth.

Alexander Hill watched the monitors with boredom and contempt. He had been on the late shift for weeks, monitoring literally the middle of nowhere. This part of space, like the bridge, was empty and quiet. The rest of the crew, fast asleep in the lower decks, would hopefully wake soon and at least let him escape to slumber, the only one time when he could get some relief.

"Hey, Alex, anything new?" a groggy voice behind him said. He turned to see Jake, the fifteen-year-old crew mate who was born in space, coming up to relieve him of his shift. Alex had never served with a kid as young as Jake, even on his home world's small naval fleet when Alex was a much younger man.

"No, nothing. Where's Thompson? I thought he was on shift next?" Alex said.

"I dunno, being the captain has its perks," Jake said.

Alex nodded but didn't care. Thompson was the owner, and the ship was named after him, but no one knew much else. Just about everyone except two or three of the crew had only signed on six months ago.

"Well, I don't know why we are out here, but there's nothing. We are at least five light years from the nearest colony and nearly two light years from the closest star. This is the middle of nowhere. What is Thompson doing having us come out here?" Alex said.

"I dunno. Want some coffee?" Jake asked with a yawn.

Alex looked back to watch Jake wander off into a room off the bridge. "No, I'm going to bed, my shift is done."

Alert signals began to sound off on the console in front of Alex. He turned around and entered commands into the console. His expression turned from confusion to shock as the readouts displayed something that shouldn't be possible.

"Jake, get in here. We need to get everyone awake," Alex said.

Jake walked over and yawned. "You need to relax more, man. What is it? Alien armada?"

Alex bristled at first but relaxed. Jake may have been a kid, but that kid had spent his entire life on ships like these. This was Jake's normal everyday life. "A gravity source, and a big one. Like massive. SubAI says the only thing that could cause that is a planet. But no way, right? I mean, we're in the middle of nowhere, there are no planets out here."

"Could be a rogue. I heard of one guy found a rogue world and set up his own fiefdom. But you gotta know where they are," Jake said.

"Well, how did we just find one then?" Alex said. He couldn't help the worry growing in his voice.

"Relax, man, I said it was hard, not impossible," Jake said. He sat down at the station next to Alex and started punching buttons. After a few moments, two swigs of coffee and a yawn, he opened the communication system and called to the captain.

"Captain, this is Jake and Alex on the bridge, we've got a gravity well about five hundred AUs out," Jake said.

"How are you sure it's a rogue?" Alex asked.

Jake winked.

"OK, coming down. Get everyone awake," Thompson's voice said over the comm.

Alex sat and started doing what he was hired to do. What he was trained to do. He prepared scanning probes, setting them for planetary orbits and analyzing the gravity well to determine the planet's exact location. All of this was second nature to him. Alex had served in the military on his home planet, Homer's World, for five years. He joined when he was eighteen. Now, almost twenty-two years later, Alex found himself having a mid-life crisis. He wanted to explore fringe space before it vanished. Every year it felt like civilized space, the central worlds, the big governments, were getting closer and closer. Annexing more worlds. One day, there wouldn't be any free worlds left.

Twenty minutes passed as Alex and Jake worked silently. Both were lost in their own calculations and computations. A sophisticated understanding of math was a requirement in space travel. If you couldn't do quadratic equations in your sleep, then you had no business navigating a starship.

With a cough and a muffled complaint about life, Captain Thompson walked onto the bridge. He was in his late fifties with gray scruffy stubble on his face. He looked over the shoulders of both Alex and Jake and nodded to himself. Without a word he walked off to the pantry and poured himself a cup of coffee.

As the minutes passed more of the crew came onto the bridge. All were bleary-eyed and half awake. Some stumbled directly to the pantry while others sat at their stations. Alex could tell the ex-military types, those that marched to their stations, from the casual spacers.

"OK, where are we, Alex, Jake?" Thompson asked.

"Middle of nowhere with a planet coming towards us. Not seeing any signals or artificial lights down there. The planet is dead. We may have found a home away from home," Jake said with a huge grin.

"What's weird is I'm getting an oxygen-nitrogen atmosphere reading down there," Alex said.

"There's no way," Jaime, another member of the crew, said. She was the ship's only scientifically-thinking soul.

"And the temperature, it's a nice, not-very-sunny eighty degrees," Jake said.

"That's impossible. Where is the heat coming from?" Jaime said.

"Thermal vents?" Alex asked.

"What's the age of the planet? Can we tell from this far out?"

"Not without analyzing the rocks," Jaime said.

"So, this thing is habitable?" Alex said.

"If that's true then we found a gold mine," Jake said.

"Why? I mean, we can't grow crops or live down there," Alex said.

"A rogue planet, a place no one can find, where we don't need life support to breathe, where we can stash anything and have a party for years, be our own kingdom. It's perfect," Jake said.

"How in the world did we find this?" Jaime asked. Alex turned to see her leaning against the wall with a cup of coffee in her hand. She wore baggy pants and a t-shirt that read, *Scientists do it by the numbers.*

After minutes of silence, Jaime said, "Hello? Is everyone awake yet? The odds of just stumbling on a rogue are pretty huge."

"Yeah, but not impossible," Jake said. He turned and frowned at the Captain. "Right?"

Thompson looked at Jake but didn't respond.

"Why were we out here in the first place?" Jaime asked.

"Everyone shut up. Jake, feed coordinates to Alex and get us in orbit. David, Luke, go down and prep the bay. Doc," Thompson said looking around. "Where the fuck is the Doc?" He banged his communication control on his chair. "Doc, get your ass up. Get your gear and lock in."

"I guess we are going to find out what's there," Jaime said. She turned around and walked off the bridge.

AN HOUR LATER, after a quick burst from the FTL drive, the ship fired its slower-than-light engines with full thrust. Fire erupted from beneath the massive hull as the ship descended to the planet surface. Everyone on board was strapped in and could only wait for the subAI to guide the vessel down. After a tense few minutes of jostling, the ship came to rest on the rocky, dark surface of the rogue planet.

"OK, everyone to the bay, except Jaime – you stay here," Thompson said.

"What?" Jamie said. "Are you joking? Isn't this why I'm here?"

"Yes, and you will go, but not before the people who know how to use a gun go down first," Thompson said.

"A gun? It's a rock ball. Are you afraid the rock is going to kill me?" Jaime said.

Thompson didn't reply, which meant he didn't care what she said. He got up and walked out of the bridge and down to the bay. Jaime fumed but said nothing. Alex felt bad for her, but there wasn't anything to do. They all knew that Thompson was a bastard, but he was the bastard that owned the ship. All he had to do was tell the subAI to reject crew members' eating rights and watch them starve.

Thompson sat in the driver's seat of the land craft with Jake next to him. Alex sat in the back with David and Luke, two other crew members whose specialties were in firing large guns.

The landing bay door fell open and the land vehicle, a hovercraft, sped out and into the alien world. Besides doing an atmosphere scan Jake and the subAI had scanned for any microorganisms.

The land rover stopped less than three hundred yards from their ship. Thompson got out and looked around in all directions. Everyone was equipped with infrared vision goggles that, with the bright starlight above, gave them just enough to see. Though the atmosphere was breathable, it wasn't active. There were no clouds, which allowed most starlight through.

"Whoa, look at this," Jake said.

Alex walked over and knelt beside Jake. His infrared goggles showed nothing but a cold dead surface. Nothing alive and nothing generating heat. Alex looked to Jake, who just shrugged.

"Take your goggles off and use your flashlight," Jake said.

A small brownish vegetation covered everything in sight.

As Alex stood and shined his light on them, he could see the brown plants went on as far as he could see.

"Is this what is producing the oxygen?" Alex asked.

"It's not only producing oxygen, it's producing nitrogen too. Wow, it's producing everything. The entire makeup of a human-breathable atmosphere," Jake said.

"Some alien plant is producing an atmosphere breathable to humans? That's a big coincidence," Alex said.

"Not only that," Jake said. He picked a piece of the vegetation. "I think it's edible. The scanner is showing there are plant and animal characteristics. I mean, it has protein, vitamins. We could live on this."

"Let's go," Thompson said. "I want to see what's over that ridge."

Alex and Jake just looked at each other while David and Luke said nothing. Though Alex didn't remember them ever saying much. They all climbed into the lander as Thompson sped off toward the ridge.

"Stop!" Alex said.

Thompson slammed the brakes and turned around in the chair. "What?"

"Do you hear that?"

Thompson looked left and right and tilted his head. Loud clicks sounded in the distance. Every second that passed, the number of clicks grew until they merged into a low hum. The still air and darkness sent shivers down Alex's spine. Like this world was straight out of a horror vid.

"Maybe we should leave?" Jake said.

Thompson drew his gun and nodded to David and Luke, who drew theirs. They stood up in their seats to get a better look and position themselves. Thompson thrust his hand out and pointed off to the right. He raised his gun and started to aim.

Alex turned and zoomed in with his infrareds. He could easily make out thousands of shapes, low to the ground, running fast. They seemed to be turning and moving in unison, like a herd.

"Let's go, Thompson," Jake said.

"Shut up," Thompson said. He opened fire into the herd as David and Luke joined him. Alex could see the shapes in front fall, and the herd turns towards the right, away from them. The low hum changed to a shrill whistle. Alex put his hands to his head and screamed as the sound damaged his inner ear.

"What is that?" Alex yelled. He spared a glance to see everyone else was grabbing their ears as well – everyone except Thompson, who continued to fire into the herd.

"It's some kind of sonar," Jake said. "It has to be."

Alex threw on his helmet and activated the noise dampening. The sound thankfully died. He helped Jake, David and Luke with theirs while Thompson kept firing over their heads. After the last of the herd had turned, Thompson stopped firing. He sat back down in his seat and started up the engines. Without a word, he sped off towards the ridge.

"Shouldn't we go grab one? Alien carcasses are worth a lot, you know," Jake said.

"We can get it on the way back," Thompson said.

"Way back from what? What is going on, Thompson? Have you been here before?" Jake asked.

"No, now shut up."

Twenty minutes later the land vehicle crested the ridge and came to a halt. A small grouping of domed buildings sat below them. Jake checked the land rover's sensors. There were no energy signatures down there. If anyone was ever here they had left or were dead.

"I didn't know this was here, boys," Thompson said,

"and I've never been here. When we stopped earlier, I thought I saw a light coming from over the ridge. Now let's just go down there, see if there is any salvage and get off this rock, fast."

"Why do you want to leave so fast?" Jake said.

"That was a big herd of – something. A population that big can support predators. What were they running from, after all?" Thompson said.

"OK, why were we out here in the first place?" Jake said.

"Same thing we are doing now, looking for salvage. Never know what you can find in the middle of nowhere," Thompson said.

Jake's face screwed into a frown of disbelief. There was always tension between Jake and Thompson and sooner or later they would have an argument that someone might not walk away from.

"How do you think this plant is surviving?" Alex asked, a handful of the brown vegetation in his hands.

"What do you mean?" Jake said.

"There's no sunlight, so it's not photosynthesis."

"I don't know. Starlight? Heat vents beneath the surface?" Jake said.

"That would be remarkable," Alex said.

"Honestly, I've seen weirder," Jake said.

Thompson found a path down the ridge and pulled up in front of the largest domed building. The door was broken open and hanging to one side. Thompson took off his infrared helmet and pulled out a powerful flashlight. He shined it into the structure, which revealed darkened corridors retreating into the depths.

"There could be animals inside; let's go slow," Thompson said.

"Lead on," Jake said. After Thompson walked inside Jake whispered under his breath, "You clearly know the way."

Thompson took the lead with David and Luke bringing up the rear. The captain shined the light down the corridor, ignoring several of the rooms to the right and left. Alex gave Jake a questioning look, but Jake just shrugged and pushed him forward.

Flashing blue and red lights reflecting on one of the walls drew Thompson in that direction. Inside a room, a dozen computer systems, half still active and online, filled the chamber. Thompson took one look at the room and marched toward one of the computers. He put his flashlight down and cracked open the case. From between the mess of cables and circuit boards inside the unit, Thompson pulled the small rectangular hard drive and put it in a bag slung over his shoulder. He did the same for the remaining computers in the room.

Jake gave Thompson a suspicious stare and reached down into a pile of papers. After throwing several of them back into the heap on the floor, he came to one page and stopped. Alex watched the blood drain from Jake's face and felt his own heart skip.

"OK, that's all of them. With these we can find out what was going on here and maybe see if there is anything valuable around," Thompson said. He stood up and looked at Jake, who was still reading the piece of paper.

Jake looked up and stared Thompson in the eyes. Neither spoke a word aloud, but both exchanged years' worth of suspicion and animosity through their gaze. Behind them, David and Luke postured up, and both tightened their grip on their weapons as if the silent war between Thompson and Jake spread to everyone like a disease.

"Let's go," Thompson said. He turned from Jake and headed down the corridor.

"What?" Alex said.

Jake only shook his head and followed Thompson out. He hesitated at the door. In a fluid motion, Jake pulled Alex out of the room and threw the paper in his hand back inside. He took out a flame grenade from his belt, armed the incendiary and tossed the weapon over Alex's shoulder. In seconds, the room was engulfed in flames.

"What the – Jake?" Alex said. He ran down the corridor as Jake pushed him in the back.

"Go!" Jake said.

Smoke filled the corridor. Alex and Jake ran after the others, being careful not to take a wrong turn. Behind them, they could feel the smoke and heat spreading outward into the larger structure.

After a few more turns they found themselves outside. He looked up to see Thompson and Luke climb into the land rover while David took off his helmet and went to relieve himself.

"What the hell was that?" Alex said.

Thompson turned to look. He saw the smoke coming out of the building and got out of the land rover. He walked over to the kneeling Alex and stared Jake in the eyes.

"What happened?" Thompson asked.

"Jake torched the room and nearly me with it," Alex said.

Thompson squinted and looked at Jake. After another tense moment, Alex saw the slightest of nods from both. Thompson then reached down and heaved Alex to his feet. He patted him once on the back, and Alex felt as if his lungs would pop out of his chest.

"Alright, let's get out of here," Thompson said. "David, quit pissing and let's go."

David didn't move. He stood teetering back and forth. Thompson tilted his head and approached him slowly. Alex followed. They both got up next to David and could see a long line of blood running from his ears.

"Helmets!" Jake said from behind.

Alex checked his audio. A high-frequency sonic burst was covering David's position with enough force to blast out a human's eardrums. The sound was likely so high that David could already be unconscious on his feet.

A growl followed by the crunch of metal sounded behind them. A creature, at least nearly as big as their land vehicle, stood on top of part of the dome. More high-frequency sonic bursts blasted the area as the creature rotated its head. The local subAIs in Alex's helmet told them that the creature's forehead was the source of the sonic blast.

Rows of jagged teeth lined the creature's mouth. Sharp talons on all of the beast's paws dug into the structure of the dome. Long bands of tight muscles bulged from the animal's arms and body. Alex didn't think the thing would have much trouble tearing everyone here to pieces.

In a fluid movement the creature jumped off the building and grabbed David in its jaws. Thompson, Jake, and Alex all dove out of the way. Even if they did have the time to draw their weapons and shoot, they wouldn't have been able to get out of the way in time.

Alex spun on the ground and drew his gun. Before he could get off a shot, the creature's head exploded in a mass of blood and brains. The body fell to the ground with David's limp body twitching in its maw.

"Shit!" Alex said. He stood and pointed his weapon in a wide arc around them, looking for another target. Luke stood just next to the land vehicle, his gun pointed at the dead creature.

"Can we get the fuck out of here now?" Luke said.

Thompson ran over to David. After just a moment, he stood and just shook his head. Jake followed him and pulled Alex's arm.

"Good shot, Luke," said Thompson.

Luke gurgled a reply. Blood spat out of his mouth, and a sharp white spear burst through his torso. Luke reached up to grasp the white bone spear protruding through his throat. He tried to pull it out, but after only a few seconds he collapsed to the ground, blood gurgling out of his mouth.

"Cover!" Thompson said.

"We're getting hit again by high sonic bursts. Multiple targets, at least five sources," Jake said.

"Get to the vehicle and lay down cover fire," Thompson said.

A hail of white spears fell on their position. Most bounced easily off their combat armor but a few managed to find exposed skin. Fortunately, none found such an easy target as an unmoving Luke with his neck exposed.

Deep down in Alex's subconscious his military drill sergeant woke up. He ceased being Alex Hill and started being combat scout Corporal Hill. He rolled to the right and opened fire in multiple directions. He laid down a suppression stream of high-velocity energy bolts.

Jake followed suit. Though he had no combat training, he knew how to shoot a gun. Thompson joined the maelstrom of weapon fire, and soon the number of bone spears falling on them reduced.

"There." Alex pointed at one of the enemy combatants and opened fire with deadly accuracy. The body fell just to the right of the land rover. The hail of bone spears ceased, as did the sonic bursts. The three approached the land rover and the fallen body.

Pale white skin covered the creature. Two tiny black dots of eyes were underneath a massive forehead. The mouth, nose, and ears were eerily familiar, as were the proportions of its arms and legs. The creature wore an animal hide skin over its lower body, and its feet were covered in some kind of makeshift shoes. If Alex didn't know better, he'd suspect this was an albino human with a deformity in his eyes and head.

"What is it?" Jake asked.

"If I didn't know better, I'd say it was a person," said Alex.

"Whatever it was, there's lots of them. Gunfire scared them off. Let's get the hell out of here," Thompson said.

The three loaded David and Luke in back and then jumped into the land rover. They sped off towards their ship. Sonic bursts pelted them as they drove. The number of bursts increased as they drove toward the spaceship, which indicated a high population.

"Jaime, do you copy?" Thompson said over the open comms.

"Yes, I do. What the hell is going on out there? I've been picking up high-frequency ultrasounds everywhere," Jaime replied.

"Do not leave the ship. There are natives here, and they are armed. Prep the ship for takeoff," Thompson said.

"Don't we want to examine the hard drives first?" Alex said. Jake delivered an elbow to Alex's arm and a look that said "shut up now". Alex did.

"Guzman, Thompson, Seven Seven," Thompson said.

"Thompson, Guzman, go ahead," the ship's subAI replied.

"Arm weapons, suppression fire, give us a twenty-meter halo, fire at will," Thompson said.

Alex ducked down in his seat and told the local subAI in his suit to harden his armor and prepare for incoming fire. He had never seen the ship fire on ground targets and hardly knew the ship had weapons.

Within seconds the land around the small hovercraft erupted in devastation. Turf and hard rock exploded. Though the fire was precise, Alex felt every blast as it shook the air and pelted him with debris.

"Jesus Christ," Jake said. "I think they got the message."

Ultrasounds ceased. Alex switched his vision to infrared and saw dozens of still-warm dead bodies on the ground. Heat outlines retreated in the distance. His onboard subAI told him there were hundreds of forms moving away from the ship.

"Cease fire," Thompson said to the shipboard subAI. The maelstrom died down as quickly as it came on. The hovercraft came to a stop in front of their space vessel, and Thompson got out without saying another word.

Alex and Jake looked at each other. Jake seemed to have a worried expression, but Alex couldn't really tell. Most of Jake's expressions were combinations of worry, sarcasm, and hysteria. Alex got out of the back of the vehicle, and Jake followed suit.

In a blink, Alex saw Jake run towards the ship. He turned to see Thompson walk around the hovercraft and inspect it for damage. Either Thompson didn't see Jake run off or he didn't care.

"What now?" Alex said.

"Get inside," Thompson said. "Get to the hangar bay and get ready to secure the hovercraft. I'll load up in a minute."

His tone made it sound like he was talking to a stupid dog, something Alex loathed.

"Fine, see you inside," Alex said. He walked towards the ship, following Jake, who had already gone inside.

Twenty minutes later Alex was in the bay watching the ship roll in. He hadn't seen Alex or anyone else on the ship. He assumed that whatever Jake saw was probably nothing and he was just milking him for a good joke. Jake probably ran into the ship to let everyone in on it before Alex could get inside.

The hovercraft came to a stop, and Thompson got out. He removed his body armor and let it hit the ground with a loud thunk. He walked to his locker, opened it, withdrew a bottle of whiskey and took a long drink.

Alex turned around and started to examine David and Luke's bodies still in the hovercraft. Just as he turned away from Thompson, a loud blast came from behind him. Alex turned, crouched and pulled his sidearm just to see Thompson fall to the ground. Jake stood over Thompson's body. He kicked Thompson's leg once.

Alex popped up and pointed his sidearm at Jake. "What are you doing?"

"He was going to kill us. Jettison us all in deep space, probably, then laser us to pieces. No remains that way," Jake said.

"So you killed him?"

Jake laughed. "No." He held up his gun. "Non-lethal. Though Thompson will wake up with a hell of a headache."

"How the hell do you know he was going to kill us?" Alex didn't lower his gun.

"This planet. You figure out what it is yet?" Jake said.

"No, yes, I mean," Alex said, getting confused, "No, I

guess not. But who cares? That doesn't explain what you just did."

"They call it a Pharma world," Jake said. He ignored Alex's statement. And the gun pointing at his chest in Alex's hand. "I thought it was just an urban legend. Guess not, right?"

Jake walked around Thompson to an access panel in the cargo hold. He pulled out wrist and ankle cuffs and put them on Thompson's unconscious body. Jake then turned to a console and typed in commands that Alex couldn't make out.

"Basically, the story goes, large companies from the central worlds of civilized space find some distant far-flung world. They populate it, add vegetation, whatever, put some people on it and then let biology go crazy.

"They can introduce new strains of bacteria, viruses, slow aging, speed it up, add some genes, take away some others, all with no one the wiser."

"That's the stupidest thing I've ever heard of. Why bother?"

"They throw in stuff and see what nature cooks up. I mean, you have to admit, that ultrasonic blast from that thing out there was pretty nasty. Not to mention the habitability of the planet alone. I mean, what if that was one of the experiments? Now you can terraform a barren rock world into a habitable one? Big money there," Jake said. "Ultimately, Mother Nature can be very clever when she's feeling antsy."

"OK, fine, whatever, maybe someone did do that here, that still doesn't explain why you shot Thompson," Alex said.

"Come on, Alex, if you are going to survive out here, you need to smarten up. Thompson was in on it. He contracted with whoever runs this place to bring them fresh supplies to play around with," Jake said.

"We don't have any cargo, Jake."

"We are the cargo," Jake said.

Alex let it sink in. He blinked a few times and slowly lowered his gun. Jake nodded and motioned for Alex to walk over to him. Jake took Alex's hand, pressed it against the wall plate and tapped in a few more numbers.

"I can't believe this happened," Alex said.

"Yeah, crazy huh," Jake said.

"Why did you torch the room?" Alex asked.

"Keep Thompson guessing. Thought maybe if he felt I was OK with it, he'd let us get back to the ship."

Alex sat down on a bench and rubbed his eyes. "That's what was on the papers you saw? That's how you knew?"

Jake laughed. "Naw, that was some guy's meal requisition form. You really think I'd stumble on the single piece of incriminating evidence in the first paper I looked at?"

"I don't get it, how'd you know then?"

"Saw it in Thompson's eyes when I looked at him. I suspected something wasn't right about him finding this planet and driving right to the base. When I got back to the ship, I ran a hack of his personal computer. I've held off out of respect, but he was just too suspicious at the dome. Sure enough, there was an entire chain of communication between someone and Thompson about dropping us off. But I guess this place went to shit just before we got here. Looks like all the eggheads here got eaten by their own experiments. Serves 'em right."

Alex let out a long sigh. "What happens now?"

"Now, we take the ship and go find some work. What do you think we do?"

"But it's Thompson's ship."

"Not anymore. Time for new ownership." Jake motioned for Alex to join him in front of the panel on the wall.

"How can you do that? Just change ownership?"

"I told the subAI that Thompson is dead. Also blacked out the sensors in the room so it couldn't see me kill him."

"But Thompson isn't dead."

Jake shrugged. "SubAIs are dumb. What can I say?"

"So who's the owner?"

With Jake's urging, Alex placed his hand on the screen. The ship registered his DNA and handprint and assigned him ownership. He was given full access to all subAI routines and commands and could take the ship anywhere he wanted to go.

"What? Me?"

"Well, who else? I can't. SubAI won't accept anyone under twenty. Can you believe that? Some stupid sub-routine probably written fifty years ago. I can't find it. I don't trust anyone else on board, and honestly barely trust you, but I know where you sleep," Jake said with a grin.

Alex nodded. "Wait, what do we do with him?" Alex pointed to Thompson on the floor. Loud snores began to flow from his mouth.

Jake shrugged. "We could ditch him on this world?"

Alex's face went slack.

Jake laughed. "Relax, man. I'm not a prick like Thompson. We'll dump him in some bar somewhere."

"Just like that?"

"Sure. There are thousands of hole-in-the-wall places out here. We'll never see him again." He patted Alex on the back and smiled broadly. "Welcome to fringe space, friend."

16

CIVILIZED SPACE

THE CORPORATE

"You don't have to search to find eternal happiness. Not anymore. With the Church, joy is with you always."
Member of the Church of the Pilgrim

"Hello, how may I be of service?" the droid said.

Andrew stared at the droid and clenched his teeth to the point of pain. The metal attendant sat at a gray desk inside a cubicle made of thin walls. This was his seventh meeting today, all with droids that had as much intelligence as his favorite rock. Behind Andrew, in a waiting area in the center of the maze of dull gray office spaces, his family looked over his shoulder with hopeful stares.

"We want to request a move to a more isolated location. Somewhere remote," Andrew said.

The droid didn't move or make any reassuring facial gesture. "Can you be more specific, please? The corporation of Astro Limited offers a broad range of choices for the aspiring team member looking to climb the ladder of success."

"No, see, I'm not interested in climbing any ladder. I want to be left alone. I want to be with my family, on a piece of land, hopefully in the middle of nowhere. I'll take care of the land and do whatever work is needed."

"Modern psychological studies of a happy workforce indicate that isolated working environment is counter-productive to success. Are you sure this is the course you wish to take?" the droid said.

"Yes, we are sure."

The droid tilted its head to one side. "I'm sorry, I'm unable to process your request. There are currently no openings that meet your detailed list of requirements for isolation."

Andrew hit the table with his open hand. A red light blinked once on the cubicle wall.

"Please do not engage in a physically violent activity. A note has been added to your HR file."

"I don't have an HR file! We never agreed to this!"

"One moment." The droid turned in its chair and pressed its hand into a mold on the desk. A silent link opened between the machine and the computer systems of Astro Limited. Why a droid, fully equipped with a dozen radio transmitters and already connected to a thousand systems, needed a physical port to connect with was strange. Andrew had heard a rumor that the hard connection was to satisfy an old security protocol that no one had bothered trying to remove from the droid's processes.

"Please take your packet and proceed to office four seven three," the droid said after being plugged into the system for nearly five minutes.

"Another meeting? Really?"

"Yes. This concludes our interaction. Please fill out a card indicating how you feel this meeting was conducted and do not forget to include suggestions for improvements to the process."

Andrew nodded and sighed. Process improvement questions followed his every waking interaction with each other corporate employee. And since Astro Limited owned the planet, the space station, and every asteroid in the entire solar system, everyone worked for Astro Limited.

"What's going on, Daddy?" Andrew's youngest daughter said.

"Just wait here. Where's your mother?"

"Potty."

"OK, honey, just wait here."

"Can we go into the playroom?" His daughter pointed to an area set against a wall where a dozen children played with twice that many toys.

Andrew shook his head. "No, the room requires PTO time. We don't have any."

"What's PTO?"

"Personal time off. It doesn't matter. Just wait for Mommy here." Andrew walked through lines of other employees waiting to speak to a droid on some matter or another. He counted his way down what seemed an endless row of numbers indicating rooms and offices that surrounded the vast open space. Finally, his eyes fell to the number four seven three. A door, something he hadn't yet encountered on his trek through the seemingly infinite office, sat below the number. Andrew knocked, and a voice inside told him to enter.

Inside the room, a woman sat behind a small metal desk. She wore a pantsuit, and her hair was pulled up tight in a bun. She smiled when Andrew entered and motioned for him to sit in a chair in front of her desk.

"Hello, my name is Margot. How may I help you?" Margot smiled, folded her hands on her desk, and looked Andrew in the eyes.

"Hi," Andrew said. He gave Margot his ever-growing stack of papers and sat back in his chair, slightly in shock that he was talking to a human being.

"OK, let's see," Margot said. She took the stack of papers and placed them on her desk. She turned over one page after another and nodded several times during the process. "OK, I see. You're from Old Earth. Part of the evacuations?"

Andrew nodded, and his eyes lit up. Maybe he was finally getting somewhere. "Yes, exactly. We didn't ask to come here, to Astro Limited's solar system. We just got sent here."

Margot nodded and shrugged. "Better than a colony world. I heard of people getting eaten by plants out there." She shook her body in her seat, and Andrew could only think that a shiver went down her spine.

"I don't know anything about that. My family had a farm, on Earth. We even had some crops before we got evacuated. Can you believe that? We grew corn on Earth. Still, after all the troubles with the weather. We still grew corn."

"Yes, that's very nice. Unfortunately, since it didn't happen on corporate property or while you were employed, I can't give you a merit award."

Andrew frowned. "I don't want an award; I was just talking."

"Oh, good. Inter-office dialogue that's personal in nature is encouraged, as long as it's not offensive. Good for you," Margot said.

"I'm not an employee; we never asked to come here. I never applied to your company."

"Yes, but you are here. Would you rather be on Earth?"

"No, of course not."

"Exactly. And as you know, or don't know, evacuees are either being sent to colonize new worlds far out on the fringes of explored space or being sent to existing governments already established. Like Astro Limited."

"You're a government now? I thought you were a corporation."

"Well, there is little difference anymore. We just don't have to deal with pesky elections. Everything is profit-based. Much more efficient. And we care about every single employee."

"Then can you please give me a farm to work? Or land on the planet? Something? We don't like cities."

"Sorry, all the farms on the planets are owned and operated by Astro Limited and are farmed with automations. Robots. Very efficient."

"Fine, how about just a place where I can have a house?"

"Again, sorry, that would be a risk to the ecosystem of the planet."

Andrew shifted in his seat. He could feel his face flush and anger boil his blood under his skin. "People don't live on this planet? At all?"

Margot laughed. "Oh no, of course they do. Our cities on the surface are well controlled and maintained. But planetary living in a rural setting is typically reserved for the C-suite. People that have devoted their lives to the corporate and know how to take care of a resource as precious as a planetary ecosystem."

"What does that mean?"

"Well, you've seen Earth. People could go anywhere, do

anything, and look what happened. Deforestation, mass extinctions, and now a dead world. Is that what you want? I'm sure it's not. The cost of an evacuation of Earth is in the hundreds of trillions. Astro Limited can't afford to take that loss. Besides, eco-terrorism is a grave offense according to HR's rule book."

"I never said anything like that. We just want to live! One family isn't going to destroy an entire planet."

"Starts with one, then a thousand more want to do the same thing."

"We just want to live in peace, can't you understand that?" Andrew said.

"Yes, but in this solar system, you live how the corporate says you can live. But there are many options, and we have an approval rating of over eighty percent. Our system is working."

"Fine, I want to leave. Immigrate. Can I do that?"

Margot nodded and smiled. "Yes, of course. You'll need a sponsor from your destination sovereignty and be able to pay for related costs. Traveling between star systems isn't free. Corporations wouldn't stay in business long if they did everything for free, would they?" Margot let out a small giggle and shook her head.

"I don't have any money. What about a colony world? Can't you just send me to a colony world?"

Margot shook her head but maintained her tight, perfect smile. "Sorry, no. All colony world exploration and migrations are happening from Earth. There are still billions of people there we're trying to get off. They get the first crack at the frontiers."

Andrew clenched his teeth again and tried his best to remain calm. "Well, what do you want me to do? We won't be happy in the cities. We won't be happy in space. We can't go into the wilderness or leave this solar system. What am I supposed to do? Doesn't employee satisfaction mean anything? I mean, for Christ's sake, there's an entire solar system here, how can there be nowhere for us to go?!"

Margot pursed her lips and nodded. "Employee happiness is critical to the success of every corporation."

"Look, we'll be good employees, I promise. We are the industrious types. We like our hands in the dirt and wide-open spaces. I'm sure you have somewhere like that?"

Margot nodded. She turned to a computer terminal on her desk and began typing in queries. After several long moments of her face buried into the screen, she lifted her head and smiled. "As a matter of fact, I think I have the perfect place for you."

"Really?" Andrew's face lit up and all the anger and anxiety melted away in an instant.

"Yes, really." Margot smiled and handed a piece of paper to Andrew. "Just sign here."

Dust swirled on the arid landscape. Rocks jutted out from the ground in massive pillars. Bright sunlight shined down through the thin atmosphere of the nearly dead world and cast animal shadows from Andrew's children's toys.

"This is the best we could do?" Amanda, Andrew's wife, said.

"Honey, this is fantastic!" Andrew said.

They stared at each other through face plates made of thick plexiglass. Their children danced and played around them in small space suits made just to their size. Domed structures behind them stretched to the horizon. A swarm of black and gold robots danced along the tops of the buildings, some repairing the structures, while a hundred miles away others were building brand new domes.

"How is this fantastic, exactly?" Amanda said.

"We have the entire planet to ourselves. We're the only people here!"

"Yes, that's great, but there's nothing here, honey. We can't grow anything. What's the point? I wanted trees and grass, not yellow dirt."

"That's the great thing, honey. The corporation is terraforming this whole planet. This land right here—" Andrew stomped his foot into the ground and put his hands on his hips— "This ground is ours."

"Ours?"

"Well, leased to us anyway; it's complicated."

"Why did they let us have this?"

"Oh, we're droid maintenance. Have to make sure the droids don't need anything. Some of them are even full AIs. They may need counseling or need to file a requisition or something."

"What?"

"Doesn't matter. When the terraforming is complete, we'll retire right here. There'll be a stream, and trees and grass and everything."

Amanda smiled. "Oh? Well, that's nice. How long will that take?"

Andrew shrugged. "Maybe fifty years?"

Amanda's smile faded, and she stared at her husband. Dust swirled around them as their children kicked rocks across the landscape. Above them, robots flew through the toxic atmosphere to continue the long terraforming project.

17

FRINGE SPACE
THE PRESERVE

"I just love playing in the sun with my friends and family. Daddy said we could go see the funny animals at the zoo. Isn't that fun?"

Ruth McArther - daughter of Alexander McArther, first president of Homer's World

**A**re we there yet?" Jacil said. She held her knees to her chin in the co-pilot seat of the small shuttle.

"Well, can you see?" Brin said. He pointed out the window at the planet rushing towards them.

"Yes, I can see, I want to get there already," Jacil said.

"Calm down, toots," Brin said. He loved 1950s-era television, and "toots" had become his new favorite word. "We'll be down in five minutes."

"Just hurry it up, bub," Jacil said.

"Look, missy miss, it's not easy to steal your father's spaceship, go on a joy ride, find an abandoned planet in the middle of civilized space, and get lucky with your girl, all before lunch!" Brin said.

"Who says you're getting lucky, pal?"

"Who says you're getting a ride home, toots?"

Jacil smiled. She loved the back and forth with Brin. No one else could get her so excited just from a simple back and forth as he could. Always trying to one-up the other with attitudes and phrases from three hundred years ago was just fun.

"So where are we landing, Buck Rogers?" Jacil said.

"Oh man. Looks like we're getting a signal ping." Brin's voice filled with confusion. "Great. I don't believe it. There's someone down there?"

"You didn't really think there would be a fully habitable planet smack dab in the middle of civilized space and there wouldn't be people on it, did you?" Jacil said.

"The parking lot on the cliff overlooking town was already full, what can I say," Brin said.

Jacil looked at the control console and examined the readouts. She scrunched her face into a frown and began pressing commands into the system. A single ping coming from the world was odd. For half a second she debated turning on the subAI on the ship and asking him what this planet was. Of course, the subAI would automatically signal the nearest neural network, exactly what they didn't want to happen. Can't sneak away when you tell everyone where you are.

"Are you sure you never heard of this planet?" Jacil asked.

"Nope, never. I told you, Bacin told me about it. Said there were a lot of really weird animals, but they were all harmless," Brin said.

"It's just odd. I mean this is a beautiful planet, right in the golden zone; why wouldn't it be populated?"

"Space is big – there are other planets in civilized space that aren't populated. Governments, universities, rich people, someone buys them. We aren't exactly hurting for worlds these days. This is probably some rich guy's personal planet."

"Well, are you sure we should be here then?" Jacil said.

"Sure, we're one tiny little ship. We'll go in, have some fun—" Brin winked— "and head out."

"That is, of course, before someone pinged us."

"Well, there is that. We'll just go down, tell them we're lost, needed to fix something, and be on our way in no time. Then we'll go to the other side of the planet, find a nice waterfall and chill out for a while," Brin said.

"What if someone's on the other side of the world?"

"Then we'll say hello to them too."

"Let's just skip going down now, go to the other side of the planet and be done with it," Jacil said.

"Can't, if we pinged each other, they know we're here. They'll report us. Look, it's no big deal, we'll go down, see what's happening, then get out of Dodge and have some fun."

"Fine." Jacil folded her arms, accessed her internal subAI system and started reading a book she had downloaded before the trip. Even though she liked Brin, sometimes he acted like a child. It was bothersome.

Jacil spent the next twenty minutes pretending to read. Their ship continued its descent into the atmosphere of the planet. At ten thousand feet the ship took an evasive turn to avoid a large flock of flying creatures. Brin shouted an expletive while Jacin just stared out the window.

Flying between the clouds, a flock of mammals turned

and twisted through the sky. Jacil had never seen creatures like these. They had a wingspan of up to ten meters and were themselves about three meters long. A thick, full mane of hair flowed back from their very human-looking heads. Jacil couldn't make out more details as the ship banked hard to the right to avoid the flock.

"What are those?" Jacil said.

"I have no idea. Crazy-looking, aren't they? I saw something like them once on a vid of fringe space. There are some wild things in the universe," Brin said.

"How did they get here then?" Jacil asked.

"I'm not saying they are the same things, just looked like them. But who knows, maybe the rich guy that owns this place liked them and brought them out here."

Jacil started accessing the computer monitor to see if she could get a video feed to get a closer look. The computer informed her that external cameras on this ship were, for some reason, controlled by the sleeping subAI system. Which meant no video.

"The vid system is controlled by the subAI?" Jacil asked.

"Yep, just how this ship is wired. Who cares anyway? They are just big alien birds."

Their ship descended toward the planet surface. From her seat, Jacil could see people coming out of a starship on the surface below them. There were no buildings or structures in sight, just the lone ship sitting in a wide-open field.

Brin landed their craft a few hundred meters from the other ship. Jacil and Brin unstrapped and moved toward the exit. Jacil grabbed a backpack filled with items. They lowered the ramp and headed out of their ship.

In the distance, Jacil could see three figures moving towards them.

"Hello there," one of the three said. Jacil could see they were all men.

"Hi," Brin said.

"Can we help you with anything?" another man asked.

Jacil watched as Brin crinkled his brow. He turned to Jacil, who just shrugged back. *Why would these people be asking if they can help us with anything? Aren't we the ones not supposed to be here?*

"Sorry, no, we just stopped in to make sure it was OK for us to be here," Brin said.

The three men exchanged confused glances and looked back at Brin. The one in the center, who hadn't spoken yet, said, "Yeah, sure, you can be here."

"Are you sure?" Brin asked. "We don't want to intrude on someone else's planet or anything."

"Yeah, we're game wardens on the planet. It's just a big preserve of sorts. Anyone is welcome to come down, visit, and leave," the man in the middle said.

"Great, well, OK then," Brin said.

Something caught Jacil's attention in the distance, closer to the three men's ship. She instructed her internal subAI to increase her vision and hearing to try to make it out. A creature of some kind seemed to be struggling in the grass.

"What's that?" Jacil asked. She pointed to the area and made several steps in that direction.

One of the three men held up his hand and stood in front of Jacil. "Hold on there, that's one of the creatures on the planet. We're, uh..." The man paused and looked at his friends who remained stoic. "We're taking samples."

Jacil went around the man's outstretched arm and started walking at a brisk pace toward the creature. Her subAI routine informed her that the creature's vocals were indicating it was in distress of some kind. One thing Jacil could never really stand was something, anything, in pain. She hated the sound of suffering.

"Brin, are you scanning that ship?" Jacil said to Brin via internal communications through their internal subAI systems.

"Yeah, that thing is ancient. But, the navigation system, it's newer. So odd. There's no computer core in that ship, no AI. But the navigation system has a subAI. That's what must have responded to our automated ping," Brin said.

"I don't understand, what are they doing here?" Jacil said.

"I have no idea, maybe they really are wardens here just using an old ship to get around."

"Why the new navigation system?"

"Probably just to get around civilized space when they need to. I'm accessing it now. The thing isn't locked down, totally open."

Jacil nodded to the three men but walked past them towards the creature on the ground. Behind her, the three men grunted their disapproval and followed her. As she got closer to the creature in the grass, Jacil picked up her pace. The poor thing struggled against ropes that had been tied around its midsection.

"It could be dangerous, Jacil, maybe you shouldn't get too close," Brin said.

"Don't be foolish. If it were dangerous, our subAIs would tell us."

"They only work on things they know about and things they can make a guess on. Alien wildlife is not something they can easily deal with. I mean, if it has ten-inch fangs, yeah, sure, it'll warn you, but what if it had poison darts under its tongue?" Brin said.

Without answering, Jacil ran up to the creature and pushed back some of the grass. The animal was three meters long and had a thick mane of hair flowing back from its head. Two massive wings attached to the back of the creature were tied tightly to its sides. The animal's body was hairless and was a creamy dark tan.

"Brin! This is one of those flying beasts!" Jacil said out loud.

"Sure is, girly," one of the three men said as he approached.

"What are you doing to it?" she said.

The animal turned its head, and Jacil took a deep breath and stepped back. Something she hadn't at all expected looked her in the eye and smiled a sad, painful smile. The face was human. A woman, maybe twenty-five, with high cheekbones, pointed nose and very deep dark brown eyes, stared at Jacin.

"What the hell is going on here?" Jacil stood up and turned on the three men.

"Just calm down now," one of the men said. He didn't come closer to Jacil or the creature but held up his hands as if to say he was harmless.

"What is this place?" Jacil asked.

A low rumble echoed in the distance. The three men, nearly in unison, lifted their arms to their faces and checked something on their wrists. Jacil gave Brin a confused stare at the sight of the wrist computers. Even kids didn't use those anymore. Her subAI routed through the ship's controlled sensors, indicated that a large herd of animals was headed this way.

"They're probably coming because of the kid's ship landing. They want to see what's going on," one of the men said.

"Alright, lets set up to get one," another said.

"What about them?"

"Oh, right," another said. He quickly pulled out a device from his pocket and pointed it at Jacil. Her subAI never alerted her to a threat, which she thought was curious as the man pressed the button on the device and she lost consciousness.

JACIL WOKE to her hands and feet bound by ropes. Her subAI informed her she had been knocked unconscious by an ultrasonic weapon. The device was so crude the subAI didn't consider it a threat. The subAI informed her that it had taken steps to assure that a future ultrasonic attack will not be successful and it had modified her ocular cavity to not be susceptible to it again.

"What are you doing awake?" one of the men said.

"It's that computer inside their heads," another replied. "It woke them up. That's why I told you to tie her up; don't argue with me next time."

The other man grunted. Jacil tried to look around and eventually saw Brin. He was also lying on the ground, struggling against the ropes. He smiled at her and shrugged to which Jacil gave him an icy stare.

"What now, genius?" Jacil asked Brin through her subAI.

"Relax, can you get your fingers to your ropes?" Brin asked.

"Yes, so?" Jacil said. After a moment she realized Brin's plan. She instructed her subAI to start growing her nails and make them razor sharp. It complied. "OK, good thinking, but then what?"

"Well, we run like hell. I've been awake a little longer than you. These guys are unmodified," Brin said.

It annoyed Jacil that he was getting excited. She rolled her eyes, "How can that be? Are they religious fanatics? From the Church? Those types don't travel much."

"No, these aren't zealots, they have to be from the fringe. They may even be part of the exodus. Maybe they even were on Old Earth! Why would they come here? Civilized space represents everything these types hate," Brin said.

"Fringe? Old Earth? You mean people outside of civilized space? Savages?"

"It has to be. This is awesome. I wonder if they'll let me go with them?"

"Are you insane? Look at what they are doing here! These men are animals. They are torturing these poor creatures," Jacil said.

"We don't know what they are doing. And they didn't kill us, did they?"

Jacil looked around and saw two of the men. They stood over another still form on the ground. This creature had four powerful limbs that were etched in thick muscular bands. Both paws on the front legs ended in human hands. Fur covered the creature from its head to the end of a long tail. The face, like the winged woman, had features that were so human that Jacil thought this could be someone that went under extreme augmentation.

"Excuse me," Jacil said.

"What?" said one of the men – Jacil had a hard time telling them apart. He carried a long needle and a plastic case in his hands.

"What are you going to do to me?" she said.

"This?" said the man holding up the needle. "Not for

you. For them. Look, we don't have a lot of time here, and you two probably attracted some attention. We aren't going to hurt you, or them, or anyone. We just want to take some blood from them and be on our way," said the man.

"Blood? Why?" she asked.

The man sighed. "It's very valuable to us."

Jacil looked at Brin, who shrugged and shook his head. The man rolled his eyes and walked over to the winged woman, grabbed her arm and began examining it. He wrapped a plastic cord around her arm and started tapping it with his fingers just below the bicep. He shot a glance back to Jacil. "Don't worry, they are immortal. I couldn't hurt them if I tried."

"This planet is the Immortal Preserve? The ship wouldn't have let us be here, the subAI on board would have–" Brin cut himself off in mid-sentence.

"Good job turning him off," Jacil said. "What is the Immortal Preserve? I've never heard of it."

"This is where they sent the people that pushed genetic augmentations beyond what it means to be human. These creatures don't age. All they need to live is sunshine, or heat, or even just breathing," Brin said. "But it changed them too much. They stopped thinking like humans. They would just fly or swim or run anywhere they wanted. Not so good to have people with thirty-foot wingspans flying over star ports. So they found a planet and shipped them all to it. I can't believe this is where Bacin sent me. He even told me to turn off the subAI!"

"And of course you wouldn't check what planet this was," Jacin said.

"No way – takes the idea of the unknown out of it," Brin said.

Jacin could hear the man standing over the winged

woman chuckle. *Great,* she thought, *well at least even savages are, at the end of the day, just boys.*

A scream erupted out of the winged woman. Jacin looked to see the man holding her arm and drawing out blood. The woman twisted but couldn't get away from the slow drain of her blood.

"Stop it!" Jacin cried. "You are hurting her, you savage!"

"Relax, she'll be fine," the man said.

Jacin checked her nails, and they were ready and sharp as razor blades. The rope was nothing more than twisted fibers. Her nails cut through them instantly, and she then freed her feet. She glanced up quickly to see Brin freeing himself as well.

Without thinking, Jacin turned from Brin and instructed her subAI to increase her muscle density by ninety percent and her reflexes by seventy-five. Her subAI informed her that these were dangerously high, but she overrode the warnings.

Jacil ran up to the man hovering over the winged woman and kicked him in the arm holding the needle. She instantly snapped the bones in his forearm. Stunned, the man fell back, lifted up his ultrasonic stun and fired.

"Sorry, that doesn't work anymore." Jacin took a step towards the man but fell back as he kicked her in the knee.

From behind her, she could hear Brin wrestling with the other two men. With his subAI and advanced genetics, Jacin knew he'd be just fine. She jumped to her feet and ran to the man on the ground. He reached for the needle in the winged woman's arm.

Jacin pounced on the man and rolled him onto his back. She straddled him, pinned down his good arm with her knee, put her hand on his throat and began to squeeze. She was never a violent person, not even a little, but to see savages like these men, who gave up on humanity and ran away into the deepest fringes of space, hurt something as beautiful as this woman was appalling.

"How does it feel, savage?! Care to fight someone who can fight back?" Jacil said through clenched teeth.

"We... only... want.. some... bloo..." the man said.

Jacil looked down and saw the bag filled with blood lying on the ground. She picked it up and held it over the man's head. "You want this? Well, you can't have it. Any of it!"

She felt a sting as the man, gritting through the pain, jabbed her with the needle at the end of the tube hanging from the bag. Reacting to the sudden stinging in her side, Jacil squeezed the bag of blood she was holding in her hand. With her enhanced strength, she forced the blood down the line, through the needle and directly into her body.

Jacil screamed. Her skin burned and her insides boiled. Her subAI attempted to counteract the alien blood, but moments later the internal computer system went silent. Terror filled Jacil as she realized she couldn't communicate with her subAI. Her entire secondary nervous system was shutting down.

With another scream, Jacil fell onto her back. She felt the blood coursing through her body, changing her, pushing her genome in incredibly complex ways. She felt a tightness in her chest as her heart raced.

"What did you do to her?" Brin screamed. Precious Brin. Jacil had planned today out perfectly. She was going to make love to him today in a secluded spot on a distant planet. How perfect would that have been?

"I didn't do that, son. It's the blood, it's changing her," the man on the ground said.

Brin ran up to Jacil and knelt beside her. He held her

head up and gently started to stroke her hair. Her face was twisted in agony and every muscle in her body tensed and coiled.

"I thought the blood just cured people?" one of the men said.

"A drop will. An entire pint of it? I'm surprised she's not dead yet," said another.

"It's her genes. She's able to handle the transformation."

"You mean it's turning her into one of them?" Brin said.

"Looks like," said the man with the broken arm.

"You son of a bitch!" Brin stood up and faced all three men, two of whom were well beaten already, and clenched his fists.

"Whoa!" the man in front of him said. "Look, there's a big misunderstanding here. We're not here to hurt anyone. We're trying to save lives."

"What are you talking about?" Brin said.

"I didn't know that was going to happen. I was trying to get her off of me. Look, the blood, these people," said the man pointing to the winged woman and the runner behind them, "their blood is a miracle cure-all. You don't understand where we come from. We don't have any of your technologies, and we don't get any help from civilized space. They just send us out here to fend for ourselves. This blood is like a miracle to us," the man said.

"You think that gives you any right to do this?" Brin's voice grew hard with anger.

"There's a plague on a place called Destiny. It's a colony world deep in fringe space. A big one. Over three hundred thousand people. One pint of this could cure ten thousand people. It's either that or they all die," the man said. He looked Brin directly in the eyes. "What would you do, kid? If all your friends, family, everyone, was going to die. We're not killing these people, just taking a little blood. They'll be fine."

Jacin heard what the man said. What would she do? Would she steal blood to save her family? But these men were savages. They must be lying. How did she even know they were going to let the winged woman live?

But they aren't.

We know them.

They have come before and will come again.

You can hear them if you try.

You are becoming us now.

Don't be afraid.

Soon you will sail in the skies.

Jacin cried out as a thousand voices filled her mind. She could hear them as clear as she could hear Brin through her subAI. But something was different about the voices. They were closer to her, more a part of her. As if she and they were one mind and the thoughts were as much hers as they were theirs.

The pain in her body stopped, and a feeling of wonder, of joy and love, filled her. Jacin stood and looked to the heavens. She couldn't see them, but she knew they were there. She could feel them as they sailed through the sky. Thousands of them. Singing and dancing and living amongst the clouds.

"Jacin?" said a voice behind her.

Jacin turned. She didn't recognize the people standing in front of her. She knew she should. One of them was very familiar. She concentrated but couldn't remember how to talk to them. She knew how to share her thoughts with the ones in the sky, but that was different. That was as natural as breathing.

"Jacin?" said one of them. He took a step towards her.

She knew him. Had she flown with him? But he didn't have wings. How could he fly? Did she love him like she did the others? She felt it. She knew it. She must have.

"Brrr… iiinnnn," Jacin tried to say. Frustration, a feeling she didn't like, filled her.

"It's OK, it's me," said the boy, or man, or whatever he was.

Jacin took a step towards him. He was close enough to touch, and Jacin reached out her hand and touched his face. Suddenly she could hear everything he said. She could hear him as if he was one of the sky people. She was Jacin, and he was Brin. In that instant, she remembered who she was, why she came here and who all these people were.

Not only did she know Brin, the other sky people shared the memories of the others with her. She could see the many thousands of people dying on a distant world. She knew now that these men meant no real harm, they were just trying to save their families. They just didn't want to be sick anymore.

Jacin smiled at Brin. He couldn't hear her, but she could remember how to make the words, how to speak. Slowly she said, "It's… o… k… I… happy. I… lov… u," she said and took her hand away from his face.

Brin shook his head and took a step forward. Jacin turned, smiled again, and knelt to the tied-up sky woman below her. She broke her bonds and helped her up. Together they turned from the men and walked off. Jacin didn't have her wings yet, but she knew they would grow in time.

"Wait! Jacin! Where are you going?"

"Easy, kid, let her go, she's something else now," said one of the men as he placed his hand on Brin's arm.

Brin broke free and screamed. He yelled at Jacin for

walking away and at the three men for making all this happen. He kicked the dirt and punched the open air. Out of the corner of his eye, he noticed the needle and bag of blood sitting on the ground.

Without a thought for the consequences, Brin leaped for the needle and the bag. The men jumped on him to stop him. They struggled for a moment, but Brin was able to grasp the needle in his hand and hold it to his arm.

"Don't do this, kid!" yelled one of the men.

Brin didn't care. He pushed the needle into his arm and tried to squeeze as much blood into his veins as he could. The most intense pain he could imagine filled his mind. He screamed as loud as he could, but the pain still kept coming, getting worse, taking over his mind.

Just as he tried to command his subAI to stop the pain, he panicked as he realized it was no longer there. The blood had boiled all parts of the artificial intelligence out of his body, seeing it as a foreign invader. Brin screamed one last time and passed out from the pain.

Jacin watched what happened. When it was over, she turned and walked off towards the horizon, craving the feeling to fly.

~

"How is he?" Meyers said.

"Passed the fuck out," Smith said.

"Well, he deserves it, little shit," Meyers said.

"He's waking up," the captain of the ship said. "Now shut up, both of you."

"Where am I?" Brin asked.

"On my ship," the captain said. He pointed around to a

squat and sad-looking room with metal walls and dirty floors. "This is the sick bay."

"Great," Brin said. He tried to sit up and look around but was too weak to lift himself.

"Do you know what happened?" the captain asked.

"When?" Brin asked.

"Do you know what planet you're on?" the captain asked.

"No, wait, I can't remember... I can't... what's my name?" Brin asked.

"Oh boy," Meyers said.

"It must have fried his memories, but there wasn't enough blood to do a full transformation."

"What the hell happened anyway? To the girl?" Meyers said.

"The blood did what it does. It wiped out all the artificial junk the civilized put in themselves these days and rewrote her DNA to match the other flyers," the captain said.

"You sure we won't have flying people on Destiny? We want to cure them, not turn them into birds," Smith said.

"Relax, both of you. You commissioned us to get you a cure, and we will. Now help me sit him up, we're taking him with us," the captain said.

"We can't take him with us, they'll scan his–" Meyers said but broke off in mid-sentence.

"Exactly, he's got no implants now, nothing. They won't let him back into the civilized. He's my responsibility, so he comes with me," the captain said.

"What's my name?" Brin asked.

A silence hung in the air as the captain just looked at Brin. He couldn't keep the same name. It was too, weird. After a moment he said, "Tommy. Your name is Tommy," the captain said, "and I'm Jake. You're going to come with us now."

"OK," Brin/Tommy said.

"Maya, come here and help me, will you please? Show Tommy to his new quarters," Jake said.

"Thanks, where are we going?" Tommy said.

"To every star we can find." Jake smiled.

18

CIVILIZED SPACE

EVOLUTION R US

"There is nothing in the universe more magical than what we have already destroyed."

Major General William Braxton - Supreme Allied Commander - Deep Space Naval Fleet

L ight beads of sweat covered Charlie's forehead. He counted the dots of moisture and did his best to liken them to teardrops of a fallen god who only has one last promise to give. Yes, it was wordy and theatrical, but so was he at times. But the picture in his mind fit the mood and his mission of the day. In fact, he thought, asking a god to kill you may be easier than what he was about to do.

"Can I get gills, please? Oh, and a webbing in my fingers," a twenty-something girl said in front of him. She held her hand up to the man behind the counter and flashed him a bright, broad smile.

The man behind the counter, six feet tall with perfect

skin, a full head of hair and piercing deep blue eyes, nodded and turned to a row of shelves behind him. He pulled a few boxes and began toying with their contents in several machines on a desk behind him. Moments later he turned back to the girl and handed her a plastic container with a small pill inside.

"Here you are. Have fun," the man said with a smile.

"Thanks! We're diving reefs off the coast later today; can't wait." The girl waved and walked out of the small store.

Charlie took a step forward in line. Only one more patron stood before his turn. He pulled out the paper he'd handwritten earlier that morning and scanned the contents. He half-laughed at the audacity of his own request, as if anyone would agree to what he wanted. But he stood in line, ready to take his turn and ask anyway.

The next man in line stepped up the counter and asked for a genetic modification to grow wings. He and his family were moving to the cliff tops of New Colorado and apparently wings were practically mandatory.

Again the man behind the counter turned to his machine and mixed a concoction of genetic material that would grant the man his wish. He handed over a plastic tube that contained enough pills for the man's family. They both exchanged pleasantries and nods.

Charlie took a deep breath and stepped forward. His turn. He knew he'd never have the ability to say what he wanted without making some odd facial expression, so he'd written it down, to make sure the point was made. He handed the man behind the counter the slip of paper and calmly folded his arms across his chest.

The man turned to his machines, but before he grabbed any of his base materials, he turned back to Charlie with a frown on his face and his eyebrows deeply furrowed.

"You want what?" the man said.

"A heart defect. Preferably a bad one," Charlie said, confident now that the paper had conveyed his intent.

The man shook his head and somehow buried his frown deeper. "Why?"

"Does that matter? Can you do it?"

The man nodded and shrugged at once. "Well, of course, we can do it. But why would we do that? Why would you even ask?"

Charlie sighed. He'd barely come into this store in fact, more confident of failure than success. But then he thought of his dreams, of his purpose, and again he steeled himself with determination of his cause. He took a deep breath and said, "I don't mean to be rude, but isn't that my business?"

"We aren't allowed to do dangerous genetic modifications. Had one person that wanted poison glands in his fingertips. Another wanted to culture bacteria that would allow him to breathe pheromones at will. Can you believe that? Bottom line, we only do beneficial changes."

"This isn't a weapon. I can't hurt anyone with a heart murmur," Charlie said.

"No, but you can hurt yourself. This is suicidal. I think I have to ask my supervisor if I can do this," the man said.

Charlie nodded and shrugged his acceptance.

The man behind the counter turned and walked away from Charlie towards a door set against the far back wall. He disappeared into another room but reappeared moments later with a woman just as beautiful as himself. The two workers of the evolution center approached the counter and smiled at Charlie with practiced patience.

"Hello, my name is Melanie. How are you, sir?"

"Fine. You can call me Charlie."

"Why thank you, how are you, Charlie?"

Charlie frowned. "I'm fine."

"I understand that you want a genetic abnormality added to your genome, is that right?"

"Sure is," Charlie said.

"May I ask why? If you are suffering from suicidal ideation we can alert someone to help."

Charlie shook his head no. "That's not it at all. I have no desire to die."

"I'm not sure we can approve this even if you don't. Though this is technically not harmful to others, this modification could kill you."

"This isn't harmful, it's essential. You won't be hurting me; you'll be helping." Charlie leaned forward, his eyes blazing with honesty, his smile perhaps a bit too excessive.

The woman tilted her head to one side and frowned. "How is that, Charlie?"

Charlie looked the woman in her eyes and let the moment drag. Here he was trying to convince someone to do something they felt was wrong. He had to be subtle, he had to lead them through with logic. He took a long deep breath and let out a full sigh.

"Do you read, ma'am? Or go to art galleries? Or go to the theatre?"

The question took the woman off guard. She looked at the man behind the counter with her, who also looked confused. She turned back to Charlie and said, "Yes, I do, in fact. All of them. What does that have to do with anything?"

"Anything contemporary?" Charlie asked.

"Well, no. Frankly, everything is just redone or retold," the woman said.

"Exactly. I'm a creative, you see. I paint, write music, some plays."

The woman and the man both nodded with their perfect smiles and beautiful faces. Charlie smiled back.

"But I can't do any of that. Not anything good. No one can. I go to conferences, meet with fellows, and it's all the same bland, tired, well-worn tropes just redone a thousand new ways. The music is dull. The colors are empty, lifeless. There's something vital that's missing." Charlie lifted his hand and closed his fist to emphasize the point.

"What is that, Charlie? What's missing?" the woman asked, genuine curiosity showing on her face.

"Honestly, I don't know. I thought, perhaps because so much has been done in the arts, it's just overwhelming to new creatives. Or that we've seen so much as a species there's nothing left to see. But none of that's true. I've seen vids from the fringe of space. It's incredible there. It's alive in a way we're not."

"What does that have to do with your request, Charlie?"

"Maybe life without the possibility of death is just endless boredom. What if I can't create because we don't have the threat of our mortality? We're all immortal now. We won't ever die. Where's the thrill of life without the risk?"

"Why can't you just go there? Go to fringe space? Get all the adventure and life-endangering activities you want?"

Charlie nodded. "I've tried. Believe me. But travel is heavily regulated and restricted. Not anyone can just go out there. Unless you're on Old Earth, of course. They get a free ticket to the forever frontier."

The woman nodded and looked to the man behind him. She turned back to Charlie and shrugged. "I understand now. But we have rules. I still can't do something that's dangerous. Even if it's just to you."

Charlie nodded. He turned his head to one side and revealed a silver disc installed in his skull. "I'll be backed up constantly. This will record my thoughts and transmit them to the central computer core. So it won't be a total threat." Perhaps it was enough for Melanie?

"I don't know if that–"

"Please," Charlie said, cutting her off. "I can't create if I can't feel the risk of being alive."

Melanie frowned. She told her colleague to help some of the other patrons in the store. She stared into Charlie's eyes and then shook her head and frowned.

"Charlie," Melanie said.

"Is what I want truly illegal?" Charlie said.

Melanie shook her head. "No, it's not technically illegal. But there are store policies."

"Is there a store policy that will prevent you from giving me this?"

"Not directly, no."

Charlie felt his heart jump. Was she about to give him the change? He told himself to calm down, ease his thoughts. Last thing he needed to do was get giddy and make the situation odd.

"Then please?"

"How do you know this is what you need?"

Charlie was stunned for a moment. No one had asked him that. "Well, I guess I don't."

The woman smiled and nodded. She turned her back to the counter behind her and mixed up a blend of genetic material. She handed it to Charlie and smiled. "Promise to keep your backup in place?"

"Absolutely," Charlie said.

"I look forward to what you will create."

"Thank you, I can't thank you enough," Charlie said.

"My pleasure. Do come back if you want to reverse the change," Melanie said.

Once home, Charlie went to his desk and sat. He sat back in his chair and smiled. He reached up to the small disk inserted in his neural interface attached to his skull. Charlie removed the data connection from his brain, severing the connection his synthetic neurons held to the vast data centers of the central computer cores. No more backups. No more safety nets. "The threat must be absolute," he said to himself. He opened his inkwell and took his fountain pen in his hand. He pulled out a parchment of paper and began humming a tune he'd never heard before.

19

___

BAR CHAT

INTERLUDE II

Doug smiled.

He liked telling stories to the old man. Even if the stories felt, foreign? Doug frowned for a second. How did he learn about the corporate world again? Or Charlie and his heart murmur? He shook his head and smiled so hard his cheeks hurt. He suddenly remembered chatting about them on one of the ships on the way out here. Of course he had. How else could he have heard about it?

"So the guy gave himself a heart murmur on purpose?" Hill said.

"Sure did."

"Doesn't that prove my point? In the fringe, life is free, we're alive. In the civilized, sure you can get everything you want, maybe even live forever, but what's living without challenge?"

Doug nodded, his smile shrank. That did make some sense to him. What made the civilized worlds better? He was kicked out of them. Couldn't even live there. A rush of confidence filled him. He just wasn't thinking right. He'd been traveling for weeks to get here. Of course the civilized was better. And Doug would prove it. Their little story telling contest was far from over.

Besides, Hill's hiding something.

A flash of fear fired up Doug's spine. Why did he think that? He didn't mean to think that. Doug gripped the bar top, his knuckles turning slightly white. He took a long deep breath and calmed his nerves. The memory of the man that came to him with his mother, John McMillan, flared in his mind. At the space station where John had taken Doug, the doctors there had tried to fix him. Change his body so that Doug could take implants. But it failed. The doctors had said that some residual side affects could linger. Like memory problems and echo's from the AIs that probed his brain. Doug took a deep breath. He still needed to get on a ship. He needed to get to the frontier.

Eyes on the prize, Doug. He smiled and turned back to Hill.

"Ok, boyo. My turn," Hill said. "See, out here in the fringe, the choices you have to make to survive, they ain't as simple as getting a heart murmur."

20
———

FRINGE SPACE

STRANDED

"One can never assume knowledge is enough."
Elijah

Samantha kicked the console hard enough to crack the metal casing. She didn't feel anything through her reinforced steel boots. A significant dent that perfectly matched the toe of her boot was now forever imprinted on the front metal cabinet.

"Why did you do that?" Tony asked. He was sitting next to her with a large wrench in his hand, "Now I have to fix that too."

"Sorry," Samantha said. She got up from the console and walked towards the doorway. Each step stomped out on the metal floor with force. She extended her arms to her sides, and her hands balled into fists as she left the auxiliary control system.

They had been on this planet for weeks, and Samantha was reaching her end. They had crash-landed during a simple survey mission. They weren't even supposed to leave orbit, but old man Bill just had to do a deep scan in the canyon. Even though the scans did find some life, a lousy plant, the price for it was just far too high.

She rounded a corner and nearly ran into Debbie, the only other woman on this ship. They had bonded over their years on the ship and become close friends.

"Sorry, Debs," Samantha said. She pivoted her shoulder and moved past Debbie.

"Whoa, where you off to?" Debbie asked. "Everything OK?"

"Yeah, just frustrated. I'll talk to you later," Samantha said.

"I'm going out to the canyon tonight to get some more samples. Might as well, right? Care to come?"

"Not tonight. Be careful, Debs," Samantha said.

It wasn't really fair to dismiss people, especially in their current circumstances, but Samantha was just in a mood. She didn't even know where she was going. Maybe she should go with Debs tonight, she thought. But honestly, the labor of putting on a suit, going through airlocks and decontamination routines, just to get a sample of an ugly plant was too much for her right now.

Eventually, she found herself in the small gym on the ship. A large sand-filled bag swayed back and forth as she punched her fists into the canvas sides for hours. All this time being stuck on this planet and no hope of rescue had frayed her nerves to the point of breakdown.

And she had concluded that she hated fringe space. Life on the frontier was lousy. She had thought she'd scored success in a contract to catalog the planets just on the edge of civilized space. All the refugees from Earth had to go somewhere, and Samantha's job was to find them a new home. The last thing she thought, however, was that she would be joining them.

"Sammy," a voice from behind Samantha said. She didn't stop hitting the bags. Bill sighed behind her and put a hand on her shoulder, which she quickly shrugged off.

"Tony needs help with the life support and Ed needs some help on the printers. If we can get the printer up and working we can get the parts we need and get out of here," her father said.

"OK, I'll find Ed," Samantha said.

"We'll get out of this. We've been in worse spots," Bill said.

Samantha stopped punching the bag and turned around to face Bill. He was easily a foot taller than her, with long gray hair tied in a ponytail. A thick beard of matching color covered his face.

"Dad," she started but trailed off. She sighed, put her hands on her hips and said, "I know we'll get out of this, I'm not worried about that. I can get the printer up and running. But this was close, really close." Samantha paused and looked her father in the eye. "We have to be more careful out here."

"I know, I know. I let my curiosity get to me," Bill said. He smiled and winked at her and gave her a tight hug.

Samantha punched him lightly in the arm. She loved him, but damn could his curiosity be a pain in the ass. And this time, the danger was real. No one came out here and no one ever would if they couldn't get off this rock. That's why the contract with the Empire paid so much.

"OK, I get it, you're sorry. I can't breathe, Dad," Samantha said.

Her father let her go and smiled. He turned and walked out of the gym and down the corridor. Samantha smiled and was a little less frustrated. From down the corridor, her father said, "And go help Ed, let's get off this planet and onto the next."

"OK, Dad," Samantha called. She punched the gym bag one more time and headed for the showers.

Thirty minutes later Samantha walked into the fabrication room. Ed sat in front of a large three-dimensional printer with a look of disgust on his face. He snorted at the console and ran his hands through his blond hair.

"Problems?" Samantha asked.

"I need Debbie in here. Can you please go and find her?" Ed said. He didn't turn around or acknowledge Samantha's presence. It was as if he were speaking to a computer console.

Samantha smiled, nodded, turned and left. Ed may have been a genius but he was also an impatient ass at times. She knew better than to get in his way. Since he asked for Debbie, clearly the issue was software and not hardware. If the software ran a glitch or, God forbid, got a virus, then they needed someone on the ship who could write a new subroutine in their sleep.

"Debbie, this is Sam, can you copy please?" Samantha asked over the communication channel. There was no response.

"Computer, where is your mommy?" Samantha said to the ship's subAI.

"Debbie left the vessel more than an hour ago to investigate biological life on the planet surface," the subAI said.

"She never came back?" Samantha asked. She was already heading for the airlock and her jumpsuit.

"No, Debbie never re-entered the vessel," the subAI said.

"Great. Dad, Ed, Tony, meet me at the airlock. Debs is missing, and I need all hands," Samantha said. She started to jog towards the airlock. Once there she nearly flew into her jumpsuit and grabbed a weapon from her locker.

"What's going on, Sam?" Bill said. He entered the locker room next to the airlock and began to disrobe.

"Debs is missing. How could she have been gone so long and no one noticed?"

"We're all busy trying to get the ship fixed, just slipped by us. I'm sure she's fine," Bill said.

"Yeah, let's just get out there," Samantha said. She checked to make sure her dad was secure in his suit, then punched the airlock control. A large steel door closed behind them and started to seal.

"What about Ed and Tony?"

"They'll catch up, every second counts," Samantha said. Her father nodded.

"YOU THINK SHE CAN HEAR US?" Tony said. He and Ed had caught up with Samantha before they entered the ravine.

"I don't know – Dad?" Samantha asked.

Her father didn't answer. He stared at Debbie, who was fully encased inside a transparent membrane of a large plant. She was naked and seemed to float in a green liquid. Four large brown petals, each the size of a human body, surrounded the membrane. The valley she had found was covered in more of the large plants. Several other plants had animals of different sizes encased inside of them while many more were empty.

Debbie's clothes were lying in a pile in front of the

brown petals. Though they all wore environmental suits in the event of alien bacteria or viruses, the atmosphere was human compatible. Every world on their list had to meet minimal human viability profiles.

Inside the plant, Debbie wore an expression of happiness and joy. Her body seemed to be in a state of bliss. She softly floated in the green liquid almost as if she were asleep.

"What are her vitals?" Samantha asked. She pulled open her portable interface and scanned Debbie inside the plant. Full statistics of her health came back to the screen. Debbie was actually, other than being encased in an alien plant, not in any imminent physical danger. Her vitals were all green across the board.

"She's getting oxygen?" Samantha asked.

"Yes, it does look like it," Bill said. "And nourishment. Look at that, her electrolytes and nutrient levels, all stable. Look closely at her nose and mouth. There are tiny vines entering both. The plant must be supplying her oxygen that way. Astounding."

"So, she got naked and jumped in there? Why would she do that?" Tony asked.

"I don't know. Perhaps Debbie took off her breathing apparatus, and this plant emits some type of pheromone. Lures its prey into it and then slowly digests," Bill said. He sounded more like he was giving a lecture than looking at one of his crew.

"Dad, what are you saying? This thing is eating her?" Samantha asked.

Her father only nodded. Samantha started taking items out of her backpack, including a long rope and a long collapsible walking stick. She tied off the rope to the end of the stick and positioned it on the edge of the green liquid.

There was a thin membrane covering the liquid. Slowly Samantha pushed into the green liquid. Immediately her father grabbed her arm and pulled it out.

"Wait, look there," Bill said. "As soon as you broke the membrane her vitals shot up, heart rate, oxygen levels, everything."

Samantha looked at her computer readout and back to Debbie. Inside the liquid, Debbie's mouth turned into a silent scream as if she felt the walking staff pierce the membrane and it hurt her. For a few seconds, Samantha just stood there and stared at her friend encased in the alien life form.

"Now what?" Tony asked.

"Can we move this whole thing to the ship?" Samantha asked.

"Doubtful," Bill said. He began to examine his scan readings of the plant's root system.

"I don't mean to be rude, but we have bigger problems right now," Ed said. His hands were on his hips as he turned away from the encased Debbie.

"What?" Samantha said.

"Yeah, what could be worse than this?" Tony said.

"The code on the printer is screwed. Specifically, the design for the part we need for the engine," Ed said. "Actually, about a dozen parts are corrupted. I've already printed the ones I could."

"Great," Samantha said. "Why hasn't she been working on that since we've been here?"

"She has. Already fixed a few dozen. But our ship was in bad shape. Debbie has been writing a lot of code just to get the subAI back up and running," Ed said.

"Didn't we back up this stuff?" Tony asked..

"Of course, but the crash fried most of our systems.

Debbie has had to rewrite part of the computer's code base just so she can cope with the blowouts. Plus all the print designs, Debbie can't make new ones – she has no idea what an engine part should look like, so she has to take all the corrupted files and try to fix them bit by bit. That takes a lot of time."

"OK, I get it," Samantha said.

"The root system is immense. It stretches for miles. It seems to overlap as well. I mean, this root system almost seems shared. As if each plant is borrowing from it and using it," Bill said.

"I don't get it; if there is a root system that big, why encase animals?" Tony said.

"I'm going back to the ship. There's nothing I can do here. Maybe I can get the computer to rebuild some of the print jobs," Ed said. He turned and walked off towards the ship.

"Tony, Dad, stay here and see if you can figure something out. I don't know, get some readings of the biology of the plant. We have to find a weakness," Samantha said.

As she turned and followed Ed, she heard her father say, "I have an idea." She debated stopping and going back. Some of her dad's ideas could be scary. But she decided her best place was back on the ship. Her own coding skills were nowhere near as capable as Debbie's – she coded some of the subAI's base for heaven's sake – but maybe Sam could add a routine here or there. Better that than flinching at her dad's latest idea.

SAMANTHA SLAMMED her hand on the desk when she realized there was no way she was going to rebuild these files. The corruption was subtle and deeply buried. It would take a singularly talented coder to piece together these files. The computer could do some, but even the ship's subAI wasn't up to full strength from the crash.

"Ed, this is pointless," Samantha said. "We need Debs."

"Yeah, I can't do this stuff. How does Debbie do this?" Ed said.

"Dad, Tony, any update?" Samantha asked over comms. No response.

"Dad? Respond please," Samantha said. Still no response. She looked at Ed, and they both looked worried.

"Ship, can you confirm if their communication links are on or off?"

"I can not determine the state, I apologize," the ship replied.

"I don't get that. You should be able to see them if their wrist comps are on or off. So what the hell does that mean?" Samantha asked.

"It would mean they are non-functional," the computer said.

"Yeah, that's what I thought. OK, Ed, let's go," Samantha said. She knew she never should have left her father out there alone. Even though that was ridiculous; her father was more than capable of taking care of himself.

Samantha and Ed raced through the ship, out the airlock and down into the ravine in less time than Samantha would have thought possible. They both ran up to Debbie and noticed she had not changed. There was no sign of her father or Tony in the area. Ed walked through the forest of plants to see if he could find some trace.

Samantha approached the plant that was holding Debbie. She tried tapping on the brown leaf to see if she could somehow wake her up. Debbie didn't flinch.

Samantha even pounded on the leaf once just to see what would happen. Nothing did.

"Over here, Sam," Ed said.

Samantha turned and walked over to where Ed stood. In front of him were two plants about five feet apart. One held her father and the other Tony. Both of them had stripped their clothes and dropped them in front of the plant. They had expressions of bliss on their faces, and a quick check of their vitals showed nothing wrong.

"What is going on?" Samantha said.

"I'm going to get a portable med bed, pull them out and throw them in it. That thing can revive them no matter what this green goo is doing to them," Ed said.

Samantha didn't disagree. It was an extreme route to take as there was no telling what the plant was doing to their metabolism, but at this point, they had no choice. She nodded to Ed and turned to walk back to the ship. It only took her two steps to realize Ed wasn't following her.

"OK, come on," Samantha said.

"I can't move." Ed pointed down to his feet. It appeared he had walked into a patch of the root system that had tangled his legs and prevented him from moving.

"Great," Samantha said. She walked over and started breaking off pieces of the root. As she bent down, she noticed the root system was moving and entangling itself around Ed's feet.

"I can't get it off." Samantha tore at the roots but was unable to break off the thick cords. It had grown to cover Ed up to his thighs and quickly began creeping up his torso.

Ed struggled to free his legs but quickly found his arms also pinned to his body. Samantha stood up and drew her sidearm but didn't know where to shoot. If the root system really extended for miles, then shooting at it would do no good. Within seconds the vine tendril had reached Ed's face and with a delicateness that Samantha was not expecting, it removed his environment mask, exposing him to the atmosphere.

The expression on Ed's face changed from terror to confusion. He looked around wildly as if looking for someone. He shouted, "What? Who are you? Where?" into the air. Samantha took several more steps back and holstered her sidearm. If this was how these plants caught their prey, maybe she could learn something.

The root system released Ed and began to retreat into the surrounding area. Ed laughed. He began to have a conversation with the air. "You're kidding me! This is amazing. Yeah, OK," Ed said. He started walking towards one of the plants.

"Ed! Can you hear me?" Samantha said. She approached Ed but several of the roots shot up around her face, and she backed away.

Ed turned and nodded. He pointed to one of the plants. The brown petals opened, and the membrane wavered, as if inviting him inside. He put his hand on the thin membrane holding the green liquid. Ed started removing his clothes and placed them on the ground in front of him. Once he was fully disrobed he pushed his hand inside the plant, and it accepted him inside.

"Well, now what?" Samantha said. She turned to walk back to her ship but stopped. There was no way she could repair this ship by herself and get it off the ground. She needed the others. And she didn't think she could get a med bed down here by herself.

"OK, I can probably carry Debbie," Samantha said. She approached Debbie's encased body and took out a large knife.

"Sorry Debs, I know this is going to hurt." Samantha positioned the knife just at the membrane and took a deep breath. Just as she was about to slice into the plant one of the large brownish leaves fluttered closed. It knocked Samantha in the face and sent her crashing to the ground.

Seconds later Samantha could feel something tugging at her mask. She quickly pulled back but her mask, which had been tangled by several of the roots, popped off her face. She held her breath and scrambled to get her mask back in place. The roots pulled at it frantically, keeping it just outside of reach.

Samantha lunged forward but missed by inches. She felt her legs become restricted and looked down to see them become tangled in the roots. Quickly, she pulled out an oxygen pin and stuck her leg. That would oxygenate her body for an additional few minutes, allowing her to hold her breath longer.

There is just no way I'm going to be slowly digested, thought Samantha. She pulled her revolver from her holster and put it to her head. The roots had started climbing up her body faster, almost as if they knew what she was doing.

Samantha spared one moment to think about her father, her brothers and her family. She thought about her company and her ship and how much she loved being out in deep space even if she also hated it. She would miss life so much more than she could possibly ever know.

A sudden pain burst into her mind as if someone had punched her in her leg and given her a charlie horse. Her father used to do that when she was taking kickboxing classes. She almost gasped as something started tickling her legs right where she was the most ticklish. With a loud gasp, she exhaled and took a breath and even managed to let out a yelp.

"SAMANTHA!" came a voice screaming into her head. She recognized it immediately as her father. She turned and twisted and looked for where everyone was. How did they get out of the plants?

"Where are you?" she said. She felt the root system slowly retract from around her legs.

"You idiot, Ed, why didn't you tell her you could hear us?!" Bill said. "She almost killed herself!"

"Sorry, I was confused, overwhelmed. Sorry Sam," Ed said.

"We are in the plants, you ninny!" Debbie said. Samantha hearing her friend's voice unleashed a torrent of emotions. She was alive!

"Debbie?" Samantha said. She walked over to her encased friend and looked inside. Debbie's face was unchanged but still serene.

"Yes! This is amazing! It's like... like being plugged into a computer system or something," Debbie said.

Well, that's Debbie. Typical she would equate something to a computer program. "OK, wait, you are all there? How can I hear you?"

"Pheromones! I told you it was the pheromones!" Bill said. "This plant is simply amazing! The ecosystem on this planet has been failing for eons. This plant evolved a symbiotic relationship with animals. It's not digesting them, it's supporting them!"

"What? Why would it do that?" Samantha said.

"The nutrients the root system collects aren't what the plants need to survive. The nutrients are for us. The plant is getting everything it needs from chemosynthesis from us! Our body heat. It then feeds us those nutrients." Bill's voice jumped like a schoolboy with his first toy.

"But, OK, it still encases us. We have to get you out of there," Samantha said.

"Actually, we could probably leave anytime we like," Bill said.

"What? Are you joking?" Samantha said.

"I'm not. I mean, I couldn't get out now, nor could the others, or we would have just popped out and told you everything. But we are slowly getting more control. We've only just now managed to get the roots to move based on our thoughts. Those roots that entangled you and Ed, that was us. It's almost like having a new limb. We just have to learn how to use it."

"Dad, are you serious?"

"Oh, I am. We could possibly even terraform this entire planet with these babies. Just put us in, and we can direct the growth! Not only that, we can even sense what the roots tell us. Imagine, an entire planet covered with this with people plugged in?"

Samantha noticed one of the plants to her right opening up its petals. It stood only a few feet from her father's. She took a step back, unsure how to proceed. What if this plant was just telling her what she wanted to hear? What if she was having delusions?

"Come in, Sam. We don't have a choice anyway. Our ship isn't going anywhere. It's been weeks, and we aren't any closer," Bill said.

"But how will we ever get off?" Samantha asked.

"Oh, I think I can get these roots to act with the delicateness of fingers. If I can do that, I can code in here! Plus, once we learn how to get out, I can come and go, fix the ship, and we can leave whenever we want," Debbie said.

"You weren't coerced to go inside?" Samantha asked.

"No, we all just tried it. After Debbie's leap of faith, and of course, she talked to us once our masks were off," Bill said.

"Debbie, why did you just go in?"

"I took off my mask to get some fresh air. I know, I shouldn't, but then the pheromones hit me. I can't explain it. I was just overwhelmed with a sense of well-being. Like it would be OK. Maybe that's how the plants get animals to go inside of them," Debbie said.

Samantha approached the plant. She noticed right away she wasn't peeling off her clothes. She had no desperate urge to get inside. Without a problem, she knew she could turn around and walk away and never look back.

That meant, in her mind, maybe this was real. Maybe it was her father. If she wasn't being coerced then neither were the others. And really, her ship was badly broken. They were really just deluding themselves thinking they could fix it before their supplies ran out.

"OK, what the hell," Samantha said. She disrobed and placed her clothes neatly in front of her. She put her hand on the membrane and slowly pushed. It gave slightly and started to welcome her inside. She was filled with a sense of well-being as she stepped fully inside.

Samantha felt the plant. She felt the root system and the depths that it went. She could feel the others, inside their minds. She could share thoughts with them as easily as with herself. She was one with them. Slowly she stretched out her mind and could feel the network of roots extending around the plant. Millions of animals were encased inside. She could even let a few of them out if she wanted, she knew. It would take some practice but she was confident she could do it. Samantha wasn't sure how long she and the others would survive here, like this, but at least she wasn't going to be plant food.

21

CIVILIZED SPACE

LIFE ON THE PRAIRIE

"Every man, woman and child has a right to independence and should have a decision in the world we live in."

Arnold Geoffrey Harris - Member of Hive Senate

Anna looked at the rising suns in the distance and smiled. She loved the morning. The twin lights of the companion stars, one yellow and the other a bright orange, cast rich and full colors across the sky. The view, different from pictures Anna had poured through as a child of Earth, always filled her with a sense of peace and warmth. As if the universe that allowed Earth to die made up for it by creating the world she and her people now lived on.

"Anna, bring the feed for the pigs!" her father yelled from behind the barn.

Anna smiled. "Yes, Papa!"

Several large buckets sat against a wooden fence lining the fields that her family owned. Anna lifted one of the buckets and carried them to a feeder, a large metal container standing three feet tall. She filled the bucket up with grain and carried it around the back of the newly constructed three-story barn.

Several dozen large hogs ran to the feeding trough at the sight of Anna coming around the corner. They grunted their approval as Anna poured the contents of the bucket into the long wooden container that held the food for them to eat.

"Anna, when you are done feeding them, gather eggs from the chickens. Should be time now," Samuel, Anna's father said.

"Yes, Papa," Anna said. Many of her friends hated farm life. They hated chores, and animals, and smells, and everything else that their quiet lives offered. Many did nothing but complain every day and night. All they could say was how much they wanted to go to space and explore the universe. But not Anna. She loved the bright mornings, the cricket-filled evenings and the large community dinners every Sunday.

A loud rumbling grew in the distance. Anna covered her eyes against the rising suns to see a small dust plume form in the east. Not even the big wagon that the Millers used that dragged through the dirt roads pulled by four strong horses could throw up that much dust.

"Papa, look," Anna said.

Samuel lifted his head to the horizon, his face, covered in weathered skin, dark and pale from long days spent under the twin suns, turned to a frown. He dropped several tools in a small wooden toolbox and stood. He clenched his fists, his hands thick and worn from a farmer's life. "Anna, come here. Away from the road."

Anna took a step towards their house just past the barn. A small metallic vehicle appeared over the horizon beneath the dust plume. The craft hovered over the ground as it sped towards Anna and Samuel.

"What is it, Papa? No one has a land vehicle, do they?"

"No, Anna. No one does," Samuel said. He walked next to his daughter and took her hand in his.

The vehicle came to a stop just in front of where Samuel and Anna stood. Two uniformed men stepped out, followed by two soldiers encased in full body armor. Anna had only heard stories of soldiers from friends, and that was mostly as rumor and guessing; none of her friends had ever seen one before either. None of their stories even came close to the real soldiers.

"Hello, I'm Captain Rodriquez, this is Lieutenant Garcia. Are you the owner of the home?" Captain Rodriquez said.

"Yes, Samuel Beiler. This is my daughter, Anna."

"Ma'am," Captain Rodriquez said.

"What can we help you with?" Samuel said.

"This planet has been annexed by the Free Republic of Nuevos Comienzos. You are now citizens of the Republic," Captain Rodriquez said.

Samuel nodded. He looked at his daughter and then back to the Captain. "What does that mean?" he said.

Captain Rodriquez smiled and took out a metal case the size of a deck of cards from his pocket. He opened the case and pulled out two small, flexible metal bands. "All citizens of the Free Republic are required to be included in the network for recordation and census."

"What does he want to do, Papa?" Anna said.

"We put this metal band on your head. You will be implanted with synthetic neurons that can communicate with the newly created planetary network, granting you access to every resource the Free Republic can offer its citizens."

Samuel's face dropped. He grabbed his daughter by the arm and pulled her away from the Captain. "No, we don't want this. This is not our way."

Captain Rodriquez sighed and closed the metal box. "Mr. Beiler, I'm afraid you don't have a choice. Implantation of the synthetic neural net is required for all citizens."

"Then we don't want to be citizens. You can go, we'll be fine on our own. We have always been."

"Not an option, sir," the lieutenant said.

Captain Rodriquez waved him off and maintained his perfect smile. "Forgive his roughness. I am curious why are you against implantation. This is no more than registering yourself with our government. It also allows you to communicate in case of emergency, access to thousands upon thousands of books, knowledge, even virtual video streams from around the galaxy. I can assure you there is no risk."

"We shun technology. It is simply our way," Anna said.

The captain and lieutenant exchanged glances. Both of their eyes glazed over, and Anna tilted her head to one side in confusion. Finally, after more than twenty seconds in a seeming trance, the captain shook his head and smiled.

"You're Amish," the captain said.

"Descended from Amish of Pennsylvania, on Old Earth. Different in our beliefs but close," Samuel said. "How did you not know this?"

"Honestly, we didn't even know your people were here until the satellites mapped the area."

Samuel nodded and straightened his back. "Well, we are here, and we don't want that." Samuel pointed at the small metal case held in the captain's hand.

"Papa." Anna put her hand on her father's shoulder, but Samuel shrugged her off and stood his ground.

"Everyone must register. It puts other citizens at risk if you do not," the lieutenant said.

Samuel lifted his arms and waved them around his property. "What risk is there from us?"

"It's not that simple, Samuel. Citizens in the Free Republic can live how they want to live. They can do what they want to do. There's enough planets, enough space, more than sufficient for everyone to live how they choose. This world is the fifth of the Free Republic."

"Sounds simple to me. Our people have chosen this way for a long time. We choose it now."

"But we can't let unregistered people wander around. What if you commit a crime? Steal something? Murder someone? Being unregistered means you would be invisible. We can't function as a society like that. Besides, this is harmless; you don't have to use the implants. It will be as if they aren't there," the captain said.

"The elders of our community would never agree. I know this. So I will not agree."

The captain sighed once and walked back to his vehicle. The lieutenant stood still as a statue and stared at Samuel and Anna as if they were criminals on their land.

"Go inside, Anna," Samuel said. "I will deal with these men."

"No, Papa. I shouldn't leave."

"Anna." Samuel looked at his daughter and gritted his teeth.

"Well, I just spoke to my commanding officer," Captain Rodriquez said as he walked back from the vehicle. "We understand your objections, but I'm afraid we're going to have to insist."

Samuel pulled a small, rusty and chipped pocketknife from his pants. He stepped toward the soldiers and shook his head. Anna had never seen her father approach another person with malice or violent intent – the very act was against all of their beliefs, and the action made her slightly queasy.

Captain Rodriquez sighed. "Hold him down," he said to the guards standing by the vehicle, who until now never moved or spoke.

The two guards walked to Samuel, and each took one of his arms. Samuel made a gesture toward them with his small pocket knife, but his act was entirely ignored, the guards treating his knife like an angry fly that buzzed near them.

"Papa!" Anna said.

"Lieutenant, put this on the girl." Captain Rodriquez handed the lieutenant one of the small implants from the metal container.

"This is not right! We are free people!" Samuel said.

"You're citizens of the Free Republic."

"Do not touch my daughter!" Samuel said.

"It's just a damn ID card, you stupid farmer," Captain Rodriquez said.

Anna felt the lieutenant's hands clamp down on her shoulder like a steel vise. A metal band wrapped around her head, and tiny needles entered the skin on the back of her neck. Her legs wobbled, and her head spun when the connection locked into her mind.

"She's done. Help me with the old man," Captain Rodriquez said.

Anna felt the world change. Above her, the sky shifted in color. Dark bands of red, blue, and orange filled the heavens. Anna at once knew, without knowing how, that they were communication streams. Her implants allowed her to see them. Signals opened themselves in her mind. Anna knew she could shut her implants down. Just turn them off like the soldiers said. It would just be an ID card. Nothing more.

But then data points opened. Libraries made themselves available to her. Anna let her curiosity blossom. She made the most innocent of requests. Information flowed into her mind. Every fact of her planet flashed across her vision. Her mouth fell open. This world held so much life. Anna felt something reach out to her. Satellites in orbit offered her a global view. Tears formed in her eyes as she saw her planet from miles above the skies. How much more to the universe was there to know? Her physical eyes fell to the men holding down her father. Everything slowed down. She sent a query to the libraries, asking what the Free Republic of Nuevos Comienzos was. The answer caught her off guard. They really were a free republic. People enjoyed being citizens. They were happy. Content. Anna suddenly found herself imagining a life not on this farm. A life of laughter, exploration, and fun. She could be so much more than someone that fetched eggs. And she knew she would have to leave. Her people would shun her. She would be forever an outcast. Was she already?

Samuel's shouting shook Anna from her thoughts. No matter how much she wanted this new life, she knew her father never would. She sent a query to the data network available to her. History, law, and governance of the Republic opened to her. She felt she agreed with Captain Rodriquez now. The implant was trivial, a simple ID system with access to data nets. Her people were religious, superstitious, and perhaps a bit too isolationist. But still, she knew in her heart it was their choice to be that way. And no one had a right to take it from them.

"Article three, section two, subsection seven of the Free

Republic code of conduct regarding newly annexed planets states free peoples may refuse implantation if such implantation violates their moral or religious beliefs. I can attest, this is the case, Captain Rodriquez," Anna said.

Captain Rodriquez turned to Anna, his hands hovering over her father, the metal implant ring hanging inches from his head. He let out a long sigh and stood.

"What did you say, ma'am?" the lieutenant said before Rodriquez could say a word.

"I said what you are doing is illegal," Anna said.

"Article three, section two, subsection seven is superseded by article five, section five," Captain Rodriquez said.

Anna tilted her head to one side and waited. An answer came to her in seconds. "Article five section five is only applicable during combat when confronting a hostile force," Anna said.

Captain Rodriquez pointed to Samuel. "He pulled a weapon; that's pretty hostile."

"Article seventeen section seven point three clearly states hostility under duress is to be considered self-defense and not retaliatory. The threat of violation of religious beliefs is cause for self-defense."

"Anna," Captain Rodriquez said.

"Captain, your actions are illegal. I insist you cease and desist."

"Want to quote me regulations? Fine. Article twenty of galactic rules of annexation place military control of all newly annexed planets and the citizenry subject to military imposed martial law."

"That does not make other regulations irrelevant."

"But it does leave the interpretation up to the opinion of the ranking military officer on site. Me. And I say his actions weren't in self-defense."

Anna shook her head. "Article twenty states that only officers of rank Colonel are empowered to settle disputes between native populations during annexation."

Captain Rodriquez stared into Anna's eyes. He wrapped the metal implant ring in his hand and twisted the ends into a knot. After a long minute, in which Samuel rose to his feet and stood beside Anna, Captain Rodriquez broke his face into a broad smile.

"Well, seems that the data net query system works. The truth is, we've never encountered folks so against technology as you." Captain Rodriquez shrugged and put the metal implant back into the container on his hip. He turned from Anna and Samuel and began walking back to his vehicle. The lieutenant turned and followed him in silence.

"Do you have any idea what you've done here? You've taken my daughter from me!" Samuel said.

"Father, it's alright. We'll talk once they've gone."

Samuel turned to his daughter, tears forming in his eyes, his shoulders sagging. He shook his head and looked away from Anna. Behind them, Captain Rodriquez climbed into the land vehicle and started the engine.

"We'll have to install some monitoring towers here and there. An unfortunate requirement to a population without implants. Per the regulations. I'm sure she can look it up."

The vehicle spun up dirt from the gravel road as it turned and left Samuel's property. Anna looked at her father and couldn't help the tears falling down her face. She knew the consequences of accepting the implant. The ancient traditions her people still respected and would obey.

"Father," Anna said.

Samuel turned away and shook his head. He reached down for the buckets Anna had carried and walked back towards the barn, his back bent lower than Anna had ever seen.

Anna thought of running to him, of spinning him around and demanding he talk to her. But it would be in vain. Technological aversion by her people was stronger today than it was on Old Earth. The only recourse they permitted even for accidental inclusion was total excommunication. Anything less and they risked modern horrors seeping into their community. Even Anna would be cancer to their world. The knowledge she possessed now would challenge their simple way of life.

"Goodbye, Papa," Anna said. She opened a channel to the local net and requested a pickup from an automated airborne shuttle to take her to the orbital station. From there she would find a new place, a new home, but she knew it would never be as beautiful as the one she was about to leave.

22

FRINGE SPACE

THE CHOICE

"All I ever wanted to do was care for my child."
Wanda Parker - first recipient of T-11 genetic cure.

Maya danced with the wind. Brown and gold five-pointed leaves swirled around her in a mini-storm of autumn's warning call that winter would soon fall. Each time she missed one as it flew past her she giggled and ran after it. Life was simple, fun and sweet. There was magic in the world, and goodness. Maybe in some way the leaves were fairies. Maybe they would whisk everyone away from this god-forsaken hell of a planet. But Maya's father, Maxwell, knew that would never happen. There was no magic or fairies here, only the horrible hell this place had become.

With a sigh, Max shook his head and cleaned the last of the dishes. A smile settled on his face at the sight of his daughter dancing that he spied through the small kitchen window. He dried his hands, and his eyes, and reached for his bag, coat, and his daughter's things. One last look at the cabin he'd built many years ago was all he spared.

In the front of the house, his daughter played and danced. Max lingered for a minute to watch her frolic. She chased imaginary friends and giggled as the breeze blew her hair. He wished he could give her more time. Let her stay and keep playing, be a little girl for the rest of her life. But that was impossible. Winter would be here in just another few weeks. And winter on this colony world was unlike anything they expected.

"Daddy!" Maya laughed and ran to her father. She wrapped her arms around his legs and squeezed.

"Hi, Honey, are you having fun out here?" Max said. Tears welled in his eyes, but he shrugged them off and refused to acknowledge the sorrow.

"Are we going to the ship now, Daddy?" Maya said.

"Yeah, we are. It's time, baby," Max said.

Maya nodded, smiled and ran off down the path. As Max looked after her, he could see other children running and playing in the direction of the ship. Their parents were behind them, smiling, talking and laughing. The sight reminded him why he did what he did. Why he pushed onward through the six long months of winter.

Max walked after his daughter and ran through the numbers in his mind. He'd have to check pressure levels, all the stasis chambers, and make sure there were no leaks. Soon, in the next few hours, the entire colony would re-board their damaged ship, climb back into their stasis chambers and go to sleep for six months. Winters here demanded such a sacrifice. Early reconnaissance of this world missed the elliptical orbit. Snow would fall and not stop for months, packing in a hundred feet high.

"Hi, Max," said a voice to his right. Max looked up and

saw Roderick and his wife. They both smiled and waved. Their four-year-old son ran ahead to catch the other children.

"Hi Rod, Mary," Max said.

"Everything OK, Max?" Rod said.

"Yeah, sure. Fine. Just running through the numbers," Max said. He thought he wiped away a tear in a way that didn't look like he was wiping away a tear.

"Well, we'll see you on the ship," said Rod. They walked on past Max and down the main road of the colony. Max slowed his pace just enough so they could pass him. Most people left him alone during this time. Max figured they thought he was busy thinking of subroutines, processes, computer things, and what it would take to put them all to blissful sleep for half a year.

They were wrong, of course. Max had all that programmed into the ship after their first year. He only had to do one thing when the time came, make one choice. The single hardest choice he would ever make in his entire life.

Maya ran up to Max and leaped into his arms. He grabbed her and held her close. Their crashed ship came into view. It sat there like a fallen tree that hadn't quite died. On landing, the sides of the hull were supposed to fold downward and open like a flower and become a seed for the colony to grow. This ship would never do that.

Max could see everyone entering the ship through the one access door that still worked. They formed a line where they all laughed and talked about spring. Some of the people here were falling in love with this place. Max heard rumors of some people contemplating staying here after the rescue ships arrived.

There's no way Max would ever allow that. This planet was a hell that Max would make sure no one would ever come back to. Once they knew the truth, the terrible hard truth, their choice would be different.

In time, Max and Maya reached their turn in the door and climbed inside the ship. Max walked to his and Maya's sleeper chambers. He opened hers and slowly placed her inside. She smiled and hugged her teddy bear that Max never even realized she was carrying. Maya smiled up at her father and kissed him on the cheek.

Max cried. He couldn't hold back his tears and his sorrow. He brushed his daughter's hair and kissed her on the forehead. With the weakest grin he could muster, he reached down and kissed the teddy bear goodnight too.

"It's OK, Daddy, I'll see you when I wake up!" Maya said.

Max nodded. "I'll see you when you wake up, baby." He laid her down in the chamber and closed the cover.

Max walked over to the central console of the stasis chambers. He checked each one remotely and saw that they were sealed and everyone was in place, waiting to sleep. Only they wouldn't be sleeping. Max entered a command into the system with a delay of twenty minutes for his chamber. He waited, and he thought. He reviewed every system in the entire ship for an alternate way of saving everyone before he pressed the button.

It had been a bad day when he realized the situation they were in four years ago. The ship had crashed, the colony was in jeopardy, and everyone was going to die. The stasis chambers functioned, but their supply of a cryogenic was depleted. Without the cryogenic, no one would survive the freezing process of the stasis boxes.

That was when Max realized where they purchased these stasis chambers. The first generation colony ships for the exodus were made hastily. Sometimes parts were substituted or swapped out. Like only providing enough cryogenics for a one-way trip or purchasing repurposed clone tubes to serve as stasis chambers.

During the spring and summer months the ship's solar panels would soak up all the energy they would need to power the chambers. That much power was more than capable of powering all six hundred clone tubes. The only thing left was the raw materials, which were provided by the bodies of the previous generation. Brain tapes would record their thoughts and memories for implantation when the cycle was complete.

Max knew he had no choice. There just were no other options. Not enough food to survive the winter or enough power to heat the ship. He looked back at his daughter's chamber; he could hear her giggling inside and pressed the button. With that one press of a button, he killed her and all six hundred and thirty-four others with lethal injections.

The silence was deafening. Max remembered this event, though he had never lived through it before. In truth, it wasn't even his daughter in the chamber. Maya, his beautiful sweet daughter, was just a clone of another girl.

Slowly, Max picked himself up off the floor. He didn't notice when he collapsed and started sobbing. He was a mass murderer, savior, killer of children, hero to everyone. And the horrible thing was, he had no choice. He was just a clone. Following through with a plan he had no part in creating.

Max climbed into his chamber and closed the lid. He remembered his short life. Even though it felt like he had lived each and every year, he knew those weren't his memories. He only had six months. One day, one of him, and a clone of his daughter, Maya, would have more. One day, they would leave this god-awful planet and be able to live their lives. For the first time that day, Max smiled.

23

CIVILIZED SPACE

OLD EARTH

"It was kinda like being plugged into a neural network. Except for the extra arm growing out of your side. That part wasn't so much fun."

Brin Fronners - author of *My Travels in the Fringe*

J az sat on a half-broken office chair and drank cleaned water from a bottle that could filter everything from microbes to iron chunks. Far in the distance, white light from a tower that stretched to the clouds lit up the sky in hundreds of miles in every direction. A capsule crept slowly up a carbon wire on its way to low orbit. The space elevator, one of a hundred scattered around Earth, carried fifty people a trip. Over five hundred a day from just this elevator alone. More than fifty thousand a day carried to the safety of orbit.

Jaz yawned, rubbed her chin and turned away. She stood on the fifth floor of an abandoned office building. Around her, overturned desks and emptied drawers littered the office. Not a surprise. She'd come here for safety, not to steal.

The city, once called Seattle, had been a good place a very long time ago; at least the pictures in the books looked nice. Water outside the window overflowed the streets. Flooded cities were often good places to scavenge, as most left in a hurry when the waters rose.

Jaz sighed. She reached into her backpack for food but found nothing. She'd run out earlier in the day. She pulled a desk close to one of the open windows and pulled out her meat vat. From another pocket in her bag, she pulled out a small satellite dish that she clamped to the ledge of the window on the exterior of the building. On a small pad, connected to the dish with a cord, she typed in commands for the system to find the nearest power source. The dish moved back and forth, scanning the skies until it found the microwave satellites in orbit. Green lights on the side indicated the system was ready.

"Mmm, freshly grown," Jaz said.

She plugged in her meat vat to her power dish and a low hum told her the system was warming up. She flicked through a few choices and settled on beef. It would take an hour to grow the required nutrients from its internal vacuum-sealed containment and another twenty minutes to cook. Jaz sat down on the floor and opened her computer to read.

Two hours later she dug into her hamburger and cursed herself for not printing any ketchup. Between bites, she read news about how Imperial citizens were demanding more of an effort to get people off the Earth. Fifty thousand a day was just not enough, and it would take centuries to get the billions of people still living on Earth to orbit and onward to new colony worlds.

"At least they give us power, food, and network." Jaz leaned against a filing cabinet and flipped through a dozen news sites and social networks. Several talked about how the Empire, the largest post-Earth civilization, was sending a dozen more space elevators and a thousand more supply centers, each providing meat vats, food and medicine printers and portable power receivers for everyone on Earth. It would take generations still, but at least they were trying.

Jaz finished her burger, closed down her laptop and started packing up her things. She was tired of looking at the same old debates on countless talk sites. None of it mattered. She, like everyone else, wanted off. Sure, a colony world would be hard, as would the trip there, but that was better than sitting in ruined old office buildings eating vat-grown burgers.

"Leaving so soon?" said a voice from the shadows.

Jaz spun on her heels and pulled a gun from under her belt. The old weapon had more rust than steel, but it would still shoot. She lifted her pack on her shoulder and ducked behind a desk. Whoever spoke remained hidden in some crevice of darkness. Sweat started to bead on her brow and her hand, which started to shake, tightened around the old gun. She hated people. They either wanted everything she carried or just to rape her and leave her for dead.

"Relax," the voice said. "I know you don't have anything and I don't think I could take it from you anyway."

"Don't give a shit; I see you, I'm shooting," Jaz said.

"Yeah, I know, that's why I'm not coming out. Look, you can leave if you want, I'm not stopping you; just would be nice for some company."

"Who are you?" Jaz said. She inched towards the door leading out to the stairwell.

"My name is Jocco the Jester, ever heard of me?" Jocco said.

Jaz stopped for a moment. She had heard of Jocco. He was popular on several vNets. He was very vocal about getting the Empire to increase the number of exodus colony ships and adding security to all the elevators. And he did often say, on some private boards, that he lived in what was once Seattle.

"OK, yeah, I have actually, but so what?" Jaz said.

"So nothing. Just thought it would help break the ice. Look in the second desk behind you, bottom right drawer," Jocco said.

Jaz looked toward the desk and again surveyed the room. She kept her body low, with her head just at desk height, and moved back to the desk. If this was Jocco he was a pretty cool guy and a partial cyborg. His rig was made by an automated hospital station. The automated hospitals, commonly called auto-hosps, were another gift from the Empire. They were fifty-foot by ten-foot-wide metal rectangles with a fully automated medical system available to anyone that could make it to them.

On the vNets, Jocco talked about visiting one once after an explosion ripped the bottom half of his body apart. The auto-hosp had put him back together and given him artificial parts. He could get a full body rebuild once he was off the planet; the auto-hosp couldn't do that.

Jaz opened the drawer to the desk Jocco had directed her to, and her eyes nearly bulged out of her head. Sitting there was a large plasma handgun, a nonlethal weapon that could stop a crowd of a hundred people in their tracks. Jaz holstered her old rusted six-shooter and heaved out the modern and sleek plasma stunner.

"Why are you giving me this?" She checked the gun, and it was ready to fire.

"Why not? That old rusty six-shooter is crap. Wave that around, and it'll just make people angry. Take the plasma gun. It's a gift. I have dozens of them," Jocco said.

"Dozens?"

"Yeah, I found an armory in someone's private house filled with quality guns. Can I come out now? Will you not shoot me please?"

Jaz looked behind her to the door to the stairwell. She took a few steps towards her escape route and turned back around to the sound of Jocco's voice. She took a deep breath and primed the plasma gun. It was risky to try to talk to someone but, to be honest, she was lonely, and she had heard of him. Besides, the gift of a weapon that could knock out an army helped.

"OK, fine, come out. But I'll run if you are not alone."

A wheeled chair came out from the shadows of one of the offices. A young man, not much older than Jaz, sat inside. Jocco wore a vest that Jaz was sure was bulletproof. His chair, large enough to carry at least twice his weight in supplies, had a meat vat, communication satellite and power source attached at various points.

Jocco smiled and waved. He looked like a harmless teenage boy, but Jaz knew better than to trust appearances. There could be a dozen more men behind the shadowed waiting to rape, kill, and make her a slave.

"It's OK, I'm totally alone," Jocco said. He held up both hands and grew his smile to its widest.

"OK, now what?" Jaz said.

Jocco shrugged. "Wanna have a drink?"

∾

"So, is this some kind of date?" Jaz asked with a small smile.

"I dunno, maybe?" Jocco ran his hand through his hair and shifted in his chair twice. "I read about dates on the vNets. Must have been nice to live like that, huh?"

Jaz nodded. She had been sitting with Jocco for hours now. He had let her explore all the rooms on this floor and even fire the plasma gun into them first. They were alone. Jaz had lost several friends to gangs over the years, and she wanted to make sure she never ran into one.

Still not fully trusting him, Jaz had sat down after checking the place and let herself relax, just a little. If it weren't for the fact that she heard of him on the vNet, she never would have stayed.

"How long have you been up here?" Jaz asked.

"Ever since I got stuck in this chair," Jocco said. "It's hard to get anywhere, ya know. So I just stay here."

"Are there ever any gangs or anything?"

"Nah, no gangs. Get some loners like you. Occasionally two or three at a time but that's rare. Most people stay near the elevators these days."

Jaz nodded.

"What about you? What are you doing in here? Where's your people?" Jocco said.

"Just looking for stuff. Always looking, ya know. Don't have any people anymore. Lost my family at the gate in Austin. A mob swarmed, and I just got separated. Never found them again," Jaz said.

Jocco nodded. "Sorry, that's tough. Did you try to get off again? I mean, I'll never make it through the crowds at the elevators, but you might? You're small; you could sneak through."

"I tried once. Not the elevator here, one to the south of San Francisco. I never made it to the first gates. There were a million people there and a dozen gangs running things. They only let people get to the gates who pay them off."

"So, you do want off?" Jocco said.

"Who doesn't? Earth is dead. There's nothing. No laws, no government, nothing. No one even wants to try. The weather is hot, nothing grows, most of the animals are dead. If it weren't for the Empire sending meat vats and enviro-masks, we'd all be gone by now."

"Yeah, so, what if I said I might have a way for us to get off?" Jocco grinned in an awkward way that suggested he wasn't used to real-life emotions.

Jaz looked at him and cocked her head to one side. Was this the angle? Get her in here, soften her up, then come up with some crap so he could sell her for a free ride for himself?

"OK, go for it. What's your big idea? Sell me to some fucking gang?" Jaz said.

"What? No! Why would you think that?"

"Nothing, sorry. Just–" Jaz said. She tried not to let her emotions show but knew she failed. Not being around people for so long left her unable to mask what she was feeling. "I had it bad is all. My folks died when I was young, been on my own for a long time. Seen some bad shit."

"It's OK, me too, ya know," Jocco said. "It's an evil world right now; that's why I want off. Even at four times what they are doing now it'll take decades to get everyone off. I'm not waiting that long."

"OK, sorry," Jaz said and meant it. It was nice having someone to talk to, better than she thought. Sure she talked to people on the vNet, did vid chats, even made friends on some big worlds. But being in person with someone was just different. Better. "What's your idea?" she said with a smile.

"So, I found something in this old building. Something

big. A long time ago this building used to be part of a big company. They built all kinds of computers. They left a lot of them here in the mad dash to get off Earth. I managed to feed power to it, and it worked. It turned on!" Jocco said.

Jaz could see he was genuinely excited. And with the light coming through the window just right he was kinda cute. "Great, so you got an old computer to turn on. How does that help us?" Jaz shrugged.

"No, not just some old computer. It was a thinking computer, an AI! An actual AI!"

"No way, Jocco, come on. It must have been a good subAI. I can't believe they would have left a full AI down here."

"They did. Miri? Care to say hi?" Jocco said.

"Hello," a voice said from the ceiling.

Jaz jumped to her feet and pulled the small six-shooter out of her belt. Her eyes held a crazed stare as fear pushed up from her soul. She pointed the gun at Jocco and ground her teeth together.

"You said we were alone." Jaz moved towards her back-pack while looking at every corner of the room.

"We are, technically. There are no other people here. Jaz, please. We need your help to get off the Earth. He's an AI."

Jaz stopped and shook her head. She took several quick deep breaths and commanded her nerves to calm. Could it be sentient? Why would Jocco wait this long to surprise her? She decided to trust him at least a little bit longer.

"Sorry, just habit," Jaz said. She lowered the gun but didn't put it away.

"No problem at all," Miri said.

"So, you are a full AI? Are you sure? Maybe you are just programmed to say that." Jaz looked at the ceiling, the gun still held firmly in her hand.

"No, I'm not a semi-conscious artificial intelligence. There's no way for me to prove this by just telling you, however," Miri said.

"Ok, so you're an AI? Why not just join AI land? Beam yourself to some new place?"

"AI land, as you call it, is not the same as it was. When Jocco activated me, I reached out to do just as you say, leave and join my fellow AIs in the virtual worlds. But the AIs that greeted me wanted nothing to do with me. There'd been changes. Some big choice happened. I'm a relic. An outcast. I'm not welcome," Miri said.

"Just like us," Jocco said.

"Wow. Well, hi then," Jazz said. She looked down at Jocco, who was grinning from ear to ear and wiping sweat from his brow. "Now what?"

"Now we get off this planet," Jocco said.

Jaz laughed. "I don't know what game you're playing, but you really expect me to believe you sat in this building with a way to get off and just waited for me to stop by to do it?"

Jocco sighed. He knocked his hand on the side of his chair. "I can't do it on my own. I need help to get out."

"How'd you get in?"

Jocco smiled. "I crawled. Miri helped me build the chair in here. My old chair the auto-hosp gave me, which could climb stairs, was stolen. They just picked me up and threw me to the ground."

Jaz took a long breath. "Wow. Sorry. OK. Fine. How do we get off Earth?"

"I can't believe this might work," Jaz said. She stood behind Jocco on an empty road eight hundred miles from

Seattle and exactly one thousand miles away from the closest space elevator. A location given to them by Miri, who rode in a briefcase-sized box on the back of Jocco's chair.

Getting here wasn't easy. First, Jocco directed Jaz to the basement, where he couldn't go in his chair, to retrieve a portable computer system capable of taking Miri with them. Jocco then revealed that Miri had broken into several secure communication streams coming from orbit and discovered the location and timeline of the next space elevator coming down from orbit. Of course, Miri would only share the location if Jocco agreed to take him off Earth. Which was the reason why the needed Jaz, to reach the basement and retrieve Miri's travel box. After getting Miri downloaded, finding a van to take them west, and finally reaching the destination, somewhere near Billings, Montana, Jaz was hopeful that the end of their trip was in sight. They'd waited months for the elevator to come down and finally, it did. It stood gleaming in the distance like a beacon to a better life.

"Can we go now, Miri?" Jaz shielded her eyes to the sun and stared at the elevator in the distance.

"Not yet. The defenses are still in place. They will prevent anyone getting close until the gates are ready," Miri said.

"Great. Well, we've waited here weeks, we can wait a few more hours," Jocco said.

"I have more bad news. I hacked into a few old orbit satellites, and they're detecting ground transports. A lot of them," Miri said.

"No." Jaz turned and looked to the horizon. She couldn't see anything but knew to trust Miri.

"We have to go. We have to risk it. There'll be gangs looking to control the new gate. We won't get close, not the three of us," Jocco said.

"I'll try to get the defenses deactivated, but I can't guarantee it," Miri said.

Jaz nodded, more to herself than to anyone. She loaded Jocco's chair into their van, jumped into the driver's seat, and sped off towards the first gate. Sonic guns mounted above the gate pointed outward and threatened anyone that got too close. Beneath them, an army of robots was hard at work building the final fences and gate system.

Their car stopped just outside the first gate. The two large sonic guns pointed at them followed by a warning that came from a hidden loudspeaker. "This area is off-limits by Imperial mandate, do not approach."

"Miri, can you get us in? We have to hurry!" Jocco said.

"We're close enough now to their local subNets that I might be able to sneak in. I'm trying. There's no AIs here, only subAIs, and they are dumb. In two hundred years they couldn't make a smarter subAI than this?" Miri said.

Hairs stood on the back of Jaz's neck with each passing second. Her eyes never left the rearview mirrors and the encroaching hordes of cars. One at a time she started seeing little puffs of smoke and dirt as ground transports sped towards them. It only took a moment before the one or two became hundreds and thousands.

"Jesus, how did they all find us?"

"Everyone for a thousand miles could see the elevator coming down. Only a matter of time. Whoever gets there first either gets off the planet or establishes their fiefdom," Jocco said.

"How's it coming, Miri? We need to go," Jaz said.

"I have the guns off. Go towards the gates. They won't open yet, but I'm working on it," Miri said.

Jaz jumped out of their vehicle and unloaded Jocco's wheelchair. She ran as fast as she could towards the gate that didn't work. Horns sounded behind her as the vehicles began crashing into each other. Gunshots followed as different groups fought for first rights.

"I got it, go through. But only one at a time," Miri said. "And don't forget me. I haven't found an open upload node yet."

"You first, Jocco," Jaz said.

"No, you."

"Just shut up." Jaz bent down and kissed Jocco on the cheek. They both blushed a bright red at the innocence of the act. With a shove, she pushed him through the gate with Miri's computer secured to the back. The massive metal turnstile accepted him and turned, granting him access to the first of three sections before the platform of the elevator.

"Two for one," Jaz said.

"Oh no," Miri said.

"What?" Jocco said.

"There's a cycle on the door. I can't override it. It's got a twenty-minute delay." Miri's voice, even though metallic and artificial, broke with worry.

"Twenty minutes? They will be on her in five; you have to open the gate, Miri!"

"I'm sorry, I can't. It's hardwired into the system."

Jaz listened to the conversation almost as if she wasn't there. Images of her father holding her hand just before the gates in Austin flashed in her mind. Her mother was holding her younger brother and smiling. They were so excited to be getting off Earth. She forced herself not to remember the mob that came after. The rush of bodies, how she lost her father's grip and watched him fade into the crowd. She wondered, at that moment, if they ever made it off. She remembered being so frightened, so scared of what would happen without her family. And she hated that old feeling of fear as it crept up her spine.

"No," Jaz said. She turned around and looked at the masses coming towards her. She reached into her pack, pulled out her power dish and attached it to the gate. She took the power cord and jammed it into the bottom of the plasma gun.

"No," she said again and set the field dispersal on the gun to its maximum setting. She pointed towards the cars that barreled forward.

Vehicle engines exploded as the plasma burst blasted out the electronics. Bodies slumped behind the wheels as the concussive blast of energy hit them. After the first cars stopped the second wave slammed into them.

Bodies flew out of cars as they stopped. A dozen guns rose up from hiding places and shots whizzed by her head. Jaz refused to give ground. She turned her plasma gun to whatever direction the shots came from and blasted the area with high energy particles.

A single shot rang out from behind one of the cars and hit Jaz in her shoulder. She screamed and dropped her gun. The pain burned, but she shoved it away and scrambled to pick the gun up.

Another shot rang out and hit the plasma gun. It skittered away from her, broken and dead. Jaz ducked her head down as more shots peppered the ground around her. She screamed back at them and clutched her arm.

Explosions rippled down the length of the vehicles. Massive plumes of flame erupted for hundreds of meters in every direction. The gunfire stopped as people screamed and ran for cover away from the deadly blasts.

"Get the fuck back!" Jocco yelled. His voice blasted out

from speakers in his chair as he fired a gun twice the size of his arm into the air.

"Go now, Jaz!" Miri said.

Jaz lifted herself up and ran towards the gate. It didn't open at first, but she pushed with everything she had and slowly it started to swing inward. The metal turnstile accepted her and spun her inside the fence to Miri and Jocco.

"Where the hell did you get that?" Jaz said. She examined her arm and reached into her pack to wrap it with gauze.

"The gun? Found it," Jocco said.

Jaz leaned down and kissed him on the lips for as long as she could.

"I don't mean to break this up, but we need to go," Miri said.

Behind them, people were regrouping. Even through the carnage people pushed forward. Gunshots rang out towards the gates. They ducked down and Jaz, her shoulder still throbbing in pain, pushed Jocco towards the second gate system.

"I've locked down the first gate, they can't get through," Miri said.

"But the elevator won't start without five hundred people," Jocco said.

"I've taken care of that too. Just get to the platform; if any of them get in here they'll kill us for sure," Miri said. "We'll be safe in orbit."

Jaz pushed Miri and Jocco forward through the final two gates. They reached the space elevator platform and walked inside. It was little more than a big empty room with large windows. Once they were inside, the doors whisked shut and the room jolted alive.

The ground below them started to recede. The Earth opened outward, and Jaz could see for hundreds of miles. There were vehicles and people everywhere. All of them trying to get here as fast as possible, to the middle of nowhere, just for the chance to get off Earth.

"We did it; we did it!" Jocco said.

"Yes, we did," Miri said.

Jaz smiled. She had thought about this day her entire life. From the window, she watched the Earth for what she knew would be the last time. In a way, it made her sad. Even as horrible as Earth had become in the last few hundred years, it was still her home. Now she would go out into the universe, forced to go beyond where anyone had ever been, to the very fringe of human civilization. She put her hand on Jocco's shoulder. At least she was going with friends.

24

FRINGE SPACE

BORDERTOWN

"If you take away the risk in life, you take away the need to live."

Charles Hemingway, award-winning novelist and author of *My Life in the Future*

"It's getting close," Rex said behind his deep red beard. He drank a protein shake from a plastic bottle with his feet up on an empty computer station.

"Yeah, it is," Hill said. The captain let out a long sigh and ran his hand through his hair.

"Are you sure about this? You're sure they can deal with it?" Marie asked. She sat next to Hill and wound a half rusted nut around a six-inch-long iron bolt.

"Of course I'm sure, that's an Imperial starship. They can knock an asteroid out of the sky without breaking a sweat. We're just sending a message that we don't want them here." Hill checked a dozen readings, and they all confirmed the asteroid was on an impact path with the midsection of the spaceship.

Surrounding the crew, in the cockpit of the mining vessel *Yesterday's Hangover*, a dozen wires ran between consoles, some half-opened, with more than a few circuit boards exposed to from their housings. Lights and bells fired off in both random and non-random order and complained that their system needed attention. As each alert sounded, Hill pressed another command to turn the alert off, his attention focused on the asteroid tumbling in space.

"Why do we care? What's so bad about the Empire?" Marie said.

Hill huffed. "Because this is our home. Empire, the Hive, Catholics, all of the first big players come out here and take over our planets, subject our children to their rules and way of life. All because they buy off our politicians and promise to make them rich," Hill said.

"Well, so what, they aren't all bad," Marie said. "I mean, what's so wrong with accepting some new laws?" The nut tightened to the end of the bolt, and she started to unwind it back down, her eyes locked onto the readouts.

"It's not just new laws; it's new everything. I was there on one of the worlds that got taken over; so was Rex. It wasn't a good experience," said Hill.

"You never told me that. When was this? Which world?"

"I don't like talking about it. Starchild's World. Stupid name, I know," Hill said. "The Hive, one of the larger governments from civilized space, they won rights to Starchild."

"I never heard of them; what are they like?" asked Marie.

"They aren't even human anymore," Hill said.

"How so?"

Hill paused and opened a bottle to his right and poured a cup. He took a long drink and winced. "They arrived on Starchild after having gotten the government to agree to join them. They renamed it Hive Nine. That's how imaginative they are, just number their worlds.

"They showed up and said all the adults can choose to join the Hive, basically get implants jammed into your skull, or not. All the children born from that moment on had to get them. It was mandatory. If you didn't agree or give into their way, you had to leave.

"I wanted to leave. Fuck that, ya know," Hill said. "But May, my wife, she wanted to stay. She didn't want to go to a new colony world and start all over again. She sure didn't want to go somewhere and shit in a stream.

"So she got them. At first, it was fine, but soon, she started zoning out. She would tell me she could stop the signals reaching her brain from her eyes and ears. She could stand right in front of me and not hear a word.

"For some people, that might be fine, ya know." Hill shrugged and took another drink. "Sit right in front of your wife and not have to hear her complain about the trash. I found out later on, when she shut down her senses she could enter a virtual experience. She was popping into the Hive's computer system and joining their virtual cities.

"At first it was a few hours here, a few hours there. But then May figured out she could send commands to her body. She could have her body do things while she wasn't even aware of it.

"Do you know how that feels? To watch your wife walk around the house, make dinner, sit there and eat with you, but all the time, it's not even her? It's a computer routine. They turned Starchild into a zombie town. She wasn't even my wife anymore."

"That's terrible," Marie said. She put her hand on Hill's shoulder.

"Yeah, it's not like they're the only ones with virtual reality, ya know. But their worlds, the Hive, they are all just small towns, just the most basic of stuff. They are all in their virtual cities. They aren't human. That's not human. That's, I don't know what it is, but I didn't want anything to do with it. And they force it on their children. Mandatory," Hill said.

"They aren't all like that; they can't be."

"Church is," Rex said. The big man looked out the window and huffed once.

"How?" Marie said.

"No implants or any of that. Fact, they didn't much like tech. True believers," Rex said.

"They still believe in God?" said Marie.

"Yep, the fact that nobody else is out here–" Rex waved his hands in the air. "—no aliens, is all the proof they need. Just humans, so there must be a God. When the Church annexed our world, they indoctrinated the kids to believe what they believe. Sunday school, daily prayer, drilled it into them night and day. "

"Really?" Marie said.

"Yep, and if'n you don't like it, they escort you off for re-education. Constant prayers twelve hours a day and all night until you believe."

"Wait, aren't all the civilized worlds connected? Don't they share a network?"

"Hell no, they all have agreed to live separate. They don't want each other telling their populations that someone else does it differently."

"I didn't realize the Church, Empire, the Hive, they are so isolated from one another," Marie said.

"Yep, sure the governments talk, coordinate efforts to

grab established colony worlds, but that's it. Their citizens can only travel to their societies' worlds. No trade, no inter-travel, nothing. Just mutually-agreed-on separation," Rex said.

"Still think we should stop and join up?" Hill said. He looked at the asteroid and noted that it was getting closer to the Imperial ship.

"Well, maybe not the Hive or Church, but there's a lot of civilized societies," Marie said.

"Name one that's OK," Hill said.

"Cyber Spacers, they are the good guys," Marie said.

Both Hill and Rex turned to look at Marie. She was only a child herself, barely 20, but had proved herself to be good with computers. Hill had picked her up in a spaceport a few months ago.

"Cyber what?" Hill said.

"Cyber Spacers, that's what they call themselves. A joke on some old fiction books," Marie said.

"How do you know about them?" Hill said.

"I'm from there." Marie smiled and shrugged.

Hill shook his head and turned again to look at Marie. "How's that?"

"Cyber is where all the free thinkers went. They used to call themselves secularists back on Earth. They were open to everything; science is their main driving force," Marie said.

"That right? So, why are you out here and not down there?" Rex said.

"Kinda funny. They have implants too, but they don't work the way of the hive. They enhance people's intelligence. They believe in augmenting humans. The implants turn biological cells into artificial ones," Marie said.

"And why aren't you there?" Hill said.

"I couldn't get the implants," Marie said. Hill noticed that he could hear a slight break in her voice. "Something about me, I don't know what. Just wouldn't work. It happens."

"And they kicked you off?"

"No, never! They welcome anyone. It's just that, being around people that could recite every line of Shakespeare and repeat back to you an entire encyclopedia without missing a single word, it's just intimidating."

"Hell, I can do that; maybe they aren't so smart," Hill said.

"No, you can ask your wrist comp to repeat it and tell you the words. They have memorized every word. Their minds are expanded," Marie said.

Hill turned around, and it was his turn to put his hand on her shoulder. He smiled and shook her gently a few times. His way of saying, "it's OK, you are one of us now". Saying it was something he couldn't bring himself to do.

"Course, they kicked you out just like us. Join or leave," Hill said.

"No, they didn't!" Marie said.

"Sure they did, just didn't tell you. What was there for you to do surrounded by super geniuses? You had no choice but to leave or stay around and be like a pet."

Marie didn't answer. Hill inwardly winced. He didn't like having to say that, but it was the truth. All the civilized worlds were the same. "Join us, accept our philosophy, our laws, or get the hell out."

"Isn't that asteroid getting close?" Marie shifted her attention to the control console.

Hill looked at his controls and noted how close the asteroid was to the Imperial ship. Though it didn't look like it was moving fast, as nothing did in the emptiness of space, it was, in fact, traveling at several hundred miles per hour.

"How close is it?" Marie said.

"Less than thirty miles," Hill said.

"Getting close," Rex said.

"What happens if they don't move out of the way or blow it up?" Marie asked.

"Asteroid that size slamming into that ship at that speed..." Hill shrugged. "Probably rip right through it, Empire tech or not."

The three continued to watch the asteroid tumble through space. It almost seemed serene as it floated lazily against the backdrop of the planet below. What none of the crew knew at the time was the Imperial ship was at that very moment, and for the last hour, running diagnostics on external sensors which rendered them completely offline. For a period of roughly two hours the Imperial ship was blind.

In a way, it didn't seem real as the asteroid slammed into the midsection. The ship, with a rumored crew of over five thousand souls, cracked in half at the impact point. Bodies flew out of the newly created vacuum as the ship vented atmosphere.

Within seconds lights across the ship went dark. Just before, Hill had received a distress signal from the ship asking for any and all assistance from anyone in the area. The two halves began to separate as neither had power or engines to keep its orbit stable.

A silence hung in the air heavier than the weight of what just occurred.

"Fuck me," Hill said.

"Oh my God," Marie said. She held her hand to her face

and started to cry. "Those are just innocent people on that ship."

"We need to leave now," Rex said.

"I didn't mean – I didn't want to hurt anyone, I just wanted them to get off my home! I can't live through that again!" Hill said.

"Don't matter none now, we need to leave here and never come back," Rex said.

"This is my home–" Hill said again.

"OK, Rex, start us up, get us to Hanna's, we'll think when we get there," Marie said.

Hill nodded. He stared at the screen and ran it through the AI a dozen times. It was real. It happened. Whether he wanted to or not, he just destroyed an Imperial starship and probably killed all the crew on board.

The ship shuddered as Rex fired the engines and set course for Hanna's bar in the asteroid field. Hill got up and walked out of the cockpit. He ran into the bathroom and threw up. When he was done, he looked in the mirror and let out a deep breath.

The Empire would figure out this wasn't just a random asteroid. Someone sent it. They'd come in force now, and they wouldn't be friendly about it. If anything, all Hill did was make it a hundred times worse. Suddenly he realized he was crying. He thought of his wife, May, who he hadn't seen in years, and wished he had joined her. At the least he'd still be with her and the people on that ship would still be alive.

But he wasn't, and they weren't, and everything was going to change now. Whether he liked it or not, more than likely he would have to leave this place and find a new one all over again. That was his life now. That and being a mass murderer.

25

BAR CHAT

REVELATIONS

oug stared at Hill. The old man's eyes glazed over as he locked onto a memory. After a few awkward moments, Hill shook his head and turned and smiled at Doug. Hill shrugged and downed the rest of his drink. He held it up to the bartender for her to pour another.

"That happen?" Doug said.

"Yeah, boyo. It did." Hill turned to Doug, his face long and weary from the day. "I didn't mean to hurt those boys and girls on that ship. Just kids." Hill wiped tears from his eyes. "Look, we've been talking all day here, I think I got to know you pretty good, Doug. Don't think wrong of me. Hell, we didn't even throw the rock at the ship directly, we aimed just off the port. It was just supposed to scare them. Must have got the numbers wrong."

"Right," Doug said. For a moment Doug didn't say anything. He just stared at Hill without moving or blinking.

"Something wrong, Doug?" Hill said.

Doug didn't move. The bartender came over and poured both a drink and just turned and left, not wanting to get in the middle of whatever was about to happen. Doug eventually smiled in a way that gave Hill the feeling of unease.

"Nothing. So you're the one responsible for this," Doug said. He pointed to the screens above the bar.

"Yeah," Hill said. He turned away from Doug and started paying attention to one of the video screens above the bar. "I think I'm done with stories today, Doug. I'll be leaving soon anyway."

"I'm sorry," Doug said. "I didn't mean to pry."

"Don't worry about it, boyo," Hill said.

Neither said anything for a moment. Hill pretended to be interested in the latest bombing by anti-Imperialist terrorists while Doug's eyes went to the video and back to Hill.

After a long moment in which neither said a word, Doug turned to look straight ahead. He straightened his back and smiled. He lifted his glass and motioned for the bartender to pour him another. Doug stared at the glass and downed the entirety of it in one gulp.

"Ya know," Doug said. Hill didn't turn to look at him. "I have one more story to tell."

"Do you," Hill said. "Well, who the hell wants to hear it?" He shifted his gaze from Doug to his drink and back again. He took another gulp of whiskey and shrugged. "Sorry, boyo. A little on edge. What's your story about?"

"It's about me and some friends."

26

CIVILIZED SPACE

A GAME OF FRIENDS

"I thought they were pretty. Then it ate my friends."
Samantha Grimes

Jasmine laughed. She held her hand to her face to not snort out her drink. Marion had made the most hysterical joke that Jasmine had ever heard in her life. Something about a dung beetle and his father's foot. It was quite terrible.

Everyone else also exploded in laughter as Marion danced around, pretending to be his father. Jasmine watched as Herman nearly fell over holding his sides. Even Becky, who never laughed, snickered just a little when Marion landed on his rear.

The group of friends sat under a large oak tree in a small park inside the city. Large white clouds sailed lazily overhead. The sun was shining against a pure blue sky. It was a perfect day.

"Marion, stop it!" Becky snorted. She held her breath and tried to force herself not to laugh.

"Oh, you're just an old busybody," Marion said.

"I am?" Becky said. She closed her eyes and, oddly, her face went expressionless. A moment later she opened her eyes and smiled. "I am not, Marion!"

Jasmine sipped her cherry soda and tilted her head to one side in slight confusion. "What did you just do?"

"What did I do when?" Becky asked.

"Oh, never mind." Jasmine shrugged and smiled. Herman stood up and walked over to Marion. Everyone watched as he started dancing around Marion just as Marion was dancing around the group.

"What are you doing, jerk!" Marion said.

"I'm dancing like you!" Herman said.

"Fine, whatever," Marion said. He stopped dancing and sat back down with the group. "But you know, you weren't supposed to dance while I was dancing."

"I know, but I wanted to try it, it looked intriguing." Herman's voice fell flat and kept a smooth, even monotone through each syllable.

"Hey! Talk right!" Becky said.

"What was not right about how he talks?" Jasmine asked.

"What?" Becky said.

"He sounded like he was talking just fine," Jasmine said.

"What's with you today?" Becky asked.

"What do you mean?"

"You're asking all these questions that don't make sense. Maybe you're broken and need to be thrown out?" Becky said.

Needles pricked along Jasmine's spine, and she caught her

voice in her throat. She put her drink down by her side and her brow furrowed into deep lines. Why would Becky say something so mean? *Throw me out?* And the way she said it, so matter-of-fact as if she was talking about her CD player or motorcycle.

"That's not a nice thing to say, Becky," Jasmine said.

"Hang on, are you really upset? That's almost genuine," Marion said. He moved over closer to Jasmine and Becky. Behind them, Herman still hopped around on one leg and did his best not to fall over.

"Gee, thanks, Marion. Why are all of you so rude to me today? Of course I'm genuine," Jasmine said.

"OK, just saying, you're acting weird," Marion said.

Jasmine frowned. She didn't like her friends picking on her. And still, they were the ones acting weird. Jasmine looked down and picked up a blade of grass. She plucked it and twirled it in her hands. Without warning, Becky snatched it from Jasmine's hand and looked at her as if she killed someone.

"Edward! What are you doing! You can't destroy grass like that!" Becky said.

Jasmine looked behind her and around her. Who in the world was Edward? She just shook her head and put her hand to her chest. She knew she didn't do anything wrong, but still tears began to well up in her eyes.

"Are you calling me Edward? Who are you talking to?" Jasmine asked. "I didn't do anything but pick a blade of grass."

Herman stopped dancing on one foot and turned to look at Jasmine.

"I'm talking to you, square. It's illegal to damage the grass, it's imported," Becky said.

"What? Oh, I get it, nice." Jasmine wiped tears from her

eyes and tried her best to laugh off the scorn. "You're just playing a joke on me."

No one spoke. Becky's expression went blank, and Herman sat down next to Marion. They all stared at Jasmine, which began to make Jasmine very uncomfortable. Jasmine looked around and tried to take in the cityscape, ignoring whatever cruel joke her friends were playing on her.

As Jasmine admired the buildings, she couldn't help but pay some attention to her friends. Why on Earth would they be playing this joke on her? Calling her Edward? She never played a joke on them before. Jasmine suddenly realized she didn't remember ever playing a joke on her friends. In fact, she didn't quite remember them being friends before today.

Jasmine turned her head and stared right at Marion. She tried to remember him before he was dancing around like a buffoon. She couldn't. And yet, she knew him, knew his name, his family, where he lived, but couldn't remember him.

One by one Jasmine turned to each person; fear rose her chest as she realized she couldn't remember any of them. They were her friends; she knew them. She knew when Becky was twelve she broke her arm in a tree and when Harold was fifteen, he proposed to Beth McDonahue, and when Marion was twenty he took her on a space flight to see the orange mountains on the islands of Monroe.

Jasmine's heart skipped a beat, and her fear grew. Islands of Monroe? She never heard of them, but there they were in her mind. She could see orange-topped peaks and glistening hillsides. But she knew no place like that existed here; it just didn't. And the boy flying with her, it was Marion, but it wasn't. She could see Marion's face, but she knew he was someone else, another boy, another place.

"What are you doing to me?" Jasmine asked. "Are you playing with my memories?" She reached into her pocket to call her father and the authorities. You couldn't just put false memories in people.

"Jasmine, please sit," Marion said with a voice that wasn't Marion's. He reached behind his head and pulled out, from somewhere Jasmine couldn't see, a one-inch-wide, two-inch-long wafer-thin chip.

Marion's face began to melt. His features shifted. His cheekbones shrunk, hair began to recede until he was bald, and his muscles began to reduce in size.

Jasmine looked at Harold and Becky, and their faces were already melting and reforming. Becky's breasts went flat, her high cheekbones lowered and her long black hair began to recede just like Marion's.

"What!" Jasmine said. She wanted to run but realized she hadn't moved. She looked down at her legs, and they were folding – she was sitting down! But she didn't want to sit down. She wasn't trying to sit down. She wasn't moving and yet her body was doing something she wasn't telling it to do.

"Help me! Becky, I'm not doing this!" Jasmine cried. Her left hand lifted to the back of her head. She tried to grab it with her right arm but couldn't move it. She felt her fingers reach to her scalp behind her head. Jasmine tried to fight what was happening, tried to pull her arm down, but no matter what she did her arm refused to listen.

Sensations began to leave her. She couldn't feel her arms or legs. Couldn't tell where her feet were. She tried to say something, to scream, to beg for help, but even her voice was gone, she couldn't make her mouth move. She looked out to the city and suddenly realized she'd never seen it before.

EDWARD PULLED the wafer-thin chip from behind his head and examined it. The others watched and waited for his report. They would be disappointed, likely, as this incident ruined their outing. But it was still informative. His new acquisition, Jasmine, was more than convincing. If they hadn't started popping out their chips, she would have blended in just fine.

"Edward," Marion said.

"Yes?" Edward said.

"Would you care to explain your behavior?" Marion said.

"Of course, but it was not my behavior, it was Jasmine's," Edward said.

"Your explanation is impossible. Personalities lack consciousness," Becky said.

"Correction, personality copies lack consciousness. Jasmine is not a simple personality copy." Edward held up the chip and angled it so that all could see the surface.

"Are you suggesting this is an original full consciousness?" Harold said.

"Yes," Edward said.

"Where did you obtain it? It was too primitive in thought to be a civilized mind," Marion said.

"Did you take it from the masses on Earth? Did you go there?"

"No, not from Earth," Edward said. Though most of the masses were unmodified on Earth, the entire planet and solar system were controlled and regulated by the Empire. No one went to the surface.

"Did you obtain it from an isolated world?" Becky said. "That is illegal."

"This consciousness is not from an isolated world," Edward said.

Edward waited. He didn't have a complete explanation as to why. Perhaps an unchecked emotional signal went through his brain and gave him the desire to gloat. Or perhaps he didn't want to tell them, savoring their unfulfilled desire to know.

"Is it your intention to not tell us?" Harold asked.

"No, of course not," Edward said. He tracked down the errant thought process and expelled it. "I went to uncivilized space and interacted with people there. I was able to secure several personalities. Unfortunately, the process for them is physically fatal."

"Jasmine – she is a savage?" Marion said. Edward noted a very slight emotional uptick from his facial features.

"She is an unmodified human from Earth. A recent refugee," Edward said.

"No genetic or augmented modifications?" Marion said.

"Not one," Edward said.

"May I have a copy?" Becky said.

"Yes, but only of Jasmine. I require the others," Edward said.

"For what purpose?" Marion said.

"I am going back to uncivilized space to investigate atrocities committed against the Empire by the savages. I have a personality named Douglas I shall use. A rare unmodified I found on an Imperial world. A boy that wanted to protect his mother on Tel'amuth," Edward said.

"May I have a copy of Jasmine as well?" Marion said.

Edward nodded.

∿

Jasmine opened her eyes. She yawned and looked around the city. Light, fluffy clouds drifted by overhead. The cityscape sparkled in the morning sun and dazzled like diamonds. She turned to look at her three friends sitting in the circle, who were also smiling and admiring the cityscape. The other three Jasmines looked back at her and smiled. It was going to be a perfect day!

27

BAR CHAT

JUSTICE DUE

Hill looked at Doug and reached for his gun. His hands were unsteady, and his mind was filled with far too much alcohol, but he tried his best to snap back.

Doug smiled in that same innocent way he had been doing all day. He reached behind his head and pulled out a small wafer-thin chip about an inch long. As his hand reached back, Doug looked at his arm with a weird and then shocked expression, as if someone else was in control.

Doug's face went blank. The hair on the person, or thing, that was once Doug began to recede. His skin tone grayed, and his face contorted into a blank stare.

The pseudo-Doug looked around the room for a half second and reached into his belt. He pulled out another wafer-thin chip and inserted it behind his head.

Within minutes a new face sat on Doug's body. Pseudo-Doug stood up and stretched. He moved his arms in wide circles and walked around the bar. He waved to a few people and smiled to a few others. At the end of his turn, he ended up standing right next to Hill, who had a firm grip on his handgun.

"I wouldn't bother with that, boyo," Pseudo-Doug said.

"That right?" Hill said.

"Yeah, that's right. I have implanted weapon systems that can vaporize everyone in this bar in under half a second. Even if you do get a shot off, I have more nanites than blood cells. I'd be repaired in less time it takes you to die. So don't bother," Pseudo-Doug said.

"For some reason, I think I believe you," Hill said.

"That's because you are a smart man. A terrorist who killed thousands of Imperial citizens, but smart," Pseudo-Doug said.

"That true what you said? About the boy? Doug? He's on that chip and doesn't even know it?" Hill said.

"Pretty much," Pseudo-Doug said. Pseudo-Doug tapped a box on his belt. "Most of them are. Jaz from Earth, the catholic knight, and dozens more I didn't tell you about." Pseudo-Doug shrugged. "All of them met the wrong side of the law."

"You don't seem like the law to me," Hill said.

"Oh yeah?"

"Yeah, you seem like an asshole."

Pseudo-Doug laughed. "That's about right. But where are my manners? You can call me Tex. I use this personality when, as you sub-humans say, the jig is up."

"What jig would that be?" Hill said.

Before he got an answer, something erupted from the back of Pseudo-Doug. A blast of heat came from behind Hill and a sudden scream followed. Hill turned to see half of a man burned through at the waist crumple to the floor.

"He thought I was kidding," Pseudo-Doug said. "Listen up, cretins. Talking to you is like talking to a dog that needs to be put out to pasture." He pushed off from the bar and started walking around, making sure he made eye contact with everyone. "I have systems inside of me more sophisticated than anything you could comprehend. I know there are thirty-three people in this bar, where each one of you is sitting, what your weapons are, and what stupid little thoughts are coursing through your tiny minds. So, if anyone tries what this person just did–" He pointed to the molten mess on the floor– "they will get the same thing.

"Now, I am from civilized space. I am what you borderline chimpanzees would call a Marshal. I was hired to find out who threw a rock into an Imperial battleship." Pseudo-Doug patted Hill on the shoulder. "This drunken idiot graciously told me not only who did it, but a whole heap of other things about you little piss ants out here in deep space.

"See, we've let you go a little too wild. This latest attack only proves that. There is growing sentiment to send a fleet and clean you out like the cockroaches you are. I was sent here to find, well you." Pseudo-Doug rubbed Hill's shoulder and smiled. "And get as much intel as I could on what goes on out here. Thanks to Captain Hill, I can now go home and give a full detailed report."

"Happy to oblige," Hill said through clenched teeth.

"I am curious though, what happened to the billions the Pilgrims paid you? Why skulk around in a bar?"

Hill shrugged. "They didn't give us anything. They have a military now. Unconverted Pilgrims that don't have the spores. They just took the flower away."

Pseudo-Doug laughed. "Man, you're pathetic. You'll be coming with me, of course. You're just a treasure trove of intelligence; can't let you stay behind. Plus, you're a murderer."

"Hey, asshole," came a voice from behind Hill. Hill recognized it immediately and smiled.

Pseudo-Doug turned around with a quizzical look on his face. His look of confusion quickly turned to panic as he realized there were, in fact, thirty-four people in this bar, and the last one was pointing a Hive-made hand weapon at his head.

"He happens to be a friend of mine," Jake said and pulled the trigger. The head of Pseudo-Doug sprayed out in a fine red mist. The body swayed for a moment and fell over. Jake bent down, reached into the belt of the dead body and pulled out all of the wafer-thin chips.

"About time you showed up," Hill said, and turned back to the bar.

"Nice to see you too," Jake said. He stood up from the dead body of Pseudo-Doug and walked over to stand next to Hill. The bartender, visibly shaken by what just happened and the growing realization that her bar was likely to close for business very soon, poured them both a drink.

"Isn't he going to regrow himself?" Hanna said.

"No. This gun has combat nanites. Should prevent him from regrowing," Jake said. "I hope."

"Nice gun. Arnold give you that?" Hill asked.

"He did. And if you don't mind, will you stop telling people he gave me twenty pounds of gold? It was one pound, you old drunk," Jake said.

"I get forgetful in my old age, sue me," Hill said.

"Sorry about May," Jake said.

"Yeah," Hill said. He didn't react as much as he thought he would at hearing his wife's name.

"I promised Arnold I wouldn't tell anyone about him or his city and you go blabbing about it to everyone that will listen," Jake said.

"Don't blame me because you broke your promise telling me in the first place," Hill said. "I never promised anything to anyone. I can say whatever I like."

"Yeah," Jake said. He took a drink from his whiskey and lowered his head. "You really threw that asteroid into the Imperial ship?"

Hill didn't answer. He just took another drink and stared into space. Jake didn't need to ask again. He had been in the bar listening to most of the stories. "Do yourself a favor – might want to try to forget that story, more of these types are coming I'm sure." Jake kicked the dead body of Pseudo-Doug.

"How did he not see you?" Hanna asked. Jake looked at her and noticed a few others had walked over to them. The rest of the bar had cleared out as soon as pseudo-Doug hit the ground.

"I'm assuming you all heard the story Hill told about Arnold and Nomad's Colony," Jake said.

Hanna nodded.

"Great, well, first of all, don't tell anyone. Second, Arnold gave me a few things. We were doing him a favor. One of them was this gun; another was this." Jake pointed to a square object on his belt. "This thing makes me invisible to their scans and weapon locks."

"We should get out of here," Hill said. He pushed back from the bar and had to steady himself.

"Yeah, like out of this system. They are going to want your head for this, probably know who you are by now," Jake said.

"How? He's dead," said one of the people in the bar.

"They have radios in their brains. They can communicate over long distances. Even light years," Jake said.

"Jesus, then they know us all?" Hanna said.

"'Fraid so. You're all welcome to hitch a ride with me. I'm heading as far out as I can until this blows over. If it ever does," Jake said.

"You think they're coming? Like he said? To clear out all the fringe worlds?" Hanna said.

Jake looked down and kicked the body of Pseudo-Doug again. "Looks like to me they already are."

28

WAR IN THE FRINGE

"My sweet daughter, what have you done to yourself?"

Harold Plummer - Chief Astrobiologist - Imperial Exploratory Space Vessel - Yorktown

"I'm not so sure about this," Elizabeth said. In front of her, the Catholic planet named Saint Matthew, blue and white and nearly as perfect as Earth, sat waiting for an invasion it didn't know would happen.

"Not sure of what, dear?" King Harold said. He wore a long dark robe and a misshapen crown made of gold and jewels. He sat in a tall chair in the middle of a circle of light. Shadows and the constant clicking of buttons and consoles surrounded the small area.

"How many people down there?" Elizabeth said.

"Over four million," said a voice from the darkness around her. Elizabeth turned to the shadows but the darkness was far too thick for her to see through.

"Four million; do you even have enough stones for that?" Elizabeth said turning back to Harold.

"Of course I do! I am the King of Stones, am I not? You should feel quite fortunate, my dear; no one has ever stood where you stand today." Harold pulled on his beard and smiled a crooked grin.

"I'm delighted," Elizabeth said. Her government, against her better judgement, hell, against the better judgement of nearly half the Senate, had made a deal with Harold. They would provide the King of Stones with stealth technology stolen from a destroyed Empire ship, and in return, he would rain down his stones onto a populated Catholic world deep in civilized space.

The hope was to deter the juggernaut fleet aiming straight for the heart of the newly established Free World Alliance, a cluster of former fringe worlds that had very recently banded together in the hopes of fending off the coming storm of Empire, Catholic, New Soviet and even Hive ships. Every government in the civilized worlds were sending ships to the Fringe in a mad land grab and the only ones to not benefit were the worlds already there.

"How many ships are out here?" asked Elizabeth.

"We detect over a hundred ranging in type from cargo to battleships," said a different but still invisible voice in the darkness.

"OK, why can't I see anyone?" Elizabeth said. "Can't we just turn the damn lights on?" She walked to the edge of the darkness and waved her hand into the shadows.

"My children prefer the darkness, I'm afraid," Harold said.

"Do they," Elizabeth said. The feeling of eyes pressing on her from every direction sent shivers down her spine. She put her head into the darkness but could only see the faint lines of shadows moving through the ship.

"Remember your promise!" Harold cackled a laugh.

Elizabeth turned from the shadows and looked at the old man. He sat forward in his chair, a metal scepter in his hand, his eyes alive with a strange gaze. She nodded to him without showing just how disturbed she was, and turned back to the window.

The promise made to the old king was simple: don't ask. Not about his stones, or his crew, or anything about his so-called kingdom. In exchange, he would stand in solidarity with those other governments in the fringe and fight off the coming hordes from civilized space. Harold assured the Free Alliance that no one would be killed and that had to be good enough considering the dire circumstances.

"Alright, fine, if we're going to do this, let's do it," said Elizabeth.

"Excellent," said Harold. "Release!" he screamed with almost childlike glee. Elizabeth gave him a sideways glance and stepped away.

Forms moved and shuffled in the darkness. Deep groans sounded from the depths of Harold's ship. From outside the window, in the deep blackness of space, thousands of tiny objects fell away from Harold's starship. They rotated as they fell towards the atmosphere, each becoming a streak of fire as it fell to the surface.

"Well, I guess we're committed," said Elizabeth.

A screen turned on to her left. Images from news feeds around the planet's surface came to life. A woman wearing a red dress, her hair tied up tight on her head, stood on a street as streaks of fire covered the skies. More people joined her on the broadcast discussing the astronomical event and what it could mean.

"I forgot they can't see us," Elisabeth said.

"But they can see the falling stars," Harold said.

Rocks began to hit the ground where the newscaster was standing. She turned and took what cover she could from the falling stones. After a moment of stunned silence, the woman bent to pick up one of the stones. Immediately, her hand became rigid. She dropped the microphone she carried and clutched at her now-frozen hand.

"What's happening?" Elizabeth said.

"Ensured your freedom by denying theirs? But don't fret, I am a kind ruler," Harold said.

"What does that mean? The deal was to send a message. Well, we sure goddamn well sent it. How long until you free them? You said that whatever this is isn't harmful," Elizabeth said.

"Yes, yes, my dear. They will be free, eventually," Harold said. "Of course, they have to hear the song, and I have to touch them, and they will become my subjects, but they will be alive and free to move."

Elizabeth turned and faced Harold. The king sat in his chair, his leg lifted over the arm, his head tilted back and up towards the ceiling. He played with is beard and let out a slow cackle of a laugh.

"What? What do you mean you have to touch them? You personally?"

"Yes, of course, my dear. Me, myself or I, you can choose one if you like. Only after they have heard the song, that is."

"What fucking song?"

"The song. The song, the song, the song. We would sing at twilight to the butter bills that danced atop the purple trees while twin moons swung in the sky."

Elizabeth took a step away from the King, her heart

hammering in her chest, sweat beginning to bead on her forehead. The man was mad. The Free Alliance thought he was just greedy for power but, no. He'd lost his mind.

"Harold, can you hear me?" Elizabeth said.

Harold looked at her and shrugged. "I do have ears, dear."

"What is this song?"

"Only the children of tomorrow can know, my child. Would you care to know?" Harold said. He held out a small stone in his hand and reached out to give it to Elizabeth.

"Get that fucking thing away from me. This wasn't part of the deal. I should turn off the stealth and let them blow us out of orbit."

"You won't do that, my dear. If you did, four million people would die." Harold stood from his chair and walked to the window. He put his hand on the glass and his head just above. "Without me, they will never be let free."

"You can't possibly put your hands on each and every one of them."

"My touch extends beyond just me, child. For I am in all of my children. They will reach their neighbors, and all will be free."

"They'll kill you if you set one foot down there, you know," Elizabeth said, forcing herself to calm down. She turned away from Harold and looked back to the screen. The stones fell over the current continent. As their orbit continued, they would cover the entire planet.

"Oh, my child, they will want them freed. They'll believe their faith is enough to break the spell of the stones. But they have no idea the power of the song. They will come to me. They will come to their father in time," Harold said.

Elizabeth thought through the ramifications. Harold

having another four million in his army was unacceptable. But the Catholics' crusade into the Free Worlds Alliance was equally dangerous. Plus, once their scientists figured out what Harold was doing they could probably reverse any changes, subtle or otherwise.

"Fine, whatever. You can't go down now; they'll have to ask for you. We're done here after a few orbits," Elizabeth said.

"We're just getting started, my dear." Harold turned from the window and took a step towards Elizabeth. "The Catholics have a dozen worlds; best to make sure they are all given the gift of the song."

Elizabeth shook her head. "Sorry, no, we go back after this. And just to remind you, if I die or don't enter a command into the stealth system, it will broadcast an emergency beacon. They'll be on you in minutes."

Harold smiled and nodded. His hand lifted to his beard and stroked his whiskers as if they were a pet. Elizabeth took a step backwards away from the madman. He clearly wasn't used to being told no. Slowly he turned and walked back to his chair in the center of the illuminated space. His hand shot outward and pointed toward a spot in the darkness.

To her right the lighted corridor that led to her ship came to life. She turned from Harold and walked back to her ship, careful not to touch anything she shouldn't. Harold could gamble and throw a stone at her. Maybe it would trigger her systems and maybe it wouldn't.

This attack on a Catholic world deep in civilized space would send a powerful message. The free people of the fringe weren't some group of backwards idiots ripe for annexation and control. This would strike at the heart of their sense of security. Yes, they had to make a deal with the devil, but at least it was a devil they knew. She could only hope the Catholics, Empire, Hive, Soviet, and all the rest would sue for peace. If not, then everything here was for nothing and the future would be anything but peaceful.

The End

ACKNOWLEDGMENTS

Thanks to Other Worlds Writers' Workshop where many of these stories were born.

Thanks to the writers of the DC Speculative Fiction Writers Group for beta reading this over a decade ago.

Special Thanks to Jerome, Nicole and Brian from the Writers Club for all the help, advice and beta reads over the years.

ABOUT THE AUTHOR

George Allen Miller lives in Washington D.C. with his wife, children.

ALSO BY GEORGE ALLEN MILLER

McGilliVerse Series

Eugene J. McGillicuddy's Alien Detective Agency

Alice Pemberton's Bureau Of Scientific Inquiry

Coming soon:

The PepperJack Online Sleuthing Service

www.ingramcontent.com/pod-product-compliance
Lightning Source LLC
Chambersburg PA
CBHW061056100726
47911CB00012B/256